No Regrets

Also by Fern Kupfer

Surviving the Seasons
Before and After Zachariah

No Regrets

Fern Kupfer

Viking

VIKING
Published by the Penguin Group
Viking Penguin, a division of Penguin Books USA Inc.,
40 West 23rd Street, New York, New York 10010, U.S.A.
Penguin Books Ltd, 27 Wrights Lane,
London W8 5TZ, England
Penguin Books Australia Ltd, Ringwood,
Victoria, Australia
Penguin Books Canada Ltd, 2801 John Street,
Markham, Ontario, Canada L3R 1B4
Penguin Books (N.Z.) Ltd, 182–190 Wairau Road,
Auckland 10, New Zealand

Penguin Books Ltd, Registered Offices:
Harmondsworth, Middlesex, England

First published in 1989 by Viking Penguin,
a division of Penguin Books USA Inc.
Published simultaneously in Canada
10 9 8 7 6 5 4 3 2 1
Copyright © Fern Kupfer, 1989
All rights reserved

Grateful acknowledgment is made for permission
to reprint an excerpt from "Song" from
Collected Poems 1947–1980 by Allen Ginsberg.
Copyright © 1954 by Allen Ginsberg. Reprinted by
permission of Harper & Row, Publishers, Inc.

LIBRARY OF CONGRESS CATALOGING-IN-PUBLICATION DATA
Kupfer, Fern.
No regrets.
I. Title.
PS3561.U619N6   1989   813'.54   88-40403
ISBN 0-670-82459-3

Printed in the United States of America
Set in Sabon
Designed by Ellen S. Levine

In Memory of George Zyskind

No Regrets

Chapter 1

Regret can wash over you like water over stone. Regret can just wear you away.

At a college party nearly fifteen years ago, a boy I was going with said, "I have regrets but no scruples." This struck everyone as very funny because we were all high, and we kept repeating regrets . . . scruples . . . regrets . . . scruples . . . until the words became separate from their original meanings and we started to pretend that we were ordering in a restaurant: "I'll have some regrets, but hold the scruples."

The boy, Jack Silver, later asked me to marry him, but I said no. He was too thin-lipped. When we kissed, I thought I could swallow him up. Also, his family was well-connected and even though he said he was going into the Peace Corps when we graduated, I knew he'd end up being a corporate lawyer.

Lately, though, I've been thinking about regret and the choices that I made, wondering if I've been too practical to expect fantasies to come true. Driving along, listening to the radio, I daydream that I am a famous rock-and-roll singer playing to a packed house. In college I used to bring my guitar to all the parties, and once I even sang with a professional band at a ZBT weekend. Later, after I decided to major in journalism, I pictured myself off in the Third World writing Pulitzer Prize–winning articles about famine and revolution. Now I have a job for a magazine that is published September to May by the extension service at the University of Illinois. I write articles that read like a "Hints to Heloise" for institutional management. Much of my research has to do with methods of stain removal. As jobs go, it's not very important. But I don't think I had enough talent to have real regrets.

I thought my friend Barbara should have stayed with David. She said she didn't love him. "Do you think that's a reason for breaking up a marriage?" I asked. Lately I am sounding more and more like my mother.

Barbara was leaving a man she said she *didn't* love to go to a man she said she *did* love. The move struck me as frivolous.

"Easy for you to say!" Barbara was huffy. "You love your husband."

Actually, at the moment, I did not. That morning, Jesse had said, "Where are my socks?" and although I had left them in the dryer for three days, his accusing voice stirred some primordial anger in me so that I imagined myself floating, Chagall-like, from the bed, over to the empty sock drawer where he was standing, and pummeling him into unconsciousness.

Instead, I feigned indifference. "Your socks are in the dryer. You can get them."

"Thanks! I'm late and I have to go down to the basement to go look for a pair of socks," his voice boomed through the hall. "Thanks, Sharon, thanks a lot!"

"Do your own wash then," I yelled back at him. "I work, too. I'm not your damned servant!"

Our raised voices woke our daughter, who got up to pee. "Cut it out, you guys," Libby said, still sleepy-soft, padding her way to the bathroom.

Only last night, the three of us had watched television in bed, clumped together like animals in a lair. Maybe it's all right to have an occasional lapse of love.

◆

Now Barbara was leaving David. Leaving him with the house, the furniture, the antique clocks, the gerbils. She was packing up a Volkswagen van and taking the children to find a new life with a new man in California. Andrew was someone with whom she'd been having an affair for over a year. After he was transferred to California last December, he wrote her steamy letters describing the color of her nipples as he remembered them and his aching need. He begged her to join him.

Maybe it was this last winter in the Midwest that did her in. We had so much snow. Maybe if we lived someplace without a wind-chill factor, Barbara would not be leaving her husband.

But in blazing August the plan was all set in motion. In record time Barbara had found a new job, sent a deposit for a two-bedroom apartment in San Francisco, enrolled her younger daughter in an all-day Montessori preschool.

I remember that sometime her last week, Barbara was giving David a haircut under the apple tree in their backyard; their daughters were playing in the sandbox he had built. When Barbara went into the house to answer the phone, David turned to me. "She just came home one day and told me about Andrew. She said she didn't love me anymore. I feel so foolish. How could I not have known?" Without his glasses, he looked vulnerable, the white towel around his shoulders flecked with fine, brown hairs. "You're her best friend. Tell me why. Why is she doing this?"

If I had to defend Barbara, I had no words. I had tried over the past few weeks to remain loyal, unequivocal-no-strings loyal. You don't reject a best friend because you don't approve of what she's doing, right?

Last week I saw this program on the "Oprah Winfrey" show. Her guests were women who had stayed married to men who had done truly horrible things. One had molested their six-year-old daughter. One had embezzled hundreds of thousands of dollars from his company's pension fund. One had shot and killed his own mother in a drunken rage. The women on the panel all said they still loved their husbands. They said they were able to separate who these men were from the things they had done. The women all seemed so sincere, truly loving. Still, Oprah could hardly believe them. She kept shaking her head.

"I don't know, David," I said. "I can't understand Barbara all the time." This was true. Though I had known about the affair for months, what she was doing didn't exactly make sense to me. But Barbara was so headstrong; once she made up her mind to do something, she could never be persuaded otherwise.

"We are so free and we want so much," David said with some deliberation. David sometimes makes these sweeping philosophical statements, as academics tend to do. But in the next few weeks I thought about this observation quite a bit. I thought about what we want, how easy it is to get it, and how the consequences never seem quite clear at the time.

I also thought about what Barbara said later that afternoon as she walked me back to the car. She said, "Maybe you don't understand this, what it's like to live with someone who doesn't make you happy, but if I don't make this move, I might regret it for the rest of my life."

Chapter 2

*I*t was a year in the making, but I honestly didn't see it coming, except perhaps that Barbara kept asking questions about my relationship with Jesse—what was it that made me love him, why did I stay with him?

"Well, why would I leave?" I asked. I had not been talking about leaving. I took the first question as something of an insult. Barbara and I had been friends for years, so she knew Jesse's good points.

"I'm interested in what keeps people together," Barbara had said. "I mean people in general. Not you."

It was a hot July afternoon and I had just put Libby down for a nap. I pulled the shade in her room and tucked Woo-baby in beside her.

Barbara and I were sitting on the front porch drinking seltzer with slices of lime and she was still in her dress-for-success white linen suit. I was wearing jeans and one of Jesse's old T-shirts. All morning I had been grubbing around in the garden, weeding between the tomato plants while Libby splashed in her plastic pool.

"How come you don't have to go back to work this afternoon?" I asked.

"I took some time off because I'm leaving for L.A. tomorrow at eight and I wanted to spend some time with the girls."

Barbara had a job selling medical equipment to hospitals. A few times a year she went to conventions where she looked at machines that replace blood and unclog arteries.

"God, it's hot," Barbara said, reaching up under her skirt to peel off her pantyhose. Even without any sun, her legs were darker than mine—berry brown with glints of red. "I don't know if I can stand this much longer," she said.

"The heat?"

"This job. Never having any free time. Two days at Christmas and two weeks off for the whole damn year."

"The money is terrific," I said. Barbara makes more than three times what I do and the men she works with dote on her. They like her because she is not uppity and has nice legs.

"It's not *that* terrific. I could make more in a bigger city."

Clearly, she did not want to be placated. It was hot. Her feet hurt. Yesterday, the pediatrician had told them that Amanda needed to go in for a series of allergy shots. Every year she was red-eyed and runny until the first frost.

"It's just too much," Barbara said, distractedly fingering a dusty smudge on her white skirt.

"Don't rub at that. Use Woolite in a little cold water when you get home."

"I don't have Woolite. I send everything to the cleaners. Washing things by hand is one of the things I don't have time to do."

"Give it to me," I said, snapping my fingers. "I'll do it now."

Underneath, Barbara had on an exquisite slip, white and delicate as cigarette paper, edged in lace.

"If you didn't have this good job, you couldn't buy such expensive underwear," I said, walking away with her skirt. Sometimes I told Barbara how good she has it when she complained. It was part of the dynamic of our friendship. She didn't like it that David never got mad. I told her most of the women in this country would like to live with a man who never got mad. I told her we could turn all the battered women's shelters into condominiums. Sometimes she lamented the fact that David did not initiate sex as often as she liked. I told her that backrubs, at which David was adept, should count for something in the way of physical intimacy. David *touched*, and think of all the men who never touch but just grope for their wives in the dark and pump away. Is that what she wanted? Sometimes, Barbara said.

There was a longing and a restlessness that was strange to me but also exciting, because where I am always cautious and contained, Barbara sees beyond the usual limits. In another time and place (and most likely another sex) Barbara would have been an explorer, drawn to the glimmers at the edge of the horizon. Of course, here in our ordinary lives, the uncharted territory reveals itself only in trying out new restaurants or switching jobs. And Barbara used to have occasional affairs.

There were these men. They came into Barbara's life like meteors, falling from the sky—all speed and light, a burst of flame against the dark, and then they were gone, incorporeal and substanceless. But now in these times we are afraid. In these times, all single men are seen as possible sources of infection.

When I came back to the porch, Barbara was sitting in her slip talking to the mailman. "Sure is a scorcher," he said, handing me a pile of bills and requests for money from a half-dozen liberal-feminist-environmentalist organizations. On one envelope was a picture of a handsome gorilla with soulful eyes, his long-fingered hands outstretched in front of him, beseeching. Underneath it said: *"Poachers Kill Gorillas and Chop Off Their Hands Because Some People Think They Make Lovely Ashtrays. Do You?!"* The gorilla's hands were fine-fingered as a classical pianist's, the palms fleshy and vulnerable.

The mailman was all in blue, his shorts cut just above his white knees. I put Barbara's skirt along the back of a rocking chair, thinking that if I gave it to her, she'd stand and put it on in front of the mailman.

"Would you like a cold drink?" I asked him. He was swabbing the top of his bald head with a blue hankie.

"Thanks, I've got a thermos in the car," he said, motioning across the street where a Jeep sat under the shade of a linden tree. He hoisted his big satchel across his shoulders and walked across my neighbor's carefully coiffed sod.

"Andrew is going to come down to L.A. He's staying at the same hotel," Barbara said, chewing thoughtfully on an ice cube.

"Oh?" I tried to assume a neutral tone. Andrew had been divorced a few years before and his ex-wife had taken the friends and acquaintances over to her side in a clean sweep. When the affair began, he became very dependent on Barbara. I was surprised that she wanted to continue such an intense relationship.

I remember meeting Andrew that first and only time. It was right before the affair actually started, but I knew and Barbara knew and Andrew must have known, too. It was two summers ago. I was spending lazy afternoons on the front porch reading mystery novels while Libby napped. The zucchinis were voluminous that summer. I made zucchini bread, curried zucchini soup and a zucchini chocolate cake.

Medi-core, Barbara's company, was making diabetic pumps. One afternoon she called me from work and told me that two of their technical writers were on vacation and they needed someone to write up a description of the product and directions for use. "I told them I have a friend who does free-lance work. I'm bringing you in to work with me this week."

"I'm not really a technical writer," I protested. Even though I dealt with some scientific issues for my job, the columns I wrote for the home economics journal were pretty folksy.

"The money is great. And the whole thing will take you five or six days, max. You can do it. You write for a living, for God's sake. Don't be so insecure, Sharon."

"There are different *kinds* of writing," I said. "I've never done really techinical writing before. What if I mess up with instructions about something as important as a diabetic pump? Directions for taking insulin are a little more important than directions for removing mildew, you know."

"You don't have to worry about that. The researchers give you all the information. Then they check it over to make sure it's right. All you have to do is put everything in sentences. That's what the researchers can't do."

I was still skeptical. "I don't know. I'll think about it and talk to Jesse."

"You can bring Libby over to my house to stay with the sitter. Come tomorrow at eight-thirty," Barbara said. "And you have to wear stockings. It's a very conservative place."

The work at Medi-core ran almost until the end of August. I felt good because all the researchers seemed to like what I wrote, and one of the vice presidents even stuck his head in the cubicle I was in and said if I ever wanted a job with the company, he'd be happy to "have me aboard." I had written facile prose not only about diabetic pumps, but about nasal-gastric tubes and lipid suctioning devices. The reading had interested me. It even crossed my mind that maybe I should have gone to medical school.

That afternoon, my last day, I planned on taking Barbara to lunch at a new restaurant that had just opened near the Market Place Mall. "I'm sorry, I forgot to tell you," Barbara said, as we drove to work down University Avenue. "I can't have lunch with you today. I have a meeting." I remember that she was wearing a peach-colored suit of some soft, clingy material and a camisole underneath that peeked discreetly from the top button of her blouse. Her hair was wild, but around her neck she had a simple strand of pearls, so that the total effect was both professional and tarty at the same time.

I was disappointed. "Oh, damn. Can't you rearrange some schedules?" After even a short time at Medi-core, I knew that it was Barbara who usually called the meetings.

"I can't. Andrew Hally just has this one day. Then he's meeting with the board."

The name meant nothing to me. "All right," I said, looking at Barbara's hands at the wheel as we stopped for a light. Her fingernails were painted the same glossy peach as her dress. "Maybe tonight, then. We'll just go out with David and Jess for Mexican."

"Oh, not tonight, hon. I'm sorry. I know I'm going to be late." She flexed her smile in the rearview mirror. "Maybe on the weekend."

At noon, I bought a yogurt and an apple from the machines in the basement and was on the way back to eat at my desk when I ran into Barbara and Andrew. They were going in the opposite direction down the hall, but Barbara took his arm and guided him toward me. "Andrew, I want you to meet someone," Barbara said. Her voice was husky, the way it is when sometimes we speak on the phone late at night. "This is my very best friend, Sharon Burke."

I smiled, embarrassed. Somehow it seemed a childish description, to be introduced as a best friend. I offered my hand, which was damp from the yogurt container.

"How long have you been with Medi-core?" Andrew asked. He was as handsome as the middle-aged men in the daytime soap operas, tall and elegant with high, sharp cheekbones. He had very good posture. Barbara told me later that was because he had scoliosis as a child and had spent a lot of time in a metal brace.

I paused. "Just a few weeks," I said. "I'm just finishing up some free-lance stuff."

"She's *just*," Barbara said, dismissing my self-effacing usage, "the best technical writer we've ever had."

"Well!" said Andrew, raising his eyebrows.

"I wish she were here with us full-time," Barbara added.

There was something about Barbara's praise that annoyed me. I didn't know if it was the covetous use of the third person or the fact that Barbara and this man were going out to some fancy executive lunch while I stood there with a container of strawberry yogurt and a mealy apple. There was another minute or so of small talk before I watched them walk together down the corridor. Something about the way they looked next to each other sent a strange prickling sensation up the back of my neck. I went over to the window and watched them walk down the steps toward the parking lot. It was very sunny out and Barbara stopped to open her purse and put on her sunglasses. Andrew opened a button on his jacket. The white shirt he was wearing looked stiff and starched, pressed against his flat belly. He said something, gesturing with his hand toward one of the cars, and Barbara laughed, leaning her head toward him. I noticed that their hair was the same rich black. She said something to him and they were face to face, not standing very close, yet they appeared wrapped up with each other, connected in a way that seemed, even from afar, intense and intimate. Before it even all clicked into place, an unconscious part of me thought, Well, they really do make a nice couple. Then there was the moment of recognition, like looking at skywriting, seeing only white tufts in a blue sky and then in the next moment, reading the message there.

I watched them get into Andrew's car and drive away. Slowly, I walked back to my desk, sat in front of the amber glow of the computer monitor and ate my lunch.

Barbara called about ten o'clock that night. "Can you talk?" she asked. It was her husky late-night voice.

"What's doing?" I said casually. Jesse passed me in the kitchen with a bowl of mint-chocolate-chip ice cream, going up to watch the news. I shook my head, no, I didn't want a bite, nodded yes, that I would be up soon.

"He's really something, isn't he?" Barbara said, breathless. I knew that she meant Andrew.

"So I gather you had a good lunch," I said. "Get a lot of work done?"

"We did, as a matter of fact," Barbara said. "It just so happens that Andrew and I work very well together."

"Mmm. Sure," I said teasingly. I must admit that I looked forward to hearing about Barbara's adventures. Her affairs were titillating to me, but also safe.

"It wouldn't be anything serious for either of us, Sharon. This would be just a fling."

I listened to make sure the television was on upstairs. Barbara went on. "It's just something that happens sometimes. God, don't you sometimes meet men you'd want to go to bed with?"

I thought for a minute. In my office at work were only women—a secretary, another researcher, and the editor, Philomena Givens, a middle-aged marathoner who used to be a nun. Once, a man from the Environmental Protection Agency came to the office. He was a slow-talking man whose shoulders were covered with large flakes of dandruff.

"I don't think I do," I told Barbara.

"You're never attracted to other men?" she asked.

"Well, I am. I mean, I would be if I saw attractive men. I don't know. I guess I could see them as attractive . . ."

"Sometimes these things just *happen*, you know what I mean?"

"I still owe you that lunch. Let's go next week. Unless," I added tartly, "you'll be too busy with Andrew."

"Oooh. Maybe you're just jealous," Barbara cooed.

"I am," I said. "How come I never get to go out to lunch with men in suits?"

"Well, if you left that dippy extension service, maybe you would. You really could get a better job, Sharon."

I started defending myself. "I like having the summers off. And it's really easy work . . ."

"It's too easy. You're smarter than that, Sharon."

"Well, maybe after Libby is older. Maybe I'll start looking around next year," I said lamely.

"Listen, you don't have to tell Jesse anything," Barbara said. "About meeting Andrew."

"Of course not," I said.

"What I said to Andrew was true, you know. About what a terrific job you did with us."

"Thanks," I said modestly.

"And the other thing, too."

"What other thing?" I asked.

"That you're the very best friend I ever had," Barbara said softly.

Now Barbara confessed that she and Andrew had been writing steadily since he had been in California.

"How often?" I asked suspiciously. I knew she had been getting letters at work, a few she even let me read, but lately she hadn't said a word.

Barbara shrugged. "Hmmm. Two, maybe three times a week. And I've been calling him at night sometimes. When David goes back to the lab."

"So what does it mean?"

Barbara stood up to put on her skirt, bending to inspect the damp area. "Hey, thanks, Sharon. It came out."

"I used a wet-spotter," I said. (This is a stain-removal agent made up of one part glycerin, one part liquid detergent and eight parts water. This solution is good for many types of stains and can be stored permanently in a plastic squeeze bottle.)

"Do you want to be with Andrew?" I asked. When he was transferred, I thought the affair had been winding down. Then he came back in the spring for a training session and Barbara had managed to be with him almost every night.

"It was really wonderful when he was here," Barbara said. Her voice was unusually soft, and even though it was ninety degrees in the shade a little shiver ran through me.

"Barbara . . ." I began.

"Don't," she said.

"Don't what?"

"Don't try to warn me."

"Well, there are consequences. Come on, you know that, and if this becomes complicated . . ."

"It's already complicated." She slipped into her shoes and looked at her watch. "Sharon, I have to go."

"Why should this be so complicated? He's in California, you're here . . ."

"Because it is." She seemed impatient. "Because I love him."

"Oh." I felt dumbstruck and foolish. It was as if—couldn't I see, wasn't I supposed to know that?

Barbara stood at the screen door. "I need to talk to you. I'm going to call tonight after the kids are in bed."

"Can you tell me what this is about? Give me just a topic sentence?" I managed a smile, but it was stiff and forced.

"I'm going to leave David," she said.

"Oh, Barbara!" I started to rise, to put my arms around her, but something in the stern set of her jaw made me stop.

"It's something I'm going to talk about tomorrow. With Andrew."

"With Andrew?" I repeated.

"Sharon, I think I'm going to take the kids and move to California." She squared her shoulders and looked at a place on top of my head. In her heels she was a good five inches taller than I.

"You would move?" I practically squeaked. "You would actually move to California?!" My initial feeling was one of personal abandonment. All my family was in New York. Now my best friend would be in California. And there I'd be, stranded on the plains of the Midwest. Though I was thinking of myself, I said, "You're leaving David for Andrew?"

"Well, we're not going to live together. I really don't know what's going to happen. I need to give the girls some time to adjust."

"I see." I was surprised to hear a sharp edge to my voice.

Barbara sighed and pressed her forehead against the wood of

the door frame. "I know it doesn't seem right to you, what I'm doing. I'm not sure I can even explain it." Looking at me now, her eyes were sad. "Sharon, I feel *flattened* living with David. You know, when you see an EEG on a brain-dead person and the bleeps are all flattened out? Emotionally, that's how I feel with David."

"Barbara, oh, sweetie . . ." As soon as I touched her, she began to cry, but when I hugged her hard, I felt her stiffen against me. "Please," she said, pulling away. "Please, I have to go. I'll talk to you as soon as I can."

"Do you really think this is the right thing to do?" I called, as her heels clicked along the walk.

Barbara stopped and looked at me. "Maybe I don't know what I'm doing. But I know I need you to be my friend now, Sharon."

Across the street, my neighbor's teenage boy had just noisily pulled up their driveway and left the car running while he ran into the house. The car had a vibrant presence all its own— electric blue, plumped-up tires, rock music pouring out from every window. In a flash, he was back in the car and peeling down the street. I sat rocking for a while after Barbara had left. The heat pressed against me, settling me into the chair until I finally heard Libby's call.

Chapter 3

I always make compromises, as Libras are wont to do, seeking harmony and a peaceful balance. As a child, I was the girl to whom the teachers always trusted the class when they were out of the room. "Cooperative and responsible," my teachers would write on the back of my elementary-school report cards. "Sharon knows how to listen to reason," my mother said proudly to friends whose less reasonable children gave them pause. But even then, I chose someone who was not like me as a best friend, someone I saw as spirited and free.

In elementary school, it was Linda Tomalso, dark-eyed, dark-skinned, with a bright, edgy nervousness that occasionally bordered on hysteria. Linda was a tomboy and together we roamed into the far recesses of the woods behind our housing development, across streams and under roadways, climbing the sides of steep cliffs. "Follow me," she'd call, jumping from rock to rock.

Linda moved in junior high and I met Patsy Parker the first week of eighth grade. She had the locker across from me in gym class and asked if she could borrow my deodorant. I said sure, but was taken aback because it was roll-on, not spray, and there seemed something intimate about that sticky, little ball rolling around in the armpit of someone you didn't really know.

Patsy was a redhead, with exuberant freckles and one of those gummy smiles that are sometimes attractive, sometimes not. She was the youngest in a large family and by the time she came around, her parents were too tired to go through bringing up another child, or too resigned to believe that making the effort would make a difference.

I liked going to the Parkers' house after school. It was a comfortable, sloppy house with a family room tacked on to the sloppy kitchen. The addition was being built by Mr. Parker and his brother, who lived farther out on Long Island, but it was never completed in all the years I knew the Parkers, so that there was always plastic hastily taped up along an unfinished window, or cans of spray paint sitting under the television set.

Mrs. Parker read historical romances and looked up vaguely as Patsy waltzed in and out. From habit, Mrs. Parker still made huge meals, although there was only Patsy and one brother still home. As far as I could see there was never any formal dinner hour—the food was just always on the stove. People ate when they were hungry. Mrs. Parker would be sitting with an afghan over her lap, twirling her hair as she read, and Mr. Parker or his brother would come in, paint-splattered, sawdust still in their hair, and help themselves to a plate of beans or slices of over-cooked roasts.

The Parkers never asked where Patsy was going or when she'd be home, and I was shocked when she smoked cigarettes right in front of them and her mother passed her an ashtray as if it were the most ordinary thing in the world.

Patsy was not actually in the hoody crowd—the beauty-school girls who drove with boys in fast cars—but she had a rebellious streak. In school she was smart, a whiz at all kinds of math, sailing right through trig and calculus when I had decided to call it quits after intermediate algebra. But if Patsy didn't like a subject, or she didn't respect the teacher, she didn't much care. Then she copied her papers or cheated on tests with a lack of conscience I admired. "Because it's bullshit, Sharon," she used to say. "I wouldn't waste my time."

Patsy was determined to lose her virginity by the time she was a senior in high school. She thought of it as something she had to do before she went off to college, like taking her SATs.

I remember the day after she and her boyfriend went all the way. Patsy came over to my house and we flew up to my room and closed the door. I looked at her face to see if there was anything different, but it was the same Patsy. She told me that they had done it right in her own bedroom and there was blood all over the sheets. I gasped. (Blood is hard to get out unless it is soaked immediately in cold water.) Patsy said she was just going to throw the sheet away.

"Won't your mother know?" I asked. In our house my mother was fastidious about laundry and the sheets were all color-coordinated, each with matching comforters and two sets of pillow cases. Except in a motel, I had never even slept on a white sheet.

"She has no idea," Patsy said. "You know our house."

I thought of the Parkers' kitchen, a jumble of mismatched jelly glasses and chipped coffee cups. The linen supply would be equally hodgepodge.

"Well, how was it?" I whispered, listening for my mother's foot on the stairs. Facing a closed door, my mother was inclined to knock and enter, managing to do both with just one movement.

"It wasn't bad at all. I mean, I was expecting some incredible pain and it felt more like—I don't know—maybe pulling a muscle or something. I could see where it could get good, later on. I mean, if you had some time."

"Wow!" I said, hugging her in congratulations, her red frizzy hair tickling the side of my face.

I remember the particular way Patsy smelled. Her natural body scent had a pleasant piquancy to it, like some kind of cooking spice, bay leaves maybe, or rosemary. We exchanged clothing so frequently that when I stood in front of my closet, wondering what to wear, and sliding things along the rack, I breathed what I called the Patsy smell.

Years after Patsy died, I once had a little girl from Libby's daycare over to play. It was a hot afternoon and the children were out in the yard most of the morning. When I called them in for lunch, I reached down to pick up the little girl and put her on a kitchen stool. Instantly, the smell of that child's sweaty neck, the sharp sweetness of her, brought tears to my eyes. It was that same Patsy smell.

It's harder to have a best friend when you're married. All the Saturday nights are so neatly coupled, the days during the week so busy, that there doesn't leave enough room for nourishing such a special relationship. Then, too, there are jealousies, about loyalties and keeping certain things private. Sometimes I used to feel uncomfortable talking on the phone with Barbara when Jesse was home. But we were friends all together, Barbara, David, Jesse and I. At least I thought we were.

I used to like to tell people how Jesse and I met Barbara and David. "They came with the house," I'd explain. I could just see them, sitting on the front porch of what was going to be our new home. It was summer then, too. Barbara wore a sun dress, gauzy, with huge splashes of color, her thick, dark hair pulled back tightly in a braid. I thought she looked like an Indian princess. David, bespectacled and slim, sat in a hammock, holding a glass of wine.

"Along with the house, I'd like to give you our friends, Barbara and David Glasser!" Making the introductions was Penelope Avramedes, who was moving with her husband, Christos, back to their native Greece. In the midst of the chaos of packing, Penelope had decided to have a dinner party. We had just bought their house, an old Dutch colonial along a tree-lined street a few miles from the university, where Jesse had a research appointment.

The best part of the house was the porch, a huge, old-fashioned, drink-lemonade-and-swing kind of porch that wrapped all the way around the front and side of the house. "I loved this porch," said Penelope wistfully when I told her that the porch was what had sold me on the house. "I'd be in that hammock over there and nurse my babies, looking up at the stars, and I could be anywhere, in some tiny village near my home."

"Barbara is having a baby, you know," Christos said, stroking her belly in what I thought was a sensuous gesture. Barbara was only three months along with Amanda at the time and didn't show at all, so it wasn't like when you pat a stomach that is big and obviously pregnant.

"When are you due?" I asked, catching Jesse's eye. A year before, a year on July twenty-fifth, we had lost Carlie. He was a perfect baby, round-headed, chubby, like all the pictures you ever see of babies in diaper commercials. The image I always have of him is after his bath, bright-eyed and sleek as a little seal. Sometimes the thought of him stabs me like a needle in the heart.

"In January." Barbara turned to look at David.

"January fifteenth," he said.

"Both my babies were born in the winter," Penelope said, rocking back and forth in a chair as if she were soothing an infant. "It's a good time. You'd just stay inside anyway."

"I'm going back to work after six weeks," Barbara said. "I think I'd get loony staying in the house with a baby all winter."

"Well, we'll see . . . ," David began, but Barbara stopped him.

"That's all I get, David. Six weeks is the most I can take."

"American women can do it all," Christos said heartily, and raised his glass in a toast. Jesse and I raised our glasses as well, both of us glad to stop talking about babies.

It was a wonderful dinner. Penelope had stuffed vegetables—summer squash and eggplant and potatoes—with spicy chunks of marinated lamb, artfully arranged on a platter with sliced lemons and greens. There was a cold cucumber soup laced with dill, and fluffy popovers that had a sweet cheese in the center. Except for Barbara, we all got high on ouzo and kept toasting to a new home, a trip home, a new life. Then Christos raced down to the basement and came up holding the FOR SALE sign proudly over his shoulder. We went back out to the porch while he proceeded to break the sign in half, stomping dramatically on the two pieces that lay on the floor. Christos snapped his fingers and Penelope, as if on cue, went to the stereo and put on some Greek music while he hooked fingers with Barbara and began to dance. "Join us," he commanded. Penelope went into the kitchen to start coffee and Jesse sneaked out to help, while Barbara, Christos, David and I looped around the porch, out the door, and onto the front lawn in a sloppy line.

"May you have only good fortune in this house," Christos yelled drunkenly. "May you live long and healthy lives under this roof!" Then he threw a goblet against the side of the house, shattering glass into a bed of begonias.

"He does this at every party at his house," Barbara said to me. "Be careful weeding."

Jesse called us in for dessert and gave me a quick kiss before I went upstairs to the bathroom. "How you doing, Zorba?" he whispered.

"Don't you just love this house?" I said, fondly touching the oak banister, rubbing my open palm along the walls.

"I don't think you should drink any more of that stuff, Sharon."

"Thank you for your advice," I said haughtily, stumbling up the stairs. I decided to sit down on the first landing.

"I'll go with you," Jesse said, helping me up by the elbow.

"You drank a million more glasses than I did!" I was feeling up for a fight.

"Well, maybe not a million," Jesse said, steadying my shoulder as I sat on the toilet. I was veering slowly into the shower door. I peed for what seemed like five minutes and felt sobered afterward.

"Let's make love," I said, stroking Jesse's leg from my position on the toilet. "Right now. Here."

"Sharon, you're drunk," Jesse said, but he was smiling and stayed still while I touched him until he became aroused.

"I'm not drunk anymore. Look." I got up and proceeded to walk a straight line, but the bathroom was too small to really show off this accomplishment. One foot ahead of the other, I stepped past the sink and made a right angle along the bathtub. When I turned back to Jesse, I started kissing him, pressing him against the wall as I reached for the light switch. We started standing up, then eased our way down on the floor. There was a mat, but we overlapped onto the cold tile. I inched down, guiding him in with my hands. "Oooh," I said, giving a little shiver.

"So soon?" Jesse stopped moving above me, surprised.

"No, I was cold," I said.

"Here." Jesse slipped out and took down a bath towel from behind the door. "Lift up now."

I was so excited that just the smell of his neck made me groan aloud, even before he was in me again. "Shhh," he said, petting my hair back from my face. Downstairs, we could hear Christos's voice booming across the kitchen: "Penelope, get the cups for espresso. Where the hell are they?" Cabinets opened and slammed, opened and slammed. "Penelope, David wants a bigger piece than that. Yes, twice that size!" We heard David's murmur of protest and Barbara's deep laugh and more of Christos's loud instruction.

"I love you," I said to Jesse as we finished off in panting silence.

Everyone was back on the porch when we came in, apparently not missed. Christos was describing a movie he had seen recently and was talking with a wound-up intensity that seemed to feed itself as he spoke: "It was a marvelous film, *because* of this lack, not in spite of it. Because the main character had simply no moral conscience. None at all. He was totally unredeemable. So then when he *was* saved at the end, don't you see, that gave us hope for all of mankind, that everywhere all the biggest bastards in the world have possibilities for redemption." Christos gestured expansively into the night. Outside, the sky had a thin band of light around the horizon, as if we were all contained within a glowing ring. Penelope set out trays of coffee and slices of baklava, while Christos poured small glasses of a thick liqueur that tasted like sassafras. I felt sticky and warm all over, from the honeyed cake and the liquor, and between my legs, wet and sticky from sex.

At the end of the evening, Penelope took me aside, giving me the names of her hairdresser, the best places to shop, an honest auto mechanic, a good internist. And a pediatrician, "just in case." They were leaving all the cans of paint in the basement, some of which were still unopened. The washer-dryer that came with the house was old. The dryer made a rumbling sound, she confessed, and soon it might need a new motor. "My life will be harder, in some ways. I won't have all the conveniences back in Greece." She looked around a white-tiled kitchen where everything was frost-free, self-cleaning, automatic. "But I'll have my family. That, to me, is the most important thing."

I admitted that moving to the Midwest had been hard for me. That I had been used to seeing my parents when we lived in New York. And I missed my grandmother.

"You lived with them?" Penelope asked.

"Oh, no," I said. "I wouldn't want to do that."

Penelope told me that she had grown up in a huge, extended family, in a big house filled with babies and card-playing uncles. "I didn't have a clear idea who my father was until I was already in school," she said. "But when we go back, Christos and I get our own house. We are too American now," she added almost sadly.

"Every time I find someone I like, they move from here," Barbara said, carrying empty glasses into the kitchen. She was looking at me, but I didn't know if she meant that she liked me and hoped we wouldn't move, or that she was feeling sorry that Christos and Penelope were moving away.

"Well, it's a college town. That's what happens. All these adjuncts and temporary people. I knew people in New York who moved their whole families across the country for a one-semester job," I said.

"Academic migrant workers," Barbara said.

"How long have you been here?" I asked.

Barbara moaned. "Years and years. I went to school here. We'll be here forever. We're rooted as trees."

We heard a thump that shook the ceiling, then a wail. "Hercules," Penelope said, wiping her hands on a dishcloth. "We packed the crib. This is his first week in a regular bed."

"Or out of it," Barbara said as Penelope raced upstairs.

"Their child's name is Hercules?" I asked.

"You should see him. He's two and about the size of a five-year-old. We call him the Incredible Herc."

"And Ari is how old? Four?"

Barbara nodded. "Now she's trying again. She'll just keep going until she has a girl."

"Well, good luck." I started to rinse out the wineglasses and noticed that the washer on the faucet was loose and the spray of water uneven. I added a new washer to the list of things to do when we moved in. "Do you care whether you have a girl or a boy?" I asked.

"Well, I know you're supposed to say as long as it's a healthy baby and all that, but the truth is, I'd really like a girl. I think boys are more difficult, don't you?"

In my mind's eye I had a flash of Carlie in his crib, proud when he managed to turn over for the first time, and laughing deep in his belly. "I had a baby boy," I said soaping the sponge. "He died last year from sudden infant death syndrome." Just saying the words aloud gave me a kind of ballast. Before, I seemed as if I were acting, not showing my true self. I was not a happy young married, excited by the possibilities of a new house, a new job. I was a mother who grieved, so oversensitized to the pain of others that I could no longer read a newspaper or watch the news.

"Oh, Sharon," Barbara said passionately. "I'm so sorry." But she didn't stop there with her sympathy, the place where most people stop, because they are awkward in the face of someone else's grief. She kept talking. She asked how old he was when he died. What he looked like. She asked his name. Carlie, I told her. Really Carl, named for Jesse's brother who was killed in Vietnam. Carlie had been an easy baby, I said. He woke up each morning cooing rather than crying. He had blue eyes and light hair, more like my side of the family; all the women were mostly blondes. Even though my eyes filled with tears when I talked about him, I felt better, more normal about who I was, grateful to be able to share the sense of who he had been, a baby who was loved, who was real.

"What'd you think?" I asked Jesse as we drove back to the apartment we had been renting for the past month. It was about a thirty-minute drive to school, but the only place we could rent without a year's lease. I couldn't wait to get out of there. The previous tenants had covered two walls of the living room with simulated wood-grain Con-Tact paper. The walls buckled and bulged so mysteriously that I had the sense that the paper covered up something even more hideous. "I had a real good time," I said. "Didn't you?"

"I did. It was a great dinner. She really went all out, Penelope. I liked her a lot."

"He bosses her around a bit, don't you think?"

"I don't know. Some of it's show. He liked sharing his house, his food."

"His food! That *she* slaved over," I said. I couldn't get myself into a true snit over this. The fact was, Christos and Penelope seemed very comfortable in these roles. He as the grand host, refilling everyone's glass after a single sip, and she as the quiet organizer of the gala.

"They're an odd couple as friends go, Barbara and Penelope," Jesse said. "Strange." When I asked him why he said that, he shrugged, but didn't elaborate. He is a careful, measured speaker, different from New Yorkers. I come from a place where everyone speaks quickly and interrupts others often so the conversation has a kind of momentum. Jesse never interrupts anyone, so my family thinks he is very quiet. The truth is, he's never been able to get a word in edgewise.

"Well, what do you mean, *strange?*" I asked. "Because Barbara is more outspoken, assertive?" I knew in some sense he was telling me that he didn't like Barbara, and I felt a tension, as if the air had thickened between us, the way it does sometimes when you leave a movie you loved and the person you're with didn't like it at all and you both know this information and each has a secret scorn for the other. I pushed on. "I found Barbara so interesting. Bright, funny. I liked her a lot."

"Good," Jesse said, reaching over to turn on the radio, twirling the dial through static and late-night FM voices until he found a country-music station. His face in profile was impassive.

"I don't know, there's something very alive about her," I added.

Jesse drummed his fingers to an old Ferlin Husky tune, his wedding band making little clicks along the steering wheel. I knew he was doing it to drive me crazy. I knew it, even if he didn't. "Don't you think she's attractive?" I asked. "Maybe it was the glow of pregnancy. I found her very sexy."

"She looks," Jesse said, pausing for a moment as if trying to recall, "mmmm, I don't know. I guess she looks—hungry."

"What about David?" I asked.

"He's a nice guy. Very smart. You know he worked with Stanley Cohen at Vanderbilt?"

"Who's Stanley Cohen? Sounds like someone I went to school with."

"The biochemist who won a Nobel Prize in medicine. He did all the research about proteins and cellular growth. Remember, I just read that to you?"

"Oh, *that* Stanley Cohen," I said, recalling neither the man nor the particular contribution. Jesse reads me things from the newspaper. Sometimes I listen and sometimes I just pretend.

"Now he's doing research on cloning salmonella."

"Stanley Cohen?"

"Not Stanley Cohen. *David*," Jesse said a bit impatiently. "It's very important work."

"Is that what he was chewing your ear off about when we came downstairs?"

"He wasn't chewing my ear off about it. I asked him about his research, Sharon. He's very excited about his work."

We drove down a long, smooth expanse of newly paved road and I yawned comfortably, feeling as if we were floating along. A few times I started nodding off, then caught myself abruptly. If I were this tired, Jesse would be this tired, I reasoned, and I didn't want him to drive without company. "So let me just ask you one thing," I said, my voice breaking the silence.

"What's that?"

"How come anybody needs to clone salmonella? I mean, isn't there enough salmonella in the world already?"

"It's all right, Sharon. Go to sleep," Jesse said gently.

I closed my eyes, counting the months. If I got pregnant from tonight's lovemaking on the bathroom floor, the baby would be born in May. And that would be good because my job with the extension service newsletter would just be winding down. Officially, I hadn't even started it yet; the job began the week after Labor Day. But already I was reading up on stains. Tonight, for example, I suggested the club soda when Christos knocked a glass of burgundy onto the pale carpet. Summer is a good time to practice up on stains. Grass. Engine grease. Blueberries. I fell into a dreamy sleep, images of babies, smears of wine and blood like a watercolor splashed across my mind.

Chapter 4

Somewhere between breaking David's heart and boxing up her good china, Barbara got the idea that I should accompany her out to California to help with the driving. She offered to pay for the airline ticket back to Illinois. "And Libby, too," she said. "We'll camp across the country, just us and the kids."

I had three weeks before I had to go back to work. And Jesse *was* busy trying to get a grant together. He could use the time to himself. "Oh, I don't know, Barb," I said. "Let me think about it."

"Would Jesse let you?" Barbara asked.

"Would Jesse *let* me?" I said. Barbara and I were friends long enough so she knew what buttons to press. "I'll go with you to California," I told her.

It was only the other day that I told Jesse that Barbara was leaving David. His reaction had not been charitable. "What are you talking about?" he yelled, though I was right next to him in bed. We were watching a rerun of the old "Bob Newhart Show." In this episode Jerry, the dentist, was going to ask a woman he'd been dating only a few weeks to marry him. Everyone—Bob, Emily, Carol the receptionist, even Bob's patient Mr. Carlin—knew this was a mistake. The woman was too possessive. Already, she had forced Jerry to give up his season's hockey tickets in favor of the symphony.

"Barbara is leaving David," I repeated. "She got another job out in California."

"I can't believe this," Jesse said, still facing the TV. "I really can't believe this."

"She's not going to live with Andrew. She has her own place. It's very expensive, so the kids will have to share a room."

"Suddenly, she just gets it into her head to run off to California. . . ."

"She says it wasn't suddenly. She says she'd been terribly unhappy the whole year. That she's been thinking about the marriage, about what to do."

"What your friend Barbara has been thinking about is her own little self, just like always, Sharon. Her own needs always come first, before someone else, before her own children."

"She wanted to go now. So Amanda could start first grade in California. So she wouldn't be pulling her out of school here," I said. Though Barbara hadn't exactly told me this, I was trying to mount some sort of defense.

"She is actually *leaving* David for this guy? This guy she knows how long?"

"Well, actually, a year and a half. But the last half of that he was in California."

"I can't believe this," Jesse said again. "Your friend really has her head up her ass, you know that?"

I nodded in a noncommittal way.

"That's ridiculous, Sharon," Jesse said when I told him what Barbara had said about Andrew, that she wanted to start her life over with him. "She's thirty-five years old and she has two kids and a mortgage. What does she think this is? *Romeo and Juliet*?"

"She says she doesn't love David," I said, mouthing Barbara's words. "And she knows she doesn't want to spend the rest of her life living with someone she doesn't love."

"She doesn't know what the hell she wants. She never did," Jesse said bitterly. "She's a very immature person." I was taken aback by his tone. Though I knew that there were parts of Barbara's personality that Jesse did not like, I thought that he had accepted her, even liked her, and saw her as his friend as well as mine.

I said, "You know, when my brother and Alice got divorced and Sam was very conveniently living with a new woman before he got an apartment of his own, I guess I don't recall you coming on this way with all these self-righteous proclamations about selfishness and immaturity."

"That was totally different with Sam."

"It was not *totally* different. It was different because they didn't have children," I said.

"Well, that's a big difference, Sharon. You don't just run out on a marriage. If you have kids. That makes all the difference in the world."

"So you think people should stay together even if they don't love each other for the sake of the children?"

Jesse paused awhile and turned back to the TV. Emily and Bob were in bed, talking together just like we were. They were discussing Jerry's doomed relationship with the bossy woman and Emily suggested that it was up to Bob, as Jerry's best friend, to be honest and tell him that it wouldn't work out. I was about to point out the irony of our situations, but Jesse looked so solemn that I checked myself. "Yes, yes, I guess I do. I think in most circumstances, unless there's abuse or they despise each other or something, I think if you make a commitment to someone, then you owe it to them to work on the marriage. Especially, if there are children."

"You know this is all that Catholic guilt about duty and obligation, left over from your childhood."

"Guilt shows you have a conscience. There's nothing wrong with guilt," Jesse said. "Which reminds me. Your mother called.

Did you remember Grandma Lela's birthday?"

"Oh, no!" I smacked my forehead so hard that my head clanged against the post on our brass bed. "Damn, I meant to send the card. I bought one last week. It's in the kitchen drawer."

"Well, why feel guilty?" Jesse said sarcastically. "Just because she's an old lady in a wheelchair in a nursing home and you're the light of her life, and every day she looks forward to the mail. . . ."

"Stop it!" I felt terrible. My grandma Lela was one of my favorite people in the world. At eighty-five, she was still sharp, interested in politics, the women's movement, the world. Her letters to me were painstakingly written and shaky, but they revealed a lively intelligence. Currently, Grandma's heroine was Corey Aquino, whose picture she had cut out of *Newsweek* and pinned to a bulletin board amid all the family pictures of me and Sam and Marc and the many pictures of Libby, her only great-grandchild. For Grandma's sake, I hoped the Philippine government wouldn't fall. "Today's her birthday. I can't call now," I said looking at the clock. Almost ten-thirty. Eleven-thirty New York time. "It's too late."

"Call anyway," Jesse suggested. "She'd probably be happy to be woken up by you."

"Do you think I should?" Already I was up, looking around for a robe. I went downstairs and got the book out of the same kitchen drawer that I had her card in. It was one of those sentimental cards that I would never buy for anyone else but I knew my grandmother cherished each and every word, as if it had been written especially for her.

The phone was right by her bed, so I knew that after a sixth ring she must have been in too deep a sleep to hear it. Possibly, the nurses had given her a pill. I was just about to hang up when the ringing stopped and the phone banged a few times in the cradle. "Hello?" The voice was barely audible, creaky and soft at the same time.

"Grandma Lela?" I yelled. Though her hearing was still acute, she was awkward on the phone, and sometimes didn't catch on to what you were saying. It was her immigrant suspicion of the modern, as if she didn't expect a mechanical device to be an accurate transmitter of human communication. "Grandma, it's me, Sharon."

"Sharon, dahlink!" She perked right up. I pictured her sitting up in bed, adjusting her pillows. "Where are you, sweetheart?" My grandmother had a heavy Eastern European accent, which I think she exaggerated as she grew older. Most of the others in the nursing home were younger and American-born, and Grandma liked setting herself apart.

"I'm still in Illinois, Grandma. I realized it was your birthday tonight. I wanted to wish you a happy birthday. I woke you up, though."

"Yeah, well, so what. Believe me, I got time to sleep. Anyway, so where am I going in the morning? To work? I got a job here?" She laughed merrily at her own joke. "You know how old I am today?"

"Eighty-five," I answered.

"Ridiculous, yes?"

"Not if you can still laugh, Grandma. How are you feeling?"

"I'm not going out dancing, I'll tell you that. For eighty-five, not too bad, I must say. I think I look more like eighty. But enough is enough. How are you, dahlink?"

For some inexplicable reason, I started telling my grand-mother about Barbara, about her leaving to go to California. She interjected occasionally with odd, tangential questions. What did David do for a living? Would her new job pay more money? Was Andrew Jewish? It was unlike the condemning response of my parents, of Jesse. Then I told her that I was thinking that Libby and I would take the drive out with Barbara.

"It's good to take Libby on a trip across the country. Very educational," said my grandmother. "You know how old I was when I came to this country?"

Having been told enough times before, I knew. "How old were you, Grandma?"

"Sixteen. Sixteen years old and I went on a ship across the ocean by myself. Some people got sick. Not me. I looked across the water and I saw this must be the way to a new life. So that looked good to me."

"Oh, Grandma," I said affectionately. Unlike my mother, who was a studied worrier, Grandma had a way of always looking on the bright side. I remembered when I decided I was going to marry Jesse and my mother fretted over telling Grandma because Jesse wasn't Jewish. The other cousins and nephews and nieces had all scrupulously married "their own kind," as my mother put it. "I guess I've accepted it," I heard my mother saying on the phone to her sister Sylvia. "But this is just going to *kill* Mama."

Then, Grandma was in her seventies; she had just had a stroke but was getting around with the aid of a metal walker and still in her own apartment in Parkchester. When I went to see her, she kissed me on both cheeks and brought out her famous honey cake, which she had baked for my visit. She looked frail lifting the tea kettle from the stove and leaning with one arm on the walker as she poured the tea. When we sat down at the table, I saw that she had to stop to catch her breath. "So, Sharon is getting married," she said looking pleased. "All growed up." She sat back in her chair as if to take me in, my woman's face, my "growed-up" figure.

"He's a wonderful person, Grandma." I began enthusiastically listing all of Jesse's good qualities—what a hard worker he was, how honest, how polite. Old-country attributes. Talking about Jesse in this way made it seem as if I were not really involved in his life, as if I were entering him in some kind of competition. My two older cousins, Sylvia's girls, had both married Jewish doctors, one of whom was a gerontologist who later pulled the strings to get Grandma into the best nursing home on the North Shore.

"Mommy tells me he's a goy," said my grandmother. It was late afternoon and the light across the kitchen made her white skin look nearly translucent, though a circle of rose blush carefully dotted each cheek.

"Well, yes." I shifted uncomfortably in my chair as the caned seat creaked in protest. "Jesse isn't Jewish."

My grandmother slowly stirred a teaspoon of sugar around in her cup of tea, then put the spoon to her mouth, her lips pursing as if for a kiss. She sat up and looked out the window. "I don't think that matters so much anymore."

"You don't?" I looked at her, stunned. When my grandfather was alive, the holidays, the Friday night rituals, were all carefully observed. As far as I knew, my grandmother had not a single Gentile friend.

"Religion." My grandmother sighed. "I don't know. Sometimes I think the world is better off without religion. Fighting all the time, everywhere. The Jews and the goyim and the Arabs, fighting, fighting, fighting. Feh!" Suddenly her anger turned to tears. She had been like this since the stroke, her emotions quick-triggered and raw. "I thought the world would be better for you children," she said. "I thought after the camps, when we saw the evil that men are capable of . . . well, I thought we would pay some attention."

I nodded uneasily as she went on. "So you'll have in common love, which is most important, and children, which is the real reason to get married. Tell me, dahlink." She reached across the table and grabbed the skin right above my elbow, pinching until I cried out. "Tell me you are going to have a family, yes? You're not going to be like some of these girls today who want only to walk around downtown with briefcases?"

"No, Grandma, Jesse and I have talked about a family. We both want children very much." I didn't plan on getting pregnant for three or four years, but I automatically put my hands on my belly.

She sighed then and released her grasp. "I don't think it's bad to marry a Gentile boy. He is good to you? He is kind?"

I said that he was.

"You know someday you'll own your own house. And with a home you always have to call in the plumbers and the electricians. The goyim are very good with their hands," my grandmother said practically. "They always know how to fix things."

Chapter 5

"She was thrilled," I said to Jesse when I came back to bed. He was reading a science journal and his lower lip was out in a pout. "Hmmm? What's that?" He began underlining like crazy, whipping through the article so that the pen flew off the page.

"Watch it," I said. "You're going to get ink on the blanket."

"No, I'm not," he said as a slash of black ink appeared across the top sheet. Then, apologetically, "Oh, look, you can't even see it. It mixes in with the design."

I came back from the bathroom with a bottle of Clairol Final Net. "What are you doing, Sharon?" Jesse asked as I began spraying the sheet.

"Hair spray. It prevents ballpoint ink from setting," I said. "I could wash it tomorrow."

"Did you call your grandmother?" Jesse asked.

"It was a good idea. Thanks for telling me to." I brought my own book to bed, an account by a woman anthropologist who had lived with a tribe in some remote part of the Amazon river basin. Their lives had never been documented before, but then this woman did some unanthropological things—like throw away her notebooks and sleep with some of the tribesmen—and so her work was eventually scorned by the academic community. I thought the book was fascinating. I rested one hand on Jesse's flat stomach as we read together.

Jesse was back into his journal and with just a glance I could see that not a single word in the title was intelligible to me. I look at Jesse reading sometimes and sense just how *other* he is from me. It has to do with Jesse's work. It is about him being a scientist and buying into a technology I am ignorant and suspicious of. It is about not being Jewish, perhaps, but it is also about being a male and all the ordinary components— aggressive driving, emotional block-headedness, etc.—that go with the gender.

What Jesse does for a living I don't understand. It has something to do with particle physics and fields of force with pieces of something that would push and pull at each other if they could, but don't, because what he studies doesn't even happen in this dimension—it's all theoretical. He spends a good deal of time working with graph paper, making dots, like ova, in red ink along black lines.

I met Jesse in college, soon after I had broken up with Jack Silver. I was in a science lab where I almost killed Jesse by accidentally setting off a steel ball from a projectile. It was baby physics, 101—a course created for humanities students who needed to fulfill a science requirement. Jesse was the physics graduate student who had to run the lab.

The first week, when I asked him a question about torques, I noticed that his dark eyes had even darker lashes and he had a pencil-line scar along his forehead that interrupted one eyebrow. I thought he was very handsome. So did the other girls— I could tell by the way they leaned into him across the black-slate tables when they handed in their lab reports.

About a month into the class we had a lecture about velocity and studied formulas to measure the speed of flying objects in relation to mass and the force with which these objects were hurled into the air. What we were hurling at the time was steel balls. We had lines of carbon paper set up in a path in front of the room which were to be imprinted with the pressure made by the ball as it landed. Then we recorded the distance.

This was hard to understand, so I tried to follow along as Jesse explained about how the projectile was going to shoot these balls across the room. "Set the spring on either hook . . . place the ball in the cup . . . pull the lever back . . ." In order to be prepared, I did the steps as Jesse demonstrated in front of the room.

"Now, what you want to be real careful of . . . ," Jesse said, turning to face the class, his hand on the spring, "is that you don't set off the spring prematurely . . ."

Just as he said that, my spring snapped with a *pinggg,* and I looked on in horror as the steel ball flew across the room, whizzing over the heads of fluffy-haired girls, heading right toward Jesse. It hit him in the chest with a hollow thump.

"Oh, my God," said a voice from the back of the room.

"Oh," Jesse said in a normal tone. Just like that: "Oh." He put his hand to his heart and rubbed. Everyone was still and silent like in a freeze frame of a movie.

I felt my cheeks flame as I began a litany of apologies—"I am so sorry, I didn't mean . . . I was just trying to keep up with you . . ."

Jesse held up the other hand and then continued as if this sort of thing happened all the time. "So you want to make very sure the field is clear before you lift the lever here to set the spring," he went on.

After that, I kept a low profile, studying hard. In the end, I came out with a C.

The next semester, I saw Jesse at a poetry reading. The whole auditorium was filled up because Allen Ginsberg had come to read. He sat up on stage, cross-legged, chanting, "Holy, Holy, Holy, Holy." The sweet scent of marijuana drifted up and down the aisles and there was such a good, peaceful karma in the room that I thought we might all be lifted gently from our seats the way the transcendental meditators said was possible. Allen Ginsberg, balding and cherubic, read:

> *The weight of the World is Love*
> *Under the burden of Solitude, Under the burden of*
> *Dissatisfaction*
> *The weight, the weight we carry is love.*

I spotted Jesse three rows down. I saw the sharp line of his jaw and the dark hairs along the nape of his neck. He was sitting up very tall, at least half a foot above everyone surrounding him, it seemed to me. I couldn't tell if he was with the girl sitting next to him, who was pretty and wore an outfit that seemed to be made entirely of scarves. I stared at the side of Jesse's face, so somber and deep.

At the end of the reading, my heart dropped when I saw him walk out with the scarf girl, her finger hooked possessively around a loop on the back of his jeans. I tried not to look at him as we walked along in a crush of people, feeling embarrassed, as if I had made some overture and had been rebuffed.

"Taking any more physics this semester, Sharon?" He was right next to me so that when I turned, my lips brushed against his shirt. I remember that it was a flannel shirt, checkered in red and white, like a tablecloth in an Italian restaurant. I hadn't realized he knew my name.

I wanted to say something clever and nonchalant, but I just smiled and shook my head, my face hot. Later I replayed the meeting in my head, embarrassed at the memory.

Back in my room, I looked through all the pic books we had in the dorm—the pamphlets with pictures of incoming freshmen, four years' worth—but I still couldn't find her. Possibly the scarf girl had come as a graduate student. I kept seeing her leaving the auditorium; I imagined her attaching herself to Jesse, tying him to her with swaths of pink and purple silk. That night I had trouble falling asleep. There was a wind and it made me feel all loose and fluttery.

The next day, Saturday, the phone woke me at eight. "Hi ya, Cookie!" said a voice, very enthusiastic for the hour. It was my father, feeling lonely this week because my mother was visiting her sister in Baltimore. This was his third call since Tuesday. "How you doing, Sharon?"

I tried to muster up some energy to describe the Ginsberg reading and the paper I was working on for my propaganda analysis panel. We were doing a statistical survey of the elderly in mass media and I was trying to pay attention to laxative commercials. Although my father never went beyond the tenth grade, he was intensely interested in all my college work. He looked at my education as an investment.

"What about you, Daddy?" I said. "Are you glad Mom's coming home soon?"

"The house is too big," he said, sounding forlorn. In two years, all three of us left—first me and then the twins, both freshmen at Cornell. For my mother, I think, it was a relief not to have those hulking teenage boys in her kitchen, drinking up the milk and practicing wrestling holds in the living room. But Dad missed the house all filled up with life. "Any new men in your life?" my father asked. He emphasized the word "men." Everyone I went out with was a boy in my father's eyes. I thought of Jesse and the word suddenly seemed appropriate.

"I've been admiring someone from afar," I confessed. Alone without my mother's cheerful voice on the extension, these talks between my father and me had special meaning. There he was without his family, pining for us in that big house.

"What do you mean, 'from afar'? How far?" he said.

"Remember the graduate student who used to teach our physics lab?"

"The one you hit with the steel ball?"

I had forgotten I told them. Probably I made it a funny story, one which my mother could retell to her friends.

"Yes, that's the one. I saw him last night. Actually, he was with a girl. I think it's just a crush."

My father sighed raggedly. "My baby." He sighed again. I could picture him at the big oak table in the kitchen, the sunlight streaming in through my mother's starched white curtains with the yellow daisy cutouts along the edge.

"Daddy, I think as long as I'm up, I'm going to try and make it to breakfast before it closes." The clock said eight-twenty—ten minutes if I wanted to dash over to the cafeteria before they shut the doors. "What are you going to do today?"

"I think I'll go out into the yard. Do some raking and cleaning up before Mom comes home."

"Give her a kiss for me," I said, looking under the bed for my other tennis shoe.

"Eat eggs. Get some protein," he said.

I kissed into the phone and headed out, unwashed and uncombed, wearing the same cutoff sweatshirt I had just slept in. No one was in the cafeteria anyway on Saturday mornings except maybe a couple of grinds who wanted to be first in the library when it opened and who sat hunched over their cereal, noses in their books.

It was a beautiful morning—blue sky with just the first signs of spring—the big elms along the quad with their buds ready to burst, ripe and full, before the blight had wiped them out entirely. Years later, when we went back for a reunion, Jesse remarked that he felt right at home, that now the bare quadrangle looked like home, like Wyoming.

I got to the cafeteria just as the sliding door began to move. "We're closing," said the woman at the door, tight-lipped, an early-morning grouch. Most of the women who punched meal tickets in the cafeteria were nasty. They never let you in if you forgot your meal ticket even if they had seen you a thousand times all year. And they always closed up exactly on time. "Get back," this one growled at me.

I didn't answer, but jumped in before the door finished unfolding, quickly pulling back my arm as the woman slammed the partition into place.

"Cutting things a little close?" someone said. Standing next to me, pouring himself a cup of coffee, was Jesse, still in his red-and-white shirt from the night before, a day's growth of dark beard rough along his cheek.

"Hello," I said stiffly, helping myself to a cinnamon roll I knew I wouldn't eat. I was aware that my teeth were not brushed and my hair was matted and sticking out in funny places.

Jesse followed me out to a table. There was a certain intimacy because he was all stubbly, still in his same clothes. He drank black coffee and watched me eat. Probably he had spent the night with the scarf girl. I knew he didn't live in the dorms. His address was in the Physics 101 syllabus—an apartment complex north of town.

"What are you doing around here?" I asked, taking a bite of rubbery sausage.

"Just having a cup of coffee," he said innocently.

"That woman is so awful," I said, looking uneasily at the cafeteria lady, who was pushing a mop and a bucket of gray water in a little cart along the aisle. The water slopped over the edge of the pail when she jerked the cart around the corner.

"Maybe it's hard for her," Jesse said kindly, "working for minimum wage and all of these young, pretty college girls streaming by every day."

I got up to get more orange juice and as I walked back, I saw Jesse eyeing me up and down. I must have looked disapprovingly at him because he said, "Oh, was I obvious? I didn't mean that. I'm sorry."

"You're sorry for looking at me like that or you're sorry for being obvious?" I asked. It was the first time I felt I had the upper hand.

"I guess I'm sorry for being so obvious," Jesse said. He had a smile that softened me, pressed into me.

We talked until we were the only ones left in the cafeteria. Jesse had eaten my cinnamon roll and one of the leftover sausages. We talked about the Ginsberg reading and I was surprised, because for a science student, Jesse knew a lot about poetry. He liked Ferlinghetti and Robert Creeley and some of the other poets that everyone liked at the time—although not necessarily if you were a physics student who came from a ranch in Wyoming. He told me that his mother was Irish and used to be a Communist. She met his father while hitching across the country, breaking her ankle as she jumped from the cab of a truck when the driver made a pass at her. Jesse's father drove by with a trailerful of horses, found her on the side of the road and took her to a hospital. Two weeks later they were married.

I thought it was a terribly romantic story. My own parents met through formal introduction by my mother's cousin Mildred. They were engaged for a year and then were married in a synagogue in the Bronx. The bridesmaids wore mauve. That's about as flamboyant as it got.

Jesse thought that being Jewish was itself exotic. Before coming to an eastern school, he had never met any Jews. Here, more than half the physics grad students were Jewish. "They're very smart," Jesse said to me. The back of my neck prickled. I feel uncomfortable with a compliment like that because the generalization opens the door for all the other stereotypes about Jews—they're very rich, they're very shrewd, they're too loud in restaurants.

At least he didn't tell me that I didn't look Jewish, which is something I've heard most of my life. Some friends in high school envied my looks—conventionally pretty in a blond, cheerleadery sort of way—but back then, when people started to wear black turtlenecks and go to poetry readings, I wished I had one of those dark Jewish Afros and a nose with some character. And, when feminism found its voice, I wished I were not petite and perky, but an earth mother with comforting breasts—a woman of substance.

"All Jews aren't smart," I told Jesse. "I know a lot of really dumb ones."

"I don't," he said.

Together we returned the tray, and he walked me down the granite steps of the student union. "Well, it's been nice talking with you, Sharon," he said politely before he turned and walked up toward the library. I looked at the back of him the way he looked at the front of me in the cafeteria. He had one of those long, rangy bodies that look so good in tight jeans. Reluctantly, I ran back to the dorm, the image of the scarf girl passing over me like a shadow.

It was strange after that. We just kept running into each other all over. Once in the bookstore. Once in the library. Once crossing in an opposite direction on a downtown street. It was always fast—him going one way, me the other. Every time we said hello, I felt something pull, not wanting to let him go.

One night I had an erotic dream about him. I was in a physics lab when I dropped my pencil under the table. It was a long, wooden table that had a floral skirt sewn all around it, like a woman's fancy dressing table. When I went underneath to look for the pencil, I saw Jesse looking down from the other end. Then he got under the table and crawled over to me, the pencil held teasingly in one hand. He reached over to kiss me and then we lay flat out underneath the table, kissing long and deep as he began moving his hands under my sweater. "We can't," I said, showing him that we were surrounded by the feet of various students, all working on their experiments.

"They won't miss me," Jesse said, kissing me along my neck, reaching underneath to touch my breasts. Aching for him, I started to move my hand to unzip his jeans. The clanging bell that suddenly went off in the lab room was really the alarm for my eight o'clock class. I shut it off and tried to get myself back into the dream, but it was too late, like missing a train. All morning I walked around in a sexual stupor, the dream vibrating through me for hours after, like noise along the railroad tracks.

It was later in the spring that our country invaded Cambodia. There was an all-campus meeting in the student union; everyone was aflame and there were speeches into the night. Everybody was talking about student strikes and taking over buildings. Some of the young liberal professors got up to speak. They said we should petition through the town. Keep it cool, they said.

At times you could hardly hear the proposals. Everyone was milling around in their own groups, talking, shouting down each other. We finally voted with a show of hands. No classes the next day. The local news station was there, a camera whirling over the crowd.

Someone tacked up a poster of a Vietnamese woman holding a dead child in her arms. Two boys in the back started pushing a campus security guard up against one of the tables. The guard, pink-cheeked and sweaty, looked younger than the students themselves. He elbowed his way out of the crowd and stood sullenly at the door.

I saw Jesse across the room, occasionally rubbing the back of his neck as if he had an ache. He was sitting between two short, dark-haired boys—the Jewish graduate students, I presumed. When everyone got up to leave, I found myself making my way slowly over to their side of the room. I was behind Jesse when he turned around.

"Sharon!" he said, looking truly delighted to see me. Then he invited me out to have a beer with his friends, Gerstein and Schwartz.

Lucky's was a bar on the north side of the city, a "townie" bar as opposed to a campus hangout like The Grill. Lined up along the bar as we came in were middle-aged men, some still in their work clothes, watching a baseball game. There were a few women in miniskirts, and some kids in high school jackets playing pinball in the back.

Jesse slid into the leather booth next to me, and Gerstein and Schwartz sat across from us. Schwartz was delicately featured with white skin—he looked as if he'd stayed in the house all through childhood, playing the violin or conducting chemistry experiments in the basement. Gerstein was masculine, but had long, hippie-length hair past his shoulders.

Jesse, with his cowboy boots, was the only one who looked as if he belonged in a bar like this. When the waitress came over to take our order, she looked mostly at him.

Jesse asked for a pitcher, which I said I'd share, and Schwartz added a shot of J&B.

"And what about you, ma'am?" the waitress said to Gerstein. She was standing slightly behind him and couldn't see his face behind the curtain of hair. "Do you want anything?"

"I want you, baby," Gerstein shot back with a macho snarl.

Realizing her mistake, the waitress fell all over herself trying to apologize. She called Gerstein "sir" and said how she just wasn't paying any attention. For a moment I thought she was going to give us all drinks on the house.

"Dumb bitch," Gerstein said petulantly as she walked away.

"Hey, easy," Jesse warned.

I thought he said that because I was there. Sitting with the three of them drinking in that rough-looking bar, I felt a little like a gang moll.

"You know what my number is in the goddamned lottery?" Gerstein said, his eyes blazing. He had come out of the meeting filled with fury, cursing our country, cursing Nixon, cursing "all those scumbags who run the Pentagon!"

"No, what?" Schwartz said without much enthusiasm.

"Number two! I'm a fucking number two. Now this is really funny," Gerstein said with a high, bitter laugh. "Really funny. Because I was the salutatorian at my high school. Stuyvesant High. Old St. Uvesant. I was number two in the graduating class. *Numero dos*. The only one smarter than me was a Chinese kid named Harry Fong whose brain was hooked up to a computer. Now I'm number two in the goddamned national lottery. There I am next month in 'nam. How will I look? Back, Cong, back!" Gerstein grabbed a fork and got out of the booth, fencing with an invisible enemy. "Back, Cong, back! It is the mighty Gary Gerstein, United States soldier extraordinaire. Green Beret unit sixty-nine. The yarmulke division. Get back, you slimy slants!"

The men at the bar turned with amused grins to look at Gerstein jabbing the air with a fork. I was hoping he'd sit down soon. If the men at the bar found out Gerstein's real politics, we'd all get beaten up.

"Let's blow up the fucking science building," Gerstein said, finally getting back into the booth.

"Gary just doesn't want to finish his dissertation," Schwartz said primly and downed his J&B in one gulp.

"Do you have a good number, Jesse?" I asked. It all seemed crazy. Calling out numbers like it was a game of bingo. Low. High. A chance of getting killed or having to kill someone else because your birthday fell on a certain day.

"I have an exemption," Jesse said, looking into his beer.

"What do you got, big Jess?" Gerstein hooted. "Flat feet? Hem-orrh-oids?"

Schwartz looked up with interest, blinking behind his thick glasses.

"Sole surviving son," Jesse said. His face was set flat, but there was a sadness in his eyes. "My brother was killed in Vietnam the summer before I came here to school."

"I didn't know that," Gerstein said softly.

I could hardly speak. I had not known anyone who had gone to Vietnam. All the middle-class boys I knew were protected, first with college deferments, later with medical excuses about congenital heart defects, allergies, mixed personality disorders.

"He joined up," Jesse explained. "Carl was a whole lot smarter than me. Had a full ride to Princeton. But he joined up. It was his rebellion, I guess. Against my mother and her lefty ways." Jesse shrugged. "It was his own kind of protest. To become a Marine."

We left the bar a little after midnight and stood outside in front of Gerstein's car. There had been a warm spring rain and puddles of fog rose from the black street. Gerstein and Schwartz were going back to the dorm, but Jesse lived just around the corner and he was going to walk home. Schwartz got into the front seat and Jesse held the door open for me. I hesitated for a minute and stood in the crook of his arm.

"I'd like to see you again, Sharon," he said, standing so close to me that his breath was a warm, beery mist along my cheek.

"I would like that," I said, wanting to say more.

"I'll call you." He bent to kiss me. It started as a friendly, see-you-later kiss, but then something happened. Later Jesse told me that it was because he couldn't resist me, that he just couldn't help himself. But I think it was because he had had too much to drink and talking about his brother made him feel wanting.

Suddenly he enveloped me, wrapping his long arms around me, the kiss secondary to the hug that lifted me, pulling me up like there was something in me that he needed. The kiss was sweet and filled with longing. In my mind, Jesse was going off to war and we were standing on the platform of some railroad station. Afterward, I folded myself into the backseat of Gerstein's car, feeling mushy and weak, as if I had no bones.

Chapter 6

"Let's name things I like, things I don't like," Libby said when I came into her room in the morning. Though she went to sleep with hardly a fuss, she liked my attention in the mornings, needing to ease herself into the day. It was going to be difficult to go back to work in September and give up these lazy times. We'd have to get into a schedule if we were all going to be out by eight o'clock.

"Let's see," I said, pulling back the yellow sheets and getting in next to her. She was still warm with sleep and delicious. I cupped her little behind in my hand. "You like Cheerios for breakfast, and I have some."

"I like Honey Nut better than plain, though," she noted.

"Yes. Next time we go to the store we'll buy Honey Nut Cheerios."

"What else do I like?" Libby turned around and nuzzled my neck, staring up at me. Her eyes were coffee-colored, like Jesse's, and they had a sensual droop that sometimes gave her face a wise, knowing look.

"You like Becky Jorganson and Teri and Amanda," I said.

"And Shannon Groovner," Libby added.

"Who's Shannon Groovner?"

"A boy who used to hit, but now he's nice."

"What made him turn nice?" I asked.

"His father said if he ever hits again, he's going to slam him one."

"Oh." I must have sounded suspicious.

"Well, he doesn't hit anymore, Mom," Libby said evenly.

"You like having your back rubbed," I said as I began to stroke her smooth shoulders. "You like picking strawberries and you like to use your paints and you like Daddy. . . ."

"I *love* Daddy," Libby interrupted.

"Me, too," I said.

"Okay, let's do don't like," she said with some authority.

"Let's see . . . you don't like cooked peas . . ."

"I like only *fresh!*"

"Yes, and you don't like Becky's dog that jumps up, and you don't like when it thunders in a storm, and you don't like having your hair washed. . . ."

"I don't mind having my hair washed anymore. I don't *like* it, but I don't mind."

"That's because you're getting older. You don't cry about that anymore because you're a big girl now."

"Well, I still want to use baby shampoo that doesn't burn your eyes." She sounded apprehensive.

"Of course," I assured her. "You can use baby shampoo even if you're a grown-up."

"I like baby shampoo."

"You don't like to get burny soap in your eyes," I said.

"Well, *nobody* likes that, Mom," Libby said. She gave me a patronizing kiss on the cheek before she stretched and slid down from the bed.

I took breakfast out to the porch so Libby wouldn't think of turning on the TV. She had her own little table set up in the corner, with the chair facing the street. Libby clicked her tongue if the cars were going too fast or if they didn't come to a full halt at the stop sign. They had done a thorough job of teaching the children at daycare the meaning of street signs and traffic lights; Libby knew the difference between STOP and YIELD and she didn't hold with drivers who blurred the distinction.

"Libby, I think we're going to go on a special trip soon," I said, nibbling the crust of her leftover toast.

"A trip where?" She looked up with a milk mustache, her face expectant with delight.

"Well, Barbara is going to California. She got a job there and we're going to drive with her and Amanda and Jana all across the country to California."

"How far away?"

"Well, it's pretty far. We'll drive for a lot of days. And we'll go camping like we did at the beginning of the summer at Shosh-a-pee Falls. Remember when we did that? We'll drive for a while, then we'll stop and look at things and then we'll camp. Me and you and Barbara and Amanda and Jana."

"Just girls?" Libby asked, her voice rose with surprise.

"Just girls," I said, sounding casual. I told her that Daddy had a lot of work to do at school. She didn't ask about David.

"What I don't like is, if Jana gets carsick," Libby said. "She makes a stinky mess."

It was something I had forgotten about. On the trip to Shosh-a-pee Falls, Libby had ridden in the van with the Glassers, watching disgustedly as every fifteen minutes Jana vomited into a bucket. "We'll give her a pill," I said. "There are special pills for car sickness."

"I would like it if just Amanda could go. Not that baby Jana," Libby said petulantly.

I thought guiltily how I would like that as well, how difficult it would be to conceal my feelings for Jana on the long trip together. Amanda and Libby played so well together. You could give them anything—high heels, an old slip, Tupperware, and they would spend hours in elaborate make-believe, switching roles as easily as they changed their costumes: You be baby, you be Mommy, now I be the teacher, I be the person in the store. Three is a hard number, but Jana complicated things more than she needed to. Her turns were never long enough, nothing was ever enough. If I gave the girls cookies, Jana watched, eagle-eyed, that her sister did not get the cookie that was a crumb bigger or the one with a few more chocolate chips. She cried at every imagined slight and felt forever short-changed.

"We're all going together in the big van," I said cheerfully. "We're going to see mountains and desert and woods. . . ."

"What is desert?" Libby asked.

"Oh, a place that's very hot with lots of sand."

"A beach, you mean." Libby rose up from her chair to watch a garbage truck stopped up the block. There was the noise of crunching metal and breaking glass and what sounded like an enormous belch from the recesses of the truck itself.

"Sand, but no water. A desert is a place that's really dry."

Libby looked scornful.

"Cactus grows in the desert. Like the prickly cactus that you have in the plant window at daycare."

"Is David going to live in California?" she asked.

"No," I said gently. "He's not."

"Are Barbara and David getting a divorce then?" Libby asked in a matter-of-fact tone.

"I think so," I said, wishing I knew what else to add. We had been through this before, following my brother Sam's separation from his wife. We said all the usual things, how people think when they get married that they will live together for a long, long time, but sometimes people change; they aren't in love anymore and they don't want to stay together. Sam and his wife had no children but Libby had been interested in the discussion of their settlement: who got the condominium and who got Masha, their golden retriever.

"So Amanda can go with Barbara and Jana can stay with David," she said logically.

"No," I said. "The girls will stay together. They'll come back to visit. We'll see them then."

"Well, that's not fair." Libby's voice rose and her mouth had this tight, strict line. "That's not fair if all he gets is visits!"

It struck me that Libby sounded more indignant at that moment than David had ever been in all the weeks discussing Barbara's decision to leave. David was not indignant, neither angry nor vengeful. He seemed, in fact, incapable of any emotion other than the sadness that draped over him like a shawl. There was a quality of gentle contemplation in David that I had always liked. He was a quiet man, a good listener, and didn't have many strong opinions of his own. But that summer I found his passivity upsetting. I wanted to shake him, to say, "Get with it, don't take this shit from her!" Sometimes the old stereotypes spring up, where strong men reclaim their women and set things on the proper course. Then I am embarrassed to think that way, to find that old-fashioned romantic idyll such a lure.

"Barbara is my good friend," I said to Libby. "And I don't want her to be unhappy. But you're right. When you get divorced, things don't usually turn out so fair."

Jesse was out in the backyard pulling up the creeping Charlie with his bare hands; he had a primitive and difficult approach to lawn maintenance because of his refusal to use chemical fertilizers. I liked the creeping Charlie myself. To me, it looked about the same as the snow-on-the-mountain, which Jesse planted alongside the garage. It was still hot, but the air smelled different, signaling the beginning of another season.

"I'm going to run out to Penney's to get more socks," I said. "Libby's inside watching 'Sesame Street.' Do you want me to take her?" I picked a garland of leaves off the top of Jesse's head. "Are you wearing these for a purpose? Is this the day you won your town the race?"

He ran his fingers through the dark curls. "I'll be here. She can stay if she wants."

Tonight, against Jesse's better judgment, the Glassers were

all coming over for dinner. "The Last Supper," he called it. I looked at my watch. "Well, 'Sesame' will be over in about five minutes. Why don't you have her come out and help you then? I don't want her watching TV all morning." Jesse, who is meticulous about not putting toxic substances on the ground, is more free about cultural pollutants. Libby is an accomplished performer of all the fast-food and diet-soda jingles.

"All right," he said crisply, pulling up viny strands of weed one after another. When he stopped, the lawn had a bald, brown space the size of a sleeping dog.

"Don't be testy with me." I leaned toward him for a kiss. He didn't say anything, but I knew he was feeling threatened about my going on this trip. Yesterday in the mail, a letter came from my old boyfriend, Jack Silver, who was living with his second wife out in California. Well, it wasn't a letter so much as a clipping. It was a news article from the L.A. *Times*. There was a picture of a man being helped into a police car. The article said the man, identified as Dr. Graves Stuart, had been arrested for running the largest child pornography ring in the country. THE KING OF KIDDIE PORN ran the caption. I looked carefully at the photograph, recognizing Dr. Stuart's distinctive beaked nose. "Oh, my God!" I said aloud, though no one else was in the room. Graves Stuart was an English professor both Jack and I had had for an honors lit course. "Oh, my God!" I cried again—Dr. Graves Stuart as the king of kiddie porn. Jack had written across the top of the picture, "Now what's this all about?" That had been Dr. Stuart's famous refrain in every class discussion. On the bottom of the clipping was a yellow sticky sheet adding that Jack hoped I was well, he sent his love, and included his new phone number—it was unlisted—out in La Jolla.

Impulsively, I went to the phone. Though I hadn't spoken to him for a while, we had kept in touch irregularly over the years. And this was news that needed to be savored together. Jack answered with a sleepy voice (it was 7:00 A.M. in California) which rose half an octave when he realized who had called. We laughed about Graves Stuart, caught up on family histories, and right before I was about to hang up I mentioned that I'd be coming to California in a couple of days. I didn't expect it, but Jack was insistent: Libby and I would fly down to San Diego before we went home. He would pay for the tickets. At first I said no, but Jack kept on. "Really," he said, "Ellen would love to meet you."

Reluctantly, I agreed, thinking about telling Jesse. Jesse prides himself on thinking that he is beyond the petty jealousies of romantic love. But he wasn't too happy about my going on the trip in the first place. Also, he was upset about my part in Barbara's duplicity. I had known about the affair with Andrew for a long time without telling him. He said maybe going cross-country in a van with three children under six years of age would serve me right.

The night before, neither of us had slept well. Jesse had been grinding away gently at my side, pulling me out of a deep sleep the way a fisherman tugs at his line when the hook catches something along the murky bottom of a lake. "Don't," I said, still in a dream, turning away from him.

He kept on, growing hard against my thigh, reaching around to cup my breast and bring me to him. "Stop," I said, moving his hand. I don't know how long we went on like this; soon we were both back asleep. Then there he was again, all over me with his hands, his mouth, rubbing up against me. I was saying, "No, I don't want to," only in a halfhearted way, not quite awake enough to take control. He'd stop for a few minutes, then start up again. I'd protest and move his hands, just as if I were in high school in the backseat of a car with some grabby date.

Suddenly I woke up. Really wide awake. I felt Jesse trying to work his way into me. Not forcing himself, exactly, but prodding, urging, little by little as if wearing me away, I'd open up to him.

"Stop it!" I said, my voice clear and loud in the darkened bedroom. Simultaneously, I jackknifed my knees and pushed against his neck with an open palm. He gasped and I reached to turn on the bedside light.

"You hurt me!" he said, sitting upright, rubbing his Adam's apple.

"You wouldn't stop when I said no."

"We were cuddling. We were cuddling in the night."

"Look, Jesse," I said, suddenly growing tender at the sight of him in the middle of our king-size bed, naked in a tangle of pink floral sheets. "I'm sorry. But you wouldn't listen. I felt taken advantage of. I wasn't totally conscious."

"For crying out loud, Sharon. I was sleeping myself. I was just loving you."

"Well, I was trying to sleep."

"I'm sorry if I annoyed you," he said, punching his pillow and turning to the wall.

I had a hard time falling back to sleep, fluttering as I was between anger and guilt. If I am truthful, I must acknowledge that some of our best sex has been those dreamy, middle-of-the-night couplings where we are so entwined that we don't know where one body leaves off and the other begins.

At dawn, I moved over to Jesse, spooning up against the curve of his body. "Don't," he mumbled in a sleepy voice as I pressed my hand along the smooth muscles of his chest. But I knew he didn't mean it.

At six, Barbara, David and the girls came over for dinner. David kissed me on the cheek, putting a six-pack of beer in the refrigerator, just like it was any other night that the families were getting together. "Are the shutters new?" he said, pointing toward the window over the sink.

"I just painted them." I was searching for the cheese grater, opening and closing drawers. I could hardly bear to look up to see his face. "They were natural wood before."

Barbara went out to the backyard to push Jana on a swing while Libby brought Amanda up to her room to look at Barbies. Jesse chose this time to attach the training wheels to Libby's new bike. This kept him in the garage and out of touch. I heard him whistling one of his lonesome-cowboy tunes.

"I like them white," David said, releasing the flip-top on a beer can. In light of what was happening in his life at the time, there was something unsettling about this small talk in my newly painted kitchen. It was like noticing the weather at a funeral.

"Here," I said, offering him the grater and a slab of longhorn cheese as he pulled up a stool at the counter. "The kids will eat a lot of cheese. You might as well do it all."

"Barbara and I talked about the girls staying here until she was settled in California," David said as little tufts of yellow cheese appeared on the plate.

"I know. We talked about it, too." I was chopping chili peppers, which were cool and slippery between my fingers.

"But I'm leaving for the conference in Munich—I've had those tickets for six months—and then when I get back here I have to set up three new graduate students . . ." His voice trailed off.

"David, you have nothing to feel guilty about." I went to touch him, but realized my hands were coated with the viscous juices of the chilies.

"I do, though." He gave a weak smile. "I don't know. I felt all the time that there was something I should have done, something that I should have seen before it went so far. I don't even know how it got to this point. My brother called two weeks ago and asked if we were coming up to the lake for Labor Day this year and I said, 'No, we're getting divorced.' He thought it was a joke."

He was down almost to the end of the cheese and had not slowed down. Afraid he would start shredding his fingertips, I took the grater out of his hands and gave him tomatoes and a knife. "You know how impulsive she is. I don't know what she wants most of the time either," I said.

"Well, like she rewallpapered the bedroom at the beginning of the summer. She ran around to a half dozen stores to get just what she wanted because it had to have the blue in it from the carpet, and then she wanted a certain border. Why would she spend so much time wallpapering a bedroom that she's not even going to sleep in?"

I paused. "Maybe because she wanted to make an effort. That at the time when she did it she was struggling and it was her way of showing she wanted to keep the marriage together."

"But then she couldn't follow through."

"No."

"Well, I hate that fucking wallpaper," David said sadly.

We sat across from each other in silence until finally David spoke. He said, "What do you think, Sharon? What makes a marriage work?"

I told him about this therapist I heard on Public Radio who had written a book on good marriages. She said the marriages that worked were the ones where the partners agreed, not so much about ordinary stuff like money and sex and in-laws, but on a certain *idea* of what their relationship was about. That it didn't even matter if their idea of the relationship was based in reality. She said, "Families create their own mythologies."

I had thought then about my parents and a family mythology that had to do with my father being comfortable and having his needs met. He worked hard so we were grateful. My mother showed her gratitude by making our home a kind of sanctuary for him. We children were not to talk back or show up late for supper because it would "upset your father." That my parents' *idea* of their relationship (really my mother's idea) was somewhat at variance with the facts did not affect how well this mythology worked for them. It was not until I was out of the house that I realized how flawed was their vision of themselves. My father was not a high-strung man who needed protection from the irritations of the outside world. I don't think he would have cared particularly—perhaps not even noticed—if the house was not picked up, polished and free from chaos. It was my *mother* who needed the structure and order of a peacefully run tight ship. I realized later, too, when there was talk of my father retiring, how much he really liked his job. He didn't want to stop working. Why, then, had I had the impression, all through my childhood, that my father was toiling away, performing backbreaking, highly difficult, even *dangerous* work? My father sold children's clothes and one year the Mafia was supposed to be dumping loads of inferior children's sleepers—my father said he wanted no part of it. Again, it was my mother who created the scenario they both came to accept.

"I think you have to believe in the mythology," I said to David, taking the warm pile of tortillas from the oven.

"What I don't understand," David said, "is that there are so many worse marriages than ours and the people stay together."

Jesse brought the extra chairs from the hall closet and I set out the meat and cheese in little bowls; a bag of tortilla chips was open in the middle of the table. Jesse poured some lemonade for the girls.

"I don't want a blue cup. I want red," said Jana petulantly.

"Oh," Jesse said, "I poured it already. Amanda, would you trade and let your sister have the red cup?" Amanda, at six, was well into the age of reason.

"I don't want to," she said clearly, drinking seductively from the red cup. Libby had a yellow cup and did not enter into the discussion.

"Well, just drink your lemonade," Jesse said casually to Jana. "I'll give you a red cup next time."

"No!" Jana pushed away the cup he held out to her and the lemonade spilled along his hand and onto her taco.

"For crying out loud," he said with a tone that one doesn't use for someone else's child. I flashed him a warning look.

"Here, Jana," Barbara said, opening the cabinet door. "How about a special mug? How about a Big Bird mug?"

"That's my mug," Libby said, reaching out for it, her little fingers covered with taco sauce. Then, grandly, "But Jana can use it now if she wants." Across the table I kissed the air in Libby's direction and spontaneously she kissed back; her top lip formed two delicate points like the ends on a Delicious apple.

"What's that?" Amanda said, pointing a suspicious finger to a bowl of diced avocado.

"That's avocado in lemon juice. It's very good on tacos," I said, offering her a spoonful.

Amanda shook her head. "I don't like avocados."

"Honey, try some," Barbara urged. "You've never even tasted an avocado."

"That's because I don't like them," Amanda said firmly.

After the children settled on drinks, extra napkins and individual preferences for taco filling, the room became so quiet that even with the air conditioning on and the house closed up you could hear the crickets in the yard. Moths and mosquitoes danced along the window and a few times a beetle flung itself, kamikaze-style, into the screen.

"I saw Mrs. Wilcox at Penney's this afternoon," I said. "She works there now." Except for Jesse, everyone looked up expectantly, but no one said anything. "She's in the misses dress department," I added inanely. Mrs. Wilcox was our next-door neighbor, one of the many plucky widows who lived on our street. She had baby-sat once for the Glasser children when both Barbara and David were at conferences.

"Was she the grandma baby-sitter?" Amanda asked.

Instead of picking up a taco with his hands, David was cutting his meticulously with a knife and fork; then he scooped up the leftover filling, spreading it evenly on the extra chips. I wondered what he was thinking about.

I set the ice cream out on the counter to soften, and Jesse and I began cleaning off the table. The girls put on some old dress-up clothes I had from the Salvation Army and danced around the living room, moving wildly to the rhythms of Paul Simon's

Graceland album. " 'Call Me Al!' " I heard Libby singing at the top of her lungs. Through the sliding glass door I saw David out on the patio, crying, and Barbara hugging him under the moonlight.

"Oh, God," Jesse said, whipping the dish towel across the counter so that half of it landed in the sinkful of soapy water where I reached to retrieve it. "I can't stand this scene."

"Do you want ice cream?" I called after he went back to the garage, but he didn't answer.

I finished up in the kitchen and went to call Libby for her bath. I wanted to get her in bed just as soon as the Glassers left. We were going to leave early even though we were only driving a few hours the first day. There was a campground along the Mississippi River on the Iowa side, and they offered rides on a riverboat and tubing.

Outside, David was sitting on the picnic table and Barbara was standing beside him talking, using her hands in a way that made it seem as if she were explaining something to a foreign person. David nodded his head. Barbara continued. She was wearing a striped terrycloth playsuit, the kind you might buy for a kid, and it stopped in a little elastic puff at the top of her thighs. Her black hair was held back simply with combs, shorter now than when I first met her, and cut in a shiny bob that always fell exactly right. Barbara always had the best haircuts of anyone I ever knew. David looked like the kind of smart Jewish boy I went to high school with—myopic, dependable, nice. I saw them framed in the glass of the door and it seemed like they would be preserved there forever, as if they were in a museum diorama.

It was past eleven before I finally brought the last load up from the dryer and finished packing. Jesse was already in bed reading a journal, an apple and two pieces of red licorice on the night table beside the bed. Every night, as long as I have known him, he eats fruit and two pieces of red licorice before he goes to sleep. Though initially it seemed to me a ludicrous bedtime snack, I have gotten so used to it that now I see red licorice as a staple on the grocery list, like milk and eggs.

"Let's see who's on 'Letterman,' " Jesse said, putting down his journal. He pressed the remote control and I settled beside him. The first guest was the Iowa Pork Queen, a wholesome blond girl with a slightly undershot jaw. Letterman was asking her what, exactly, were the duties and obligations of a pork queen. I said to Jesse, "I don't know why girls like this go on this show. He only makes fun of them."

Jesse said, "Well, they get to be on national television. And maybe they don't feel like he's making fun of them."

"Don't you? Feel he's making fun of them?"

"I don't know. I think there's a part of him that really likes this stuff."

The Iowa Pork Queen was saying that her primary duty was to promote pork and pork products, to help show the American people how pork, "the other white meat," was healthful and nutritious. She was so sincere in this declaration that even Letterman listened in respectful silence.

"Let's see if there's a movie on cable," Jesse said, aiming the remote control like a gun. Jesse drives me crazy with that thing; whenever a commercial comes on or when there's a break in the action, he always flips through all the stations to see if he's missing anything. He also does this in the car with the buttons on the radio. A song is hardly finished before he's punching buttons. I'm never asked my opinion, so sometimes I have to yell out, "Hey, I like that song," before his hand goes up to the dash. My brothers do this, too, I've noticed. Alice, my ex–sister-in-law, said she knew the marriage was really over when Sam changed the station on Cat Stevens singing "Morning Has Broken." It was the song they had chosen to play at their wedding.

"You want a little massage, Sharon?" Jesse asked, kneading me gently between the shoulder blades.

"Mmmm." I moved down and took the pillow from under my head. We would make love soon. Both of us were superstitious about that. If one of us was leaving the next day— usually Jesse, going to a conference—we would always make love the night before. Maybe there was some sort of instinctual meaning in that, a need to mark the territory.

"I'm sorry about last night," Jesse said, kissing me gently behind my ear.

"Do you ever wish you weren't married?" I asked. "Do you ever wish you had a life like Ron Simone?" Ron Simone was a single man in Jesse's research group, kind of dashing and debonair as scientists go. He got to screw an incredible number of students.

"Of course," Jesse said, moving along my spine with the heel of his hand.

I turned my head over my shoulder to give him a dirty look. "How often?" I asked.

"Not that often. All added up, maybe only a few hours out of the year."

"Do you ever wish you were married to someone else?"

"No."

"Oh, come on!"

"Well, sometimes, if we go to a party or something, I think about what it would be like to be married to someone there. Then I'm always glad I'm not."

"Oooh. Right there," I said, as he moved down. "The small of my back. It hurts from bending in the garden." I was a little sad to be leaving when all my plump, beautiful tomatoes were ripening on the vine.

"Do those back exercises I showed you when you drive," Jesse warned me. "And the neck ones, too. Otherwise you'll get stiff." He moved his hands down and massaged my ass. "Wait a minute, this part here feels very tense to me." He pulled down my underpants and began stroking between my legs.

"I don't ache there," I said, spreading to accommodate his hand. I turned slowly to take him in my arms, warm and welcoming.

That night I dreamed we were all in front of the Glassers' house, packing the van, and everyone was carrying out pieces of furniture, laughing and having a terrific time. Somehow we had managed to fit in the sofa and Barbara's oak dining room set so the kids had to perch precariously on top of chairs and everything in the back—boxsprings and mattresses and pots and pans—was all tied together with rope so that we looked like one of those Oklahoma families leaving the Dust Bowl. Amanda and Jana waved from the van, their skinny arms sticking out of the windows. "'Bye, Daddy! 'Bye, Daddy!" they called, not sounding the least bit sad. There was David, in a haircut that was much too short, waving away his family. I watched until he was a small speck on the side of the road and felt like the unwilling accomplice to an armed robbery.

Chapter 7

Highway 74 runs out of Urbana in a lonely stretch northwest to Bloomington, then goes another forty miles until Peoria. The alternate route, 474, skirts the city and joins back with 74 going straight north where it connects with I-80 just before the Quad Cities: Moline and Rock Island on the Illinois side of the Mississippi, Bettendorf and Davenport on the Iowa side.

The family back in New York is impressed by my sense of geography since I've moved to the Midwest. They remain like all New Yorkers, forever mixing up Iowa with Idaho and thinking that everyone from Ohio can go into Chicago for a movie.

"Go to Triple A and have them plan your route," my mother had suggested when I told her about the trip. "They'll give you good maps so you won't get lost." I told her that it would be hard to get lost going cross-country since Interstate 80 ran all the way from New Jersey to California. One major highway, like a scar across the country.

In fact, the trip was well-planned. Barbara had called ahead for reservations to the campgrounds and we had arranged certain stops. We were going to the Dinosaur National Monument in Utah for the kids and the casinos in Reno for us; I had never been gambling, and the idea of roulette wheels in fancy hotels held some mystery. We were also going to spend a night outside Boulder with Barbara's father, who had moved by himself fifteen years ago, after announcing to the family that his dream was always to run a ski resort. "My father's been very sick," Barbara had told me a few weeks earlier. "It's this strange liver disease. My mother's going to move to Colorado to take care of him."

I was surprised. Barbara's parents had been divorced since she was a teenager. Her mother then had a short and unhappy second marriage to a man she had met on a singles cruise in the Bahamas. She took him back to Pennsylvania where she continued to run the family business—a mail-order house that sold build-it-yourself antique-style clocks. "What about the clock business?" I asked. The clocks advertised in her catalogues were of designs unique to Pennsylvania Dutch heritage; that—despite the fact that most of the actual parts were made in Japan—was their special charm.

"I don't think she'd mind giving it up. She had an offer to sell to another mail-order company. Pennsylvania Gourmet Foods. They sell things like shoofly pie and scrapple."

"Mail-order scrapple?" This was hard to imagine. Once on a family vacation touring the Amish country we stayed in a Holiday Inn with circular hex signs on every wall. On the breakfast menu was scrapple, which is a kind of mush made out of pork leavings and corn meal that is allowed to set, then sliced and fried. I remember that it tasted something like burned rubber bands.

"Special mustards are their big seller," Barbara said. "Dark German mustards."

"Must be good on scrapple," I said.

"God, anything's good on scrapple," Barbara said, smacking her lips. "Scrapple and eggs. Scrapple, lettuce and tomato. Scrapple and spaghetti. Mushroom soup and scrapple casserole."

"A nice fruit dessert—pan-apple scrapple."

"What to do with leftovers—scrapple à la king."

"Scrapple *is* leftovers," I pointed out.

We made lists for the trip—toys, bedding, food. Inside the van was a minisink and refrigerator behind the front seat on the passenger side. "That refrigerator is bigger than you think," Barbara said. "It goes pretty far back. We can really stock up on the scrapple."

About thirty miles before Peoria, Jana started crying. She was dizzy, sick to her stomach, her head hurt. "Oh, damn," Barbara said, pulling over to the side of the road with such a sudden lurch that I thought we might end up in the ditch. "I forgot to give her the carsick medication." Jana began the spastic thrusts with her neck that kids do right before they're going to throw up, which make them look like baby birds reaching out for worms. Amanda and Libby scrambled over to the far end of the van. In a flash, Barbara flung the back door open and pulled Jana out just as an arc of vomit landed with a splat on the gravel. "Good job," I said, impressed with Barbara's decisive action under fire.

"I said this would happen," Libby whispered in my ear. "She always throws up." Libby stood behind me with her fist under her chin, looking smug.

"It smells back here, Mommy," Amanda complained. "Can I open a window?"

"It doesn't smell," Barbara countered. "And it's too hot to open a window. It's ninety-five degrees out." I looked at Libby, thinking that as guests along for the ride we both should maintain a certain detachment. I sniffed but could only detect the faint aroma of the air conditioner's reprocessed air.

"It does, too. It smells like vomit back here," Amanda said. "I think there's some on Jana's blankie."

"There is not!" Jana cried.

"Breathe through your mouth," Barbara suggested. "We're going to stop soon anyway." Then, in a voice filled with mystery and surprise: "Look at the sign. We're almost to *Peoria*. Should we buy something special when we get to Peoria?" The way she said it made it sound as if Peoria were someplace exotic and wonderful. Like Bali or the Land of Oz.

"Yes, yes!" the girls chorused, pumping themselves up and down in the backseat. Even Jana, who seconds before had slunk over to a far corner like a pale untouchable, had come to life. "Me, too, Mommy. I want to buy something in Peoria."

"Anything you want in Peoria!" Barbara said grandly, setting a precedent for what would become the general pattern of the trip. Barbara had a certain tone when she told the girls about the mountains or the desert or even the Stuckey's just off the highway. There was always the promise that in the next city, the next town, there was something marvelous to look forward to; something that we could see or eat or buy that was unlike anything we had ever experienced before; something that would make us happy. "Almost there," Barbara said, turning to give me a little wink.

"Pe-or-i-a! Pe-or-i-a!" Amanda chanted, forgetting the smell. And for just one fleeting moment, before the van hugged the curve of the exit ramp and the ordinary strip of gas stations and fast-food franchises came into view, I got a little excited about Peoria myself.

The sign said TRUCK STOP, but there didn't seem to be any truckers inside, just older men in overalls and seed-corn caps sitting at the counter under a thick blue cloud of cigarette smoke. They sat silently with gnarled, work-hardened hands circling white mugs of coffee. Attached to the restaurant was a gift shop of sorts, a small, paneled room filled with spinning wire baskets of trinkets and postcards. "All right," Barbara said with the enthusiasm of a camp counselor, "what we're going to do is, first Jana takes her pill, then we all go to the bathroom, then come back out here and each of you can choose a special present." She blocked the entrance to the gift shop with her body while the girls tried to look around her; over Barbara's shoulder, I managed to get a peek of some dusty, stuffed bears and a T-shirt that said "Truckers Do It on the Road."

"I don't have to make!" Jana screamed, flapping her hands back and forth in front of her in a way that made her look seriously disturbed. A couple at one of the tables looked over to us and smiled sympathetically. The woman was huge, with white arms like slabs of bread dough.

"Just try," Barbara said cheerfully, opening a door to reveal one lonely toilet and an old sink streaked with rust. Despite what some of the commercials say about popular cleansers, there are certain stains—rust, bleach, dried paint, to name a few—that are impossible to get out. This sink would be a hopeless task.

"We'll wait for you," I said, resting my hand on the top of Libby's damp head. The woman at the table was eating something covered with a floury gravy, and you could tell by the methodical way she brought the fork to her mouth that she was really enjoying herself; there was an elegance about her, a dainty pinky finger held out as if she were at a formal tea.

"You're on," Barbara said, holding open the door as Amanda scooted next under her arm.

"Did you go?" Libby interrogated Jana.

"Just a little," she answered grudgingly.

"Go ahead," Barbara said, positioning herself back in the doorway to the gift shop. "Then we'll all go in together."

After Libby and I came out of the bathroom, we filed into the paneled room as if it were a church. "Okay," Barbara said solemnly. "One choice. One choice only." She looked at her watch. "You have ten minutes. Make your selections wisely."

I saw Libby tense with excitement as she started through the narrow aisle toward the stuffed animals. She couldn't have been more thrilled if she were in one of those toy warehouses that take up a whole city block. Jana and Amanda walked slowly around the room, staring with the greedy eyes of lottery winners. Libby held up a purple pony with an electric pink mane and smiled expectantly. "He's cute," I said, feeling like a phony, knowing that if I were in a place like this alone with Libby I'd be acting differently. Maybe we'd look around, but I'd also let it be known what I thought of this stuff. Junk. Crap. Garbage. Like sugared cereals and plastic toys that break and almost everything advertised on Saturday morning television. Seeing the children now aglow with anticipation made me feel like the Christmas Grinch, mean-spirited and cranky.

The men at the counter didn't move or speak, but sat under the flickering fluorescent light, their postures as severely set as if they were in a Grant Wood painting. It is something I have noticed in midwesterners, this stillness. In the men, especially. They are very friendly and nice when you speak to them, but it is as if any extra talk or liveliness might be considered showing off.

Libby picked up a little bear and sighed as she clutched him to her chest for a trial cuddle. "Two minutes," Barbara called. She started humming something that sounded like game-show music. "Dum dum dum-dum-dum-dum dum dum dum!" The cashier, a teenage girl who sat stooped over a romance novel the whole time we were inside, now looked up, her interest perked. When Barbara yelled "Time!" the children squealed and even the men at the counter slowly turned their heads.

"Bring everything here," Barbara instructed. The girl rang up the purchases, careful to use only the pads of her fingers rather than catch one of her long nails. They were meticulously manicured, spear-shaped and painted the color of persimmons. I saw Libby gaze admiringly as the girl's fingers clicked over the keys.

"Sharon, look." Amanda showed me one of those booklets with puzzlers and teasers that reveal their answers only with an invisible-ink pen—"For Ages Six to Sixty."

"That's so pretty," Barbara cooed to Jana, whose birthstone bracelet and necklace had red rubies that already looked loose in their plastic settings. Libby, loyal heart, had stuck with the purple pony.

Back in the van, we headed off to the Quad Cities and Barbara, in a lusty, off-key alto, began a chorus of "The Rock Island Line": *"Oh, the Rock Island Line is a mighty fine line. The Rock Island Line is the road to ride . . ."*

She floundered after the first stanza and made up some of her own words.

"Get your ticket in the thicket, if you buy it, you can try it, so come on to the station of the Rock Island Line!"

We moved on to a rousing rendition of another song along the same railroad track: *"This train, don't carry no gamblers, this train . . . This train is bound for glory, oh, this train."*

Then we segued into *"I've Been Working on the Railroad"* where the children joined in: *"All the live-long day. I've been working on the railroad, just to pass the time away."*

At the "fe-fi-fiddley-i-o" part, we all held our breath at the final "o" to make it last until I was the only one left holding the note, crossing my eyes and turning pink for the last fifteen powerful seconds.

"Do it again, Mommy," Libby asked.

Instead I began a solo, singing plaintively about trains and whistles and being five hundred miles away from home.

I looked out over the even midwestern landscape, just blue skies, flat fields, an occasional copse of trees surrounding an old farmhouse. Barns leaned precariously into the wind. On one side of the road were hundreds of tiny A-frame structures, shiny metal, just a few feet off the ground. I had lived in the Midwest for several years before I finally asked someone about them and learned that they were PUDS—Planned Unit Developments for swine management—where each animal had its own individual shelter. Like pig condominiums.

"Five hundred miles, five hundred miles," I sang, my voice filling up the van.

The girls had settled back quietly, Libby with the glazed look of a child about to fall asleep, and Jana sucking peacefully on her thumb.

The sun glinted against the little pig houses and sent sparks of light across the fields. Out of the corner of my eye, I saw Barbara's hand go up to her face.

"Barb," I asked, "Are you all right?"

"How far are we really, Mommy?" Amanda wanted to know; looking up from the book she had in her lap. "How far are we away from home?" I turned when Barbara answered and saw that she had been crying.

"The odometer says ninety-eight miles."

"So not even a hundred, right?"

"It just feels like more," Barbara said, reaching for my hand across the vinyl seat.

I know Barbara better than anyone else. Better than the friends she has at work. Better than her older sister, Nadine, who still lives in Middletown, Pennsylvania, where she teaches first grade. I know Barbara better than her own mother did. Better than Andrew. Probably better than David, though maybe that is just ego on my part.

I think the side of Barbara that David and Andrew fell in love with was the most obvious side—that which reflected her passion and spontaneity; there was a kind of yearning hopefulness (what Jesse had warily called "hunger"), so that when you were with Barbara, there was always the feeling that something was about to happen. What you see on the surface with Barbara is a very self-confident, *today* sort of woman, the one who brings home the bacon, fries it up in the pan and still has the energy for great sex; a woman who knows how to send food back in restaurants and who deals efficiently with the outside world of doctors and plumbers without once using the abashed, little-girl voice that rises up in so many of us.

I also know another Barbara. She has a part of her that wants to please and needs approval, a part that cares very much about what people think.

I remember a certain dinner party, the time Jesse and I were invited to meet David's parents. His father had spent years nursing the original complaint: Barbara was not Jewish. He had not gone to the wedding, and only grudgingly called after the birth of his first grandchild. Then, a few months later, Mr. Glasser had a mild stroke. Barbara wrote to him in the hospital and sent him pictures of baby Amanda and encouraged him, as she did so often, to visit. Probably it was the recognition of his own mortality that softened him.

Barbara saw the dinner party as a kind of celebration that the family was really together. Jesse and I were invited, not only because we were Barbara and David's close friends but because we were also a mixed marriage and held up as a good example. When we were introduced, Mr. Glasser took my hand and stared searchingly into my eyes. I supposed he was wondering if I were really Jewish. The rest of the evening I found myself trying to establish myself—saying things like "*Oy vey*" and going into great detail about my mother's homemade blintzes.

Barbara worked so hard that night. There were candles and flowers, with everything gleaming and polished. There was champagne, which David's mother said she couldn't drink because it gave her a headache; and lots of food, which they both sniffed at suspiciously.

David's father had a narrow, sharky face and a head of silver hair cut short as a Marine's. Everything about him looked clipped and precise. His right hand, left damaged by the stroke, lay straight down at his side, as if, at any moment, it would be ready to salute.

Pregnant with Libby, I sipped cranberry juice, fighting back the need to belch, and made observations about what a happy, smart baby Amanda was. Whom did they think she looked like?

I asked. Amanda was already asleep for the night, so I turned to the framed picture on the buffet. It was clear to me that she had David's crinkly blue eyes and pale skin.

"Babies just look like babies," Mr. Glasser replied in a tone that brooked no further discussion.

"Barbara tells us that you're having a baby, too, dear," Mrs. Glasser said. Then, without waiting for affirmation on my part, she started going into the difficult, life-threatening labor she had had with all three of her pregnancies. David, the first, was apparently the worst. "I thought I was just going to die," she repeated a number of times, looking over at David who slumped lower into his chair with each gory detail.

"That's enough, Bernice," said David's father, and Mrs. Glasser's mouth snapped shut as suddenly as if a string had been pulled at the back of her neck.

We were passing around platters and bowls when Mrs. Glasser observed that Jesse had not taken a slice of roast beef and started to put a piece on his plate. "Thank you, no," Jesse said, holding up his hand.

"You don't want any meat?" Mrs. Glasser pressed, holding the platter still aloft.

Jesse shook his head, indicating that with the salad and potatoes and cauliflower in cheese sauce, there was already plenty before him.

"I made it for you, Sid," Barbara said to David's father. "I knew roast beef was your favorite. Jesse doesn't eat meat."

"You're a vegetarian?" Mr. Glasser said accusingly.

Jesse admitted he was.

"For how long?"

"I guess since college. I'm not that strict anymore. I eat chicken sometimes and . . ."

Mr. Glasser interrupted him: "Did you know that Hitler was a vegetarian?"

I stopped with my fork in midair, not daring to catch Barbara's eye. It was one of those remarks after which you expected someone involuntarily to spit water across the table and start choking.

"Dad," David began, but you could see he was helpless.

"No, sir," Jesse replied politely. "I didn't know that Hitler was a vegetarian."

Later, I went into the kitchen to help serve the brandied fruit compote that Barbara had made from a recipe in *Gourmet* magazine. "Let me see your chest," I said to Barbara, turning her around toward me. "I want to see where to pin the medal."

That night was the beginning of David's renewed relationship with his parents, encouraged—perhaps abetted would be a better word—by Barbara. After Mr. Glasser's retirement, they moved to Chicago and were actually frequent weekend visitors. I never knew how she could stand it. The Glassers were truly awful. Ungracious, cold, maybe a little crazy, but never in the way that one could appreciate like my crazy Aunt Ceil, who spends her days crocheting for the homeless.

Barbara was the most dutiful daughter-in-law, always sending thoughtful cards and presents and making follow-up calls if she knew that either of David's parents was going to the doctor (which, in Bernice's case, was fairly often).

As for David, he laid low, his customary posture. I think he would have been happier to have his parents out of his life forever. Who could blame him? But Barbara thought that was a terrible thing. "They're his *parents*," Barbara said to me after she had remodeled a small den as a guest room just for them. Aside from the affairs and the upscale career, sometimes she acted just like a traditional girl.

The Glassers' reaction to Barbara's decision to end the marriage was decisive and immediate. Once David told them Barbara wanted a divorce, there was not a phone call or an inquiry on her behalf. Despite the years of good deeds and delicious dinners, she was back with them where she started out—in the

Book of the Dead. Later she told me that one of the things she felt guiltiest about was leaving David alone to face his parents.

It is a common saying in the Midwest that if you don't like the weather, just wait a couple of minutes. Sure enough, as we neared the Mississippi, I took off my sunglasses to see the skies grow black and dust swirl across the highway. Barbara flipped on the radio but static crackled on every station. "Oh, I hope it doesn't rain," Barbara said as several enormous drops spattered on the windshield. Along the side of the road, the wind flattened the tall grass and the green metal road sign—two miles to GAS, FOOD, LODGING—quivered against the force. In the center of the sky where it wasn't dark, an eerie yellow light beamed down.

"One good thing about California," Barbara said. "No tornadoes."

"Yes. Just earthquakes and mudslides. Did I tell you that Jack Silver's house almost slipped into La Jolla Canyon?"

"Uh-uh," Barbara said, not seeming very interested. "Sharon, did you ever meet this second wife?"

"Ellen? No. I knew his first wife from college. Marcy. I don't think I would visit if he were still married to Marcy."

"Jesse doesn't care that you're going to see Jack?" Barbara asked.

"He says he doesn't." I thought how I might feel if the scarf girl suddenly popped up for a visit after all these years.

The wind picked up, rocking the van as Barbara clutched the wheel with both hands. "Do you think we should pull off?" I asked. There are certain things you can do to protect yourself during a tornado. Driving in a van down the highway is not one of them. A basement in a sturdy, brick Holiday Inn would be my first choice. Diving into the ditch alongside the road was only a distant runner-up.

A gust of wind carried with it a sudden deluge, rain so heavy that no drops could be differentiated. Barbara reached for the wiper controls and turned immediately to the fastest speed. "I don't mind driving in a little rain," she said.

"Well, maybe you should slow down just a bit." I winced as we passed a truck and the wipers moved frantically with a blinding whoosh. "Do you have your lights on?"

"Yes, Sharon," Barbara said with the same patronizing tone that Jesse uses when I make suggestions about his driving, that "okay, just relax" voice which I thought belonged only to men.

"Are we going to go on the riverboat, Mommy?" Amanda piped up from the back. She was using her invisible pen to go through a maze that connected a beautiful princess and her missing crown.

"The riverboat place is closed when there's a storm, sweetheart," Barbara said apologetically. "It's too dangerous."

Already the back of the van was a mess, with cutout fringes of paper dolls, spilled crayons, odd cellophane wrappers. Jana said something, but the thumb in her mouth made her speech unintelligible.

"I can't understand you with your finger in your mouth," Barbara said as she rubbed the windshield with her hand to clear the fog. She turned to me. "I don't think this defroster works all that well. Do you feel anything coming out on your side?"

Jana took her thumb out of her mouth with a pop. "Are we there yet?" she asked.

I felt a weak trickle of cool air directed down at our feet. "Is there a dial or something? Can you change the direction of this air?" I rubbed the glass on my side of the windshield as the rain pelted us from every side. I saw a group of black-clad motorcyclists, drenched and miserable, huddled together as we shot through an underpass.

"Mommy, are we there yet?" Jana repeated.

"Oh, I think this is it," Barbara said, looking along the top of the dash. "Here, turn that black wheel away from you."

"Mommy!" Jana screeched, startlingly loud. We were behind

a trailer truck that swayed ominously, sending out arcs of spray. I gasped and pressed my foot against an imaginary brake.

"What is it?" Barbara yelled, exasperated, as if she had been responding each time.

"Are we there yet?"

"Are we where yet?"

"California," Jana answered, somewhere between a sigh and a whine.

"Not yet," Barbara said.

In the next few minutes, Libby said that she had to go to the bathroom really bad, Amanda's invisible ink pen was lost in the crack of the seat, and Jana said that her blankie did smell like vomit. Barbara turned to me stone-faced: "So how long do you think Kerouac would have stayed on the road with this group?"

Chapter 8

The rain changed our plans. We crossed the Mississippi and began the distance across Iowa, a straight ride west on Interstate 80. "We could go to a motel in Davenport. One with an indoor pool," I suggested. "And a sauna."

"It's not bad now," Barbara said. "Let's just keep driving for a while."

"Sure," I said amiably. There was the sense that this was her trip, so my opinions didn't carry as much weight. I asked if she wanted me to drive.

Barbara glanced uneasily over her shoulder. "I'm afraid if we stop, one of them will wake up." Miraculously, after a bathroom stop, after cheese sandwiches and lemonade, after my torchy interpretation of "Puff the Magic Dragon," the girls were asleep: Libby and Amanda were draped around each other like drunks coming out of a bar; Jana was spread out on her vomity blanket in the far backseat.

"How many miles do you think it is across Iowa?" I asked. The landscape was flat and dependable, comforting in its monotony.

Barbara chewed her lip. "If I had to guess, I'd say, oh, about three hundred."

I checked the map. "Very good. Two hundred ninety-five miles from Davenport to C.B."

"C.B.?"

"Council Bluffs. Belinda, Jesse's secretary, is from Council Bluffs and she always says how she's going home to C.B." Belinda, at twenty-two, was cute as a cupcake, with a little pouty mouth and big, round eyes encircled by iridescent pinks and purples. She was a good secretary and could easily work her way up to administrative assistant, but she only wanted to get married and have lots of babies. Politically, she was somewhere to the right of Rambo, frequently suggesting that the best way to deal with the tension in Nicaragua or the Middle East was to "blow them all away." Belinda was your basic Total Woman terrorist.

The rain had become a dreary drizzle, and the dark, threatening clouds moved over toward the northeast. "I can drive for a couple more hours," Barbara said. "I'm not tired at all."

I thought about how we had plotted all the stops and how now everything would be thrown off. "What do we do about where to stay? We'll be hours ahead and some of the reservations aren't until the afternoon . . ."

"Sharon," Barbara interrupted. "It doesn't matter. We can find other places. It's not like these are exactly Club Med reservations."

"Should we call and cancel?"

"We don't need to. They won't hold them after six anyway," Barbara said decisively.

I had an immediate flash of exhausted travelers arriving at a campground, having to push on when they were told that every space was already reserved. I pictured frail retirees in Winnebagos and disappointed families in rusted-out station wagons. I didn't say anything, though.

Looking back, I realize we were not ourselves on that trip, Barbara and I. Not the way we used to be together, easy and natural in each other's presence. She had asked me not to judge her and I was trying. But how can you not feel the way you feel? It's like someone saying, Don't be angry, don't be jealous, don't be sad, when these emotions come out all by themselves.

So I was quieter than usual. If I was going to express all the things I was thinking at the time I knew Barbara would be upset. The feelings I had were complicated. It wasn't only because I was hurt, because *I* as well as David was being left, but it was also because Barbara's bailing out revealed a kind of behavior that I had previously attributed only to men. If a *man* had acted the way Barbara did in dissolving his family, I know I would be the first to condemn him.

But this was Barbara, my closest friend, who told me she didn't love the man she was married to. And now she had the *real* thing with Andrew. She saw that it was possible. Wouldn't I want that for her? For anyone I cared about?

Yes, I thought. Of course. Go to California to be with your own true love.

But then there was the other part of me that thought: What about commitment? Working to keep the family together? And everything suddenly seemed like a cliché. Falling in love. Running off to California (of course it had to be California. No one ever runs off to Iowa or Nebraska).

Once I heard Garrison Keillor on the radio reading a letter from a friend who had moved from the mythical Lake Wobegon. The friend in middle age lived comfortably in a university town, married to a woman he thought didn't appreciate him. He contemplates an affair with a woman who does, but realizes that in a few years' time the new woman would also cease in her delight. "Adultery is like horse-trading," he had said.

Andrew had never driven with Barbara in a car, listening to the bickering of the children, watching Jana throw up. Even in wonderful California wouldn't it all be the same in the end? How could she know?

♦

"Welcome to Iowa," Barbara read from a billboard on the side of the road. "A Place to Grow." There was a picture of Iowa's governor, who, despite the bushy mustache, looked like a fraternity pledge.

I read from one of the travel books Barbara had bought:

" 'Iowa's unique vacation regions provide the traveler with a wide variety of historical places, points of interest, and celebrations throughout the year. Whether you are interested in history, man-made attractions, or natural beauty, you will find it in Iowa's vacation regions. . . .' "

"What are the main attractions?" Barbara asked, looking out the side window. "All I see are cornfields."

Like the song goes, the corn was as high as an elephant's eye, the stalks twisted into each other so that you could no longer make out distinct rows. "Mmm." I scanned the list thoughtfully. "Well, we'd have to travel for the Threshers Museum in Mount Pleasant, but the Amana Colonies are right off the highway. So is the Maytag Historical Museum in Newton."

"Maytag where they make washing machines?"

"I think so. Yes."

"What kind of museum?"

"Maybe like the history of clean clothes. Women beating loincloths against the rocks. Washboards. Pictures of the first coin Laundromats. That sort of thing. Or how about this? 'The Grotto of the Redemption: each stone in this shrine was painstakingly placed by hand in one man's tribute to the Lord.' "

"I don't think so."

"There's the Herbert Hoover Historic Site at West Branch, Iowa. John Wayne was born in Winterset, Iowa. And the birthplace of Mamie Eisenhower is in Boone, just north of Highway 30."

"Sharon, this is making me nostalgic for Peoria."

"We're too early for the fair. The state fair isn't until the last week of August. It says this year they're having the Statler Brothers and The Grateful Dead."

"On different nights, I suppose."

A few minutes later, Barbara said, "I'm looking forward to living in a city again. A real city where I don't have to keep running into my gynecologist in the supermarket." She added, as if musing to herself, "Though the apartment is small. The girls are going to have to share a room for a while. I think they might even like that. Until we get a house. We probably couldn't afford a house in the city yet. Maybe Mill Valley. Or Sausalito." Abruptly, she turned and looked at me: "You think I'm crazy to do this, don't you?"

"Oh, Barbara." I turned to her, searching for comforting words. I wanted to say, Let's go back now. Let's go home and say it was all a mistake. Summer doldrums. PMS run amok.

"I can't go back," she said, reading my thoughts. "I couldn't breathe with David. I don't mean that metaphorically. There were nights lying next to him in bed when I actually couldn't catch my breath. I tried to talk it into myself. I'd go through this list: he doesn't drink, he doesn't hit, he doesn't fool around. I'd tell myself what a nice man he was, smart and respected in his work, and never selfish with money. I'd be finished and think to myself, Well, this man would make someone a wonderful husband."

"Yes," I agreed.

"But not me."

I waited and when Barbara didn't say anything else, I added, "Do you think it will be different with another man?"

"Sharon, it has to be."

I sighed. "I like David. You know that I always have. So it's hard for me to understand why you're leaving him."

"Whenever I had sex with David, I used to fantasize that he was someone else," Barbara said almost longingly.

"Who?" I asked, turning back to check the girls. Libby had sunk into an impossibly contorted position on the floor of the van but was still sound asleep.

"Nobody in particular, not a movie star or even someone I

knew. Just some anonymous man whose parts I made up. Or sometimes some attractive man I passed on the expressway on the way to work. When I didn't fantasize, I couldn't come."

I confess that I've occasionally done that during sex, but not on a regular basis. Mostly I just try to concentrate on what I'm doing.

"I don't have to fantasize with Andrew," Barbara was saying. "Ever. We have incredible sex. He just knows, always, what I want. How to touch me."

"Did you ever try to teach David?" I asked, thinking about all the antique-style clocks he used to put together. Each clock had the tiniest, most delicate parts.

"It didn't work for us," Barbara said, her voice rising. "It just didn't. And you would understand what I'm talking about if it didn't work for you. It's not only the sex. It's the whole idea of looking forward to being with each other. Always appreciating each other. Not like you're just doing time. Crossing off one day after the other and every day the same."

"Well, some of that just has to do with being married," I said evenly, knowing what I was saying would make her defensive. "You talk about bringing in the car for a tune-up and needing to buy more milk. You decide who to have over for dinner on Saturday and what movie to see. You eat dinner and you do the dishes and you talk or watch TV or . . ."

"That's great! Why don't I just drive right into that cement truck then!" Barbara pressed a heavy foot on the accelerator and we zoomed up behind the truck before she changed lanes. "Is that what it's all about? You spend your life watching every evening turn into the night before?"

I thought of Jesse in bed, reading his science journals, a stub of red licorice in the corner of his mouth. "Some of what it's about, yes."

"Well, it's not enough for me."

"I don't know what else you expect," I said.

"I want to be with someone who will make me happy," Barbara said, her voice nearly a whisper.

I remember when Carlie died, one of the things I thought afterward was that I would never be happy again. Never happy again, ever. It was the kind of well-deep pain from which I thought no one could possibly emerge. I cried, not only for the loss of our baby whose life had hardly begun, but for the loss of who I was, the girl I used to be.

We were living in Rochester, New York, where Jesse had a post-doc at the university. We came with all our belongings in a U-Haul and picked the first apartment on the bus line that was cheap enough without being in a slum. Despite the fact that the building was advertised as "modern," our apartment was so poorly constructed that things were literally falling apart around us. You could pull a plug out of any socket and a chunk of plasterboard would come along with it.

Because the walls were paper-thin we knew all the details of our neighbors' lives. And they, of course, knew ours. It was an odd sort of intimacy. We were not friends with anyone in the building, hardly exchanging more than a nod at the mailboxes, yet we recognized their tastes in music and movies; we heard their fights; we knew when they had sex and how often.

Upstairs was a hard-looking blonde named Sunday, whose boyfriend would throw things around the apartment during their arguments. He thought that on the nights they weren't together Sunday brought men home from the bar where she worked as a cocktail waitress. He'd yell, "One of these days I'm gonna come in and surprise you, you little tramp." Then he'd throw something breakable across the room and Sunday would beg him to stop. As far as Jesse and I knew, Sunday was faithful to him the year we lived below her. If he weren't such a scary guy, I would have told him that she always came home alone.

To the right of us were a young married couple who worked at Kodak. They were both named Terry and we could hear them in conversation: Terry, blah, blah, blah; Terry, blah, blah, blah. Terry the girl came home earlier than Terry the boy and invariably when he'd come home, he'd call out just when he was inside the door: "Where is she? Where is she?" in this slow, teasing voice. There was silence, then scampering and cascades of giggles as Terry-girl finally revealed herself. For work at Kodak, Terry-girl dressed in conservative pleated skirts and Jonathan Logan dresses, but on those afternoons I imagined her popping out from behind the bedroom door, clad in feather boas and black garters. The Terrys had frequent and enthusiastic sex—never lasting more than a few minutes—punctuated by Terry-girl's sharp yips at the finish. Then Terry-boy always went to the refrigerator and popped open something carbonated. Often I wondered if Terry-girl was faking it. How could she consistently have had orgasms in under three minutes?

In the apartment on the other side of us were the Heinrichs, an elderly couple whose only distinction was that they subscribed to both *Time* and *Newsweek* magazines. Occasionally, soft strains of Bach and Mozart came through the walls. I pictured them reading side by side, quietly comparing the week's current events.

I knew I was pregnant right after we moved in. I remember I was hanging a picture on the living room wall—a spidery Miró print that we no longer have—and I felt a little *pinggg* just in the place where I thought an egg would start cleaving and dividing. My period was late and my breasts were tender. So I knew.

The next week Jesse went with me to get the test results at the Planned Parenthood in our neighborhood. The waiting room was filled with nervous young girls who all looked like teenage runaways. There were a couple of boys skulking in corners to have a smoke and tired-eyed women—the mothers of the runaways, I presumed—who stared grimly off into space.

A gray-haired woman called my name, and Jesse and I followed her into a small room decorated with pictures of diaphragms and condoms. On a side table was a clear plastic model of a female pelvis, cut in half like an open-faced sandwich to display all the internal parts.

"The test was positive, dear," said the gray-haired woman, in a sympathetic tone.

I looked at Jesse and smiled. "I knew it!" I said.

"That means you're pregnant, dear," the woman said carefully. Then, repeating as if we were slow learners: "A positive test means you're pregnant."

"Yes, we know that," I said, unable to stop grinning. Jesse grinned back, but he looked sheepish, as if we were sitting in the principal's office.

"Do you know yet what you're going to do?" asked the woman.

"Do?" I asked.

"What you're going to do about the pregnancy," she replied patiently. "About the options of terminating the pregnancy or keeping the baby. Or the possibility of adoption." She turned toward Jesse and opened a yellow legal pad. "Are you the father?" she asked.

"We think so, ma'am," Jesse said in his best cowboy drawl. "'Course we won't be sure 'til the critter gets born and we see what color he is!"

"I see," said the woman, her pen still poised in the air; nothing in her manner revealed that this was an unusual response.

"We wanted a baby," I told her, trying to sound normal. "I'm happy about being pregnant."

"I see," the woman said again.

Outside in the parking lot, Jesse picked me up and twirled me around and around, then set me down on the hood of a car, kissing me hard on the lips. Then he looked solicitous: "How do you feel, Sharon?" he asked.

"A little dizzy actually," I said, still reeling from the spin. "Are you excited?"

"I'm excited," he said, kissing me again.

"Just don't be like some of those men who call their wives 'Mommy' all the time. I just can't stand that."

"All right, Mommy," he said. Gently, he began rubbing my belly through my jeans, making round circles as if he were rubbing a magic lantern to make a wish.

I had gotten a temporary job—starting up a newsletter for the Rochester Chamber of Commerce. Eventually, I was supposed to teach the secretarial staff to take over. What they wanted was a jingo-jangle of buzz words—positive growth, the challenge of tomorrow, building a better future, that sort of thing. Everyone thought I was a terrific writer. No one seemed to realize that the Chamber of Commerce newsletter didn't actually say anything.

Two days a week I worked at the Chamber of Commerce; the rest of the time I stayed in bed, reading novels, or scavenged the city for used baby furniture. I was alone a lot that year. There was no one at the Chamber of Commerce to make friends with, and the other post-docs in Jesse's research group were studious foreign students who nodded a lot but couldn't hold up their end of the conversation.

The winter was gray and bitterly cold, as Rochester winters tend to be, but inside the apartment I kept turning down the thermostat. I was hot all the time, the force of a new life emanating from me like a space heater. After supper, I took long walks by myself into the blustery night. I was cautious only of slipping on the ice, but otherwise the pregnancy made me feel invincible.

Often I passed a worn brick storefront called the Young Men's Spanish-American Association and the men behind the glass window waved and made wet, kissing gestures; sometimes if they were in the doorway, they called out, "Hey, there, little mama! Hey, *mamacita!* You're looking good!" By the end of February, when I could no longer button my winter coat and walked with my huge belly leading the way, I waved back to the young men, smiling as if they were old friends.

Carlie was born on a March day so windy I thought the roof of the apartment house was going to blow off and we'd end up like little dollhouse people with rooms of furniture but no ceilings. I was at the stove, stirring chili, when the first pain hit, crumpling me against the wall. For weeks before, I had wondered how to know when labor really started, but I was not prepared for the pain that felt as if a giant hand were crunching my insides together.

When Jesse came home a few minutes later, I was standing in the bathtub, shaving my legs. "Where is she? Where is she?" I heard him call from the kitchen. He brought a bowlful of chili into the bathroom and sat on the toilet, watching me. "It came out great, Sharon," he said. Steam rose from the bowl and the smell of chili filled up the room.

"We have to go," I said, undramatically, careful not to cut myself along the shin.

"Go where?" Jesse asked, a red streak of tomato clinging to his mustache. He had a full black beard back then, which made him look dark and mysterious. Except when he ate. "Sharon, why are you shaving your legs now?"

"The labor has started." Saying the words aloud sent a shiver through me, as if I had become part of the collective birthing experience of women through the ages.

"How long between each contraction?" Jesse asked calmly, looking at his watch. "Should I eat first? I'm really starving."

I put down the razor and gave him a withering look. I suppose all the childbirth classes took away some of the fear, but a part of me still expected him to race us out to the hospital in a panic. "Sure. Eat. Watch the news. Take a nap for yourself," I said sarcastically. "I can wait." I grasped the towel rack as a wave of pain washed over me and the metal bar broke off in my hand.

Jesse put his empty bowl on the sink. "Sharon, get out of that tub. You could fall."

I pulled my arm back as he reached for me. I really hated him at that moment.

"Come on, we'll go now. Here, let me help you out."

Cautiously, he took the razor from my hand as if I had threatened to use it as a weapon. "Everything's going to be fine," he said, holding me gently against his hard chest. "You'll see. We're going to have a wonderful baby."

We drove off into a howling wind, the traffic lights swinging so wildly overhead that I thought they were going to snap off the cables and come hurtling into our windshield. "What a night to be born," I said, hugging my swollen belly, feeling suddenly how dangerous the world really was.

My brother Sam nicknamed Carlie "Superbaby" because if you balanced him standing up on your lap, he looked as if he were going to take off and fly. Carlie had one of those tidy baby bodies that were already muscled and strong; he was always in motion, kicking and thrusting himself into the world with exuberance. I sensed, looking into his face as I nursed him, that things would come easily to him. That he would be sunny rather than sullen, active rather than contemplative, ready rather than cautious.

I had missed the spring that year, wandering through in a maternal fog of late-night feedings, afternoon naps, the endless cycles of running baths, folding clothes, wiping up. There were times I looked at the clock and realized that it was already noon and I was still walking around in a robe, stained along one breast with a milky circle. Jesse came in and out of our lives like a doctor making rounds. He was there in the early morning, kissing me good-bye as I headed back to sleep after the five o'clock feeding. He checked in by phone in the afternoon, asking what we needed from the grocery. Then I described what had made Carlie smile, how long he had slept, the nature of his stools. Jesse was home by six for dinner. We had a lot of pizza delivered and made frequent omelets. At night Jesse was back in the lab, calling again at eleven right before the news. I tried to wait up for him. I think we might even have had sex a couple of times. I don't remember.

By summer, I was paying attention again. I bought some white shorts, got my hair cut and we were all getting out of the house. We were packing for a move to the other side of town. A professor in Jesse's department was going on leave and we were going to house-sit. One more year, Jesse said. Then a real job and a house of our own somewhere.

Jesse was at the lab that day, as usual, but he was leaving early to pick up fried chicken on his way home for a picnic in the park. At four-thirty when he called to ask if I wanted regular or extra-crispy, I told him Carlie was still sleeping. "What time did he go down?" Jesse asked.

"Right at one. This is the longest he's ever slept in the afternoon. Were you ready to leave now or do you have something to finish up?" I asked. Jesse always has something to finish up because nothing in theoretical physics is ever finished up.

"Maybe you should wake him, Sharon," Jesse said. There was something in his voice that made my palms suddenly sweaty.

"Okay," I said casually. "Why don't you leave now? By the time you get everything, we'll be ready."

"Do you want beans or potato salad?" Jesse asked.

"Both." I said, hanging up.

The air conditioner in the apartment leaked onto the gold shag carpeting and hummed erratically. Sometimes it made loud sputtering sounds and then, as if exhausted by the effort, conked out entirely. There was a special little jiggle that you were supposed to do with one of the knobs to get it going again, but I was never very good at it. So when the machine turned itself off, I realized how truly silent everything was. I had seen the Heinrichs drive off in their old Buick; the Terrys were not yet home from work; Sunday was either out or sleeping alone upstairs. I stood in the doorway to Carlie's room and listened for him.

With the shades drawn, the room was dark and cool. On the dresser, I could make out the little blue playsuit I had laid out for Carlie to wear when he awoke. He was sleeping in only a diaper and an undershirt stained with strained carrots. That week was his introduction to vegetables. Carrots had not been as successful as sweet potatoes, but better than peas. At the end of the meal, he had sneezed and strained carrots dotted the wall, my hair, his shirt. I wiped him off but decided to change him after he got up. He would need to be washed up and diapered then anyway.

I don't know how long I stood in the doorway listening to my heart in the stillness of that room. I could see the little hump of his body under the blanket, a patchwork quilt made by my grandma Lela. The room smelled sweet, like talc and baby sweat.

I went to the window and pulled up the shade. Carlie's room faced the back parking lot and there were rusty dumpsters lined up alongside a row of sparse shrubs. Just at that moment Terry-girl was pulling into her space. I stood and watched her park, then walk jauntily up the path. As I moved toward the crib, I heard her footsteps on the stairs and the jangle of keys.

Carlie had been sleeping with his legs pulled up underneath him, so his bottom was up in the air, like those souped-up cars teenage boys drive. When I pulled the blanket back, I saw a crust of dried carrots along the side of his chin. I touched his bare shoulder and felt his skin. It was like the cool plastic of a doll.

It's strange, what you think of in the midst of something horrible. I remember that I screamed for help until Terry-girl ran over and dialed 911, and we both, wordlessly, took turns trying to breathe air into Carlie—all during that time, I kept thinking only how I wanted to wash him up and put on his new playsuit. How I didn't want strangers to come into his room and see him all smeary with a dirty undershirt.

When the medics came in, two strapping men who seemed to fill up the room, I stood in the corner, waiting for them to tell me that my baby would be all right, clutching that blue cotton playsuit against my breast.

We went back to New York to be with my parents for a while and both my brothers were there. Sleeping with Jesse in the same pink room I had had as a girl made me feel as though we had tumbled together into a bad dream. In the morning, I left the house to go off by myself to cry. It was as if everyone else was behaving normally, while I was so unstrung by grief that even sitting at the breakfast table eating a meal with my family seemed like a betrayal.

At the end of August we moved into the professor's house on the lake and I took a full-time job at Kodak—though I never once saw either of the Terrys.

Jesse and I also joined a support group for parents who had lost babies to sudden infant death syndrome. We met in the basement of a Catholic church. There were three couples and one single woman who came with her mother. It was a comfort to be in a room with stained-glass windows, all of us together with the same sorrow. I had the image of our babies hovering around us, flying overhead like watchful angels.

One of the things we learned in the group was how the loss of a child often resulted in the loss of a marriage. The divorce statistics of parents whose children had died were something over 70 percent. I remember reaching for Jesse's hand, determined to hold on, as if we were survivors of a shipwreck, trying to stay afloat in a stormy ocean.

At one meeting a pretty brown-haired woman came to speak to the group. Two years ago she had lost a baby boy. She and her husband were watching TV in the next room when it happened. "I thought that I would be devastated for the rest of my life," she said softly. "I couldn't imagine that I would ever go to a party and laugh and have a good time. But please believe me . . ." The group leaned into the circle to hear her, to hold on to what she was saying, almost as if the words themselves had tangible, life-giving properties. "Something terrible has happened to us all. We will never completely forget the pain of this loss. But I'm here to tell you that you will survive this. And I can promise that you will be happy again."

Chapter 9

"Adventureland. Does that sign say Adventureland?" Amanda was already out of her seat belt and breathing heavily in my ear. From the parking lot we could see the S-shaped curve of the Tornado and hear the shrieks of terrified people as the train of cars plunged down the roller coaster's steep incline. We had driven three more hours and now were ten miles outside of Des Moines, Iowa.

"That's what it says!" Barbara answered cheerfully. I looked out the window so Barbara would not see my face. Her relentless enthusiasm with the children I thought bespoke a certain unwillingness to face up to the enormous consequences of this move, taking the girls from their home, from their father. That, and her apparent lack of remorse, had me baffled. (It wasn't until much later that I realized that Barbara was in shock. That she was behaving in some of the same ways that refugee mothers travel with children across dangerous borders. Pretending that everything is normal. Turning the journey into an adventure.)

There were campgrounds next to the park, and the clean-cut boy at the registration desk told us how lucky we were to get the last available space.

I didn't feel grateful. It was already late afternoon and the tickets into Adventureland cost too much money and it was about ninety-five degrees, too hot to wait in line to get into a bumper car.

We entered a gate flanked by a clown who was missing his bottom row of teeth. He ushered us toward a little red train that stopped at a pavilion about a half mile from the gate.

On the stage of the pavilion was a crowd of teenagers from the marching band of Oskaloosa High School. The bandleader, a man with pomaded hair and a sports jacket with big sweat stains under the arms, was hopelessly clapping the air to get their attention.

"Won't Jana get sick on the rides?" I asked, peering over to a huge barrel where centrifugal force had plastered a group of people against the wooden sides; their arms were pinned back along a rail and their hair whipped away from their faces, leaving them looking startled and strange.

"I gave her a second pill when we stopped for lunch," Barbara said, walking jauntily toward the midway. "She should be all right."

Over to one side were the more sedate rides for younger children. Libby was drawn to the boats that circled lazily on a pond of green, scummy water. "That's a baby ride," Amanda said dismissively. She was interested in some helicopters shaped like Dumbo the Elephant that were powered by the force of flapping ears. "Well, okay anyway," Amanda agreed, after Libby took Jana's hand and went over to the boat line.

The attendant on the ride was very handsome, with tight, tanned skin, brown curls with glints of gold. As each boat came to a stop, he lifted out a child, swiveling his muscled body with a slow sensuality, like an animal turning in the sun. "He's beautiful," I whispered to Barbara, as I waved Libby off.

"He reminds me of Ron Simone," Barbara answered in a normal voice. She called out, "Jana, don't put your hand in the water. Keep everything inside the boat."

I was surprised at the mention of Ron Simone's name. The first time I had seen Ron Simone across the room at a faculty party he looked at me in a way that made me drop a hot, broiled mushroom in the lap of my favorite white linen slacks. (I immediately blotted the smear with absorbent paper toweling, but unfortunately the butter left a permanent stain.) "It's those eyes," I said. Ron has slanty, sexy eyes, an incredible blue. Like the turquoise in Indian jewelry. "That look he gives you."

"It's only a look," Barbara said, smiling as the girls came into view. "Hit the bell, honey!" she instructed Jana, who was floating dully along in her boat. "Hit your bell!"

"What do you mean?" I asked. Barbara hardly even knew Ron Simone, yet her tone suggested something more than mere observation.

"Oh, that he's just a lot of pose and posture. That he really has trouble with women."

"This is conjecture on your part?" I said, playfully.

"Not really."

"Not really, what?"

"Not really conjecture on my part," she answered, laughing.

"Barbara!" I began to laugh, too. "I can't believe you. How do you know anything about Ron Simone?" I thought she had met him only once at my house—at a surprise party for Jesse's birthday. "When did you ever see him besides Jesse's party?"

Barbara was about to say something when the ride ended and we put on our good-mother smiles, welcoming the children as if they had been on a real sea journey. "Was that fun?" we both said at once. "Did you have a good time?"

The rest of the afternoon Barbara and I didn't get a minute alone. Libby didn't like the idea of flying in an elephant, so I went with her in the spinning teacups, which had an Alice-in-Wonderland mural along the wall. She clung to me as we careened wildly into Alice's smiling red mouth.

Afterward, Barbara took Amanda—who just made it over the height requirement—on the roller coaster, while Jana, Libby, and I sat on a bench and ate corn dogs. "Is this junk, Mom?" Libby asked, taking precise bites of her corn dog from both sides of the stick. Although we didn't have hot dogs at home, they were served occasionally at daycare. I told her that yes, corn dogs probably weren't a very good food. "I thought so," she said, smacking her lips. She added, sighing, "I love junk."

Amanda and Barbara went back for another ride on the Tornado while I took the little girls to the bathroom, the merry-go-round and back to the bathroom where Jana threw up into the sink. Hurriedly, I ran cold water into the basin, but undigested pink chunks of hot dog collected in a small mound at the drain. "Let's wipe you off," I said, wetting some paper towels, as Jana screwed up her face and pulled away. "Stay still a minute, hon," I said gently, at the same time digging my fingers into her thin shoulder. In truth, I was annoyed that an experienced vomiter like Jana did not even attempt to make it to the toilet bowl.

The sun was already setting by the time we met back at the pavilion, found some seats, and listened to the Oskaloosa High School marching band play a medley from *Man of La Mancha*. They were loud and competent and fun to look at, teenagers of so many different sizes: overripe girls all breasts and buttocks; small boys without a blemish or a whisker; healthy, farmer-sized young men; both boys and girls who were a gangle of long legs and arms they had not yet grown into. The band was wearing a stiff, androgynous uniform that made all of them look like headwaiters.

To the side of the band, marching spiritedly and going nowhere, were a half dozen baton twirlers in tasseled miniskirts and high-necked white blouses. Following someone's apparently questionable taste, they also wore black fishnet stockings mended so many times with neat stiches of black thread that the baton twirlers' legs appeared cruelly scarred.

The bandleader threw his head back when the alto sax and trumpets took off, nearing the finish of "The Impossible Dream"; the baton twirlers high-stepped their hearts out, oddly touching in their outfits, like peppy, eager-to-please teen-hookers.

I looked down at Libby and saw her watchful absorption. "Do you like this show?" I asked into her ear, breathing in the damp, puppyish smell of her head.

"I like that drummer boy a lot, Mommy," she answered, pointing to a teenager with spiked hair and the brutal good looks of a rock star.

"Mmm," I responded, recalling those boys from high school. Often they were the drummers in a band. There was something that drew the girls. They seemed older, and they had a physical magnetism that the other boys lacked. They never talked much—which was probably to their advantage—but they had this hooded look in their eyes that intimated a secret kind of knowledge.

Now Libby stared, riveted, as the boy shook his body and drummed wildly at the crescendo. Would she still be attracted by such a show-off when she was twirling in front of a band?

It was almost dark when we went back to the van. Parked next to us at the campground was a yellow school bus with the words "Moingona Girl Scout Council" painted on each side. The Moingona Girl Scouts, all about twelve or thirteen years old, had already set up their tents and were settled around a campfire singing softly. Our girls stood and stared, dazed from so much marching-band music.

I went into the van to get the insect repellent and saw my reflection in the sideview mirror. My hair was pulled back in a ponytail with flyaway blond wisps surrounding a face bare of makeup but with a fine line of mustard, like a scratch, along the chin. In the semi-dark, I could pass for a teenager. I imagined myself leading a parade of baton twirlers in front of the Oskaloosa Marching Band, swishing my behind in front of that punk drummer or the good-looking kid at the boats. All the excitement of meeting his eye, the air between us so charged that I could feel his physical presence in the surrounding space; leaning in together for the first kiss, the briefest pause, a short intake of breath before I felt his lips on mine.

Then I thought: I'm never going to kiss anyone again but Jesse. I'm never going to have those first-time feelings again, where everything—all the words, the smells and touches—is fresh and new. This trip with Barbara was making me think about that again.

When I came out, Barbara was talking with two Girl Scout leaders of indeterminate age. They were the athletic, competent sort of women who have short hair in a breezy, wash-and-go style and who always wear sensible shoes; they could have been anywhere from a weathered twenty to a well-preserved forty. "This is Chipmunk," Barbara said, pointing to the shorter woman, "and this is Bunny."

Chipmunk only nodded, but Bunny took my hand and pumped it vigorously. "Glad to meetcha!" she said warmly. "I was telling your friend, here, we're taking our Scouts on a night nature walk and you're all welcome to join us." Close up, I saw that Bunny was nearer to middle-age. Strands of gray streaked through her oaky hair.

"Where do you go?" I asked, looking out toward the amusement park where the neon lights from the Ferris wheel burst in the sky like shooting stars. On the other side of the camp was Interstate 80.

"Oh, right down the road a piece, when you first drive into Adventureland. Off that service road. There's a whole mess of forest there," Bunny said with a twang. She spoke with a kind of forced ruralness, like something out of "The Beverly Hillbillies."

"Thank you," I said politely, looking firmly at Barbara. "That's very nice of you and I'm sure our girls would enjoy the walk if it weren't already so late . . ." I went on, detailing the big day we already had, how we were leaving so early the next morning.

"I understand," Bunny said, raising a hand. "Tell you what, though . . ." She looked at her watch and then toward Amanda, Jana and Libby, who had been drawn over to the campfire and were now being petted by the older girls. "We're not leaving here for another half hour at least. Why don't you let the little ones sit with us at the fire and sing some songs? That'll give your girls a nice introduction to Scouts."

She looked so pleased when I agreed that I thought she was going to sign us all up to join the troop.

Barbara took out a blanket from the van and a bottle of Chablis. "Were you ever a Girl Scout?" she asked, spreading the blanket somewhere between the two camps. We were close enough so we could see the girls, but far enough so that we would not be expected to sing along. She handed me a glass of warm Chablis in a bathroom-size paper cup.

"No. I don't know why. I remember there were Girl Scouts in my school. I never thought to join. I think my mother didn't encourage it. Maybe she thought it was militaristic. Were you?"

"A Brownie. Only for about two weeks. I hated the uniform."

"Oh, God, I did, too! Especially those beanies. Maybe that's the reason I didn't join. You think that's why we're friends?" I rolled down my sleeves against the mosquitoes. It was still hot and very humid; the blanket already felt damp and smelled like the inside of a camp trunk.

"That's part of it," Barbara said seriously. "That's why I've always been attracted to Jews. Because they're basically iconoclastic."

"I'm not iconoclastic."

"Oh, you are."

"Barbara, I don't think not being a Girl Scout and not voting Republican make someone an iconoclast."

"What is an iconoclast, exactly?" Barbara asked. "Here, have some more wine."

I held out my cup, which the wine and the wet, night air had already softened in my hand. "It's someone who smashes icons. Defies traditions."

"Mmm. Well, in a sense . . ." Barbara trailed off vaguely.

"You are much more iconoclastic than I ever could be. I mean, you're the one who's giving up marriage and a stable home to choose something dangerous."

"You think Andrew is dangerous?"

"Not Andrew personally. I meant the unknown is dangerous. Risky."

"God," Barbara said, sighing. "I used to live a much more dangerous life." She lay flat down on her back, her black hair spread like a halo around her head. "When I think of all the things I did in college. Hitching all the time. Staying in those dumps in Mexico City. All the drugs we used then." She raised herself on one elbow. "Did you ever do acid?"

I shook my head. "I was afraid. I was with Jack Silver during a few of his bad trips and that was enough." I remembered one time, sitting all night with Jack in a parked car. He made me hold him, told me if I got out of the car his mind was going to fly through the windshield and he'd never be sane again.

"Anyway, that's over with. My salad days are over." Barbara refilled her cup. "What's that expression mean anyway—salad days?"

" 'Salad days' refers to the time when you were young and green—you know, before you became an iconoclast. Tell me about Ron Simone," I added. "Was he from your salad days?"

Barbara started to laugh deep in her throat.

"Now that is a salacious laugh." I added, " 'Salacious' means 'stimulating to the sexual imagination.' Lustful."

"Very fitting for Ron Simone," Barbara said.

"Did you have an affair with Ron Simone? I can't believe you never told me that after all these years."

"I didn't because, well, it had just ended when I was getting to know you and then Jesse worked with him and I thought you would be friends and that might complicate things."

"Jesse isn't really friends with Ron Simone," I said, then realized that though this was true, it didn't mean much because Jesse wasn't really friends with anyone besides me. He had colleagues at school. And tennis partners. And guys from the softball league who occasionally went out together after the games for a beer. But he didn't have someone he called just to talk, to say how are you. David probably came closest to being a friend, but I don't think they had ever spent time alone together, just the two of them, without Barbara and me. I wondered if Jesse would even call David while Barbara and I were on this trip. Maybe what I meant to say was that if Jesse wanted to have a friend, it wouldn't be Ron Simone.

"Well, then, I don't know. It never came up. I never thought much about it after I stopped seeing him. It was strange to see him at Jesse's party, though. God, he looked good!"

"He was with Kirsten Amundsen, that very blond girl from Minnesota, who looks about sixteen."

"Sharon, she *is* about sixteen. She's an undergraduate."

"I didn't know that!"

"That's the way Ron likes them. Blond and prepubescent. I was an aberration." Barbara yawned and stretched her arms. "I'm surprised he never made a little move on you, Sharon." Then added, "I mean when you first came to Urbana."

"Oh, thanks. You mean now I'm too old for anyone to make a pass."

"Not anyone. But Ron, yes. Besides, you have a child. Anyone who has a child is automatically removed from his computer list of possible conquests."

"When did you see him?"

"Okay, actually, let me think a minute. I know David and I weren't married yet, because we were still living in that apartment on Green Street. I had told David I wanted a relationship where I had some freedom, and he told me he just didn't want to know. I only saw Ron for a couple of weeks. We were together that spring when David went to a conference in Europe." Barbara crumpled her cup, which had wilted into a papery sog, and took a swig of wine from the bottle. "We might as well kill this," she said, passing the bottle back to me. I glanced over to the singing Girl Scouts and, turning my back, surreptitiously downed the rest. "You're not going to believe where I met him," Barbara went on. "You'd never guess."

"Murphy's," I said. Murphy's had been a notorious pickup place some years ago.

"No," Barbara said. "Not a bar."

"The student union? The women's bathroom in Gregory Hall?"

Barbara shook her head. "No, not at the university."

"Where did you meet him?"

She put her hands up to her face and giggled as if embarrassed. Barbara didn't usually giggle, nor was she the type of woman to put her hands in front of her mouth if she did. I continued: "Carle Park? In line at the IGA? A truck stop on Route 74?" I sat cross-legged in front of her, holding the neck of the empty wine bottle, pointing it at her like a microphone.

"Your house," Barbara said, sitting up and composing herself. "I met Ron Simone at your house."

"Before Jesse's party? Well, when? I don't understand."

"Your house, before it was your house. When Penelope and Christos lived there. It was years ago. They had this great party with all their friends—it was some Greek holiday, I think—and everybody got really plastered and danced all over the house. Dancing in every room."

I pictured drunken Greeks dancing on my kitchen counters; in the attic, stomping on the insulation; in Libby's room with the "Sesame Street" posters.

"It was so wild," Barbara said longingly. "Everyone dancing

and kissing on piles of coats in the bedrooms. How come we don't have parties like that anymore?"

"Baby-sitters disapprove when you come home stinking drunk," I said.

"Ron was gorgeous then. He always wore these blue work-shirts that brought out his eyes and his hair was longer . . . and he had this way when he looked at you across the room."

"I know," I said, recalling the dropped mushroom.

"And then, we just got together somehow. He took me home and we sat kissing in the car for a long time before he came up. He has this incredible slowness about him—I think that's why that boy at the rides reminded me of Ron, the way he moved. Ron never breathed hard, or put himself where you didn't want him to be. Everything was slow and seductive, in this kind of teasing way. He used to do something with my hands that drove me just crazy."

"What?"

"He would make these soft, circular strokes on my palm, and then bring my hands to his mouth and kiss the fingertips." Barbara held her hands out in front of her as if they were the objects of evidence at a courtroom trial. They were sexy hands, all right, with elegant long fingers and polished nails with professionally squared-off tips.

"Yes," I said, wanting her to go on.

"And he was a very good kisser. Also spending a lot of time working his way down. My neck. Behind the ears . . ." She paused.

"Yes?"

"So, the only thing he couldn't do was fuck."

"No!" I said, feeling almost a physical letdown, the sudden disappointment that must have been hers after all that slow kissing.

"Well, he was impotent with me, but he said it wasn't always a problem. He had this thing—oh, this is really crazy—about body hair. I didn't shave under my arms, then. But it was more about pubic hair if it was dark. That repulsed him. The minute he saw me naked he couldn't do it. It was so insulting. Sharon, close your mouth, there's a lot of mosquitoes out."

"Like John Ruskin! You've heard about John Ruskin and Effie Gray?"

"Who are they?" Barbara asked.

"Ruskin was a famous Victorian writer. His marriage was annulled—it was never consummated for that very reason."

"What reason?"

"Well, that he was repulsed by a grown-up woman's body. Pubic hair, specifically, I think."

"Well, Ron is grossed out by even stricter specifications. *Black* pubic hair. The sight of it makes him limp as a noodle. Brown he still has trouble with. It's a toss-up with brown."

"But even natural blondes often have darker pubic hair," I noted, myself being a case in point.

"Right. They have to be blond all over for him."

"It must be a strange question to ask on a first date," I said. "What about redheads, though?" I had a flash of my friend Patsy Parker, the first time I saw her naked in gym class, how shocked I was at seeing that thatch of fiery red hair between her legs. For some reason I didn't expect that she would match.

"I think redheads were okay," Barbara said, beginning another giggle. "I think he could get it up for redheads."

"You know, he's almost forty now. What's he going to be like as he gets old?" I pictured Ron Simone coming to parties with a succession of younger and blonder girls, and as he aged they would become more nubile and hairless.

The Girl Scouts were singing "Michael, Row the Boat Ashore," one of Libby's favorites. I looked over to see her sitting cross-legged by the fire, all glowy and part of the gang. She was only yards away, but was so clearly separate from me that I felt a small swell of pride at seeing her singing there with those older girls. Just a few months ago, she started to get up by herself in the night to go to the bathroom without calling "Mommy" and waiting for me to come and take her. The first time I heard her solitary footsteps down the hall and the sound of her urine streaming into the bowl, I had such a poignant sense of how that baby part of her—that part that called out for me, toward which I would fly, blindly, in the night—was forever gone.

Chapter 10

Though both have an agricultural landscape, there is a real difference between Iowa and Nebraska; I'm not sure where the change begins, but Nebraska seemed to me flatter, drier, harder-edged, and the grasses grew together in isolated clumps.

In the afternoon I called Jesse collect from a gas station. The hot wind whipped the dirt around my feet, stinging my bare ankles. "Where are you?" he asked, sounding sleepy.

"Henderson, Nebraska, population 1072," I said, looking at the brownish-green weed that grew along the ice machine. "Where are you?"

"I'm in the bedroom. I just came home for a nap."

"I know. I called the lab first. Belinda told me. She sounded a little pissed off, actually."

"Oh, she and Ron Simone had it out this morning. She said she was tired of being seduced into doing him personal favors."

"Like what?" I asked, my interest piqued.

"Oh, I don't know, Sharon. I try not to get into it with them."

"Well, good for Belinda, anyway." I knew she still made all the coffee and brought in treats for everyone on Friday afternoons; I wondered about what further amenities Ron Simone received. Belinda had hair the color of corn silk, but I had always suspected it was not her original hue.

"Never mind that. How's it going, honey?" Jesse asked.

"Wait a minute." Libby was hanging on to my leg so I let her talk. She took the receiver and held it up to her ear with both hands. Immediately, she reverted to her baby-talk voice and answered monosyllabically. "No," I heard her say. "Yes. Yes. Some milk. Yes. Jana did. Yes. I love you, too. Bye-bye."

When I got back on, Jesse was all sappy and soft. "God, she sounds so sweet on the phone."

"So do you," I said. "What are you wearing now?"

"My blue boxer shorts and my Stanley Kowalski ripped undershirt. It's real hot here."

"Yes. Here, too. There was a storm yesterday, though."

"I know. I was worried; they said there were tornadoes in Iowa."

"Well, that was north of us, in Waterloo," I said, casually. "We just had some rain."

"I'll be all finished with the grant by next week. When you come home, we'll celebrate." He added huskily, "I miss you, Sharon."

"I miss you," I said, as Barbara honked from the van.

"Where will you be tomorrow?" Jesse asked.

"Well, we'll be in Boulder by tomorrow. We called Barbara's father and said we'd make it by afternoon."

"Uh-huh."

"Do you want me to call from there?"

"If you remember," Jesse said quickly. "Give Libby a kiss from me. Drive carefully, okay?"

Barbara already had the motor on and looked at her watch. "I want to get moving," she said as I climbed in next to her.

"I don't see what the big rush is," I said snappishly.

We drove down the highway in silence. Nebraska, I thought, watching as the vegetation became rougher looking, scrubbier.

It took three more states before Barbara and I had a full-fledged fight.

A few hours later, we pulled into a campsite just outside of North Platte, emerging from the van into a choking heat that made the children immediately whiny and irritable. "Look," Barbara said, pointing to a swimming pool set incongruously alongside a barn and a field of soybeans. When a hot breeze picked up, the scent of chlorine and manure wafted over. "Nobody's in it. This could be like our own private pool!"

I touched Barbara's arm. "What do you think? Do you really want to stay here?" The campground had a sleazy feel about it, with trailers and tents practically on top of one another. Wash was strung up to dry on clotheslines that crisscrossed between each site. The word "Office" was painted above the door of a rickety wooden building where there were vending machines for Coke, candy, chips and live bait.

"I want to go swimming, Mommy," Jana said, attempting to pull her T-shirt over her head. It got stuck so that all her hair was pulled back and the shirt draped over her shoulders like a nun's habit.

"I just made Five-Yard Floaters in swimming class," Amanda said to Libby. "What are you in?"

"I'm in Duckers." Then, for verification, "I'm in Duckers, now, aren't I, Mom?"

"Yes. You just made Duckers before we left," I said. "The teacher will send everyone badges at the end of the summer."

"Jana is a Guppy," Amanda said simply, though there was enough in her tone to make Jana begin to pout.

"In California, I'm going to be a Ducker," Jana said with bravado.

We walked across a dusty path toward the office and went in to face a heavyset woman sitting in front of a fan; her broad face had a sheen of perspiration, like the sugar coating of a glazed doughnut. "How you all doing today?" she asked dully. She seemed rooted in the chair, immobilized by the heat.

"Do you have any vacancies for tonight?" Barbara asked. "We don't need any hookups."

"Uh-huh."

"Oh, good," Barbara said. When the woman didn't respond Barbara added, "We'd like to stay here tonight."

"Just one night then?" the woman asked.

"Yes, just tonight," Barbara said, taking out a pen to sign a tattered guest book. Overhead there were masses of flypaper strips hanging from the rafters like party decorations. Hundreds of little fly bodies dotted each gummy roll. I wondered if anyone stayed longer than one night. Or if anyone would come if they were not on their way to somewhere else.

The woman showed us a gritty map and X'd out a place in the far corner. "There's your site," she told us, "right by the swimming pool. It's number nineteen. That's right next to number eighteen."

"Uh, how come no one's in the pool?" I asked hesitantly. "Can we swim in it?"

"Sure. Go ahead."

"I mean, is it clean?"

"Clean?"

"I mean, has it been chlorinated and vacuumed . . . you know," I thought specifically of ear and vaginal infections.

"Gol . . . I think so," said the woman. She turned around and called to a closed door in the back of the office, "Verne, that pool cleaned out? Verne?" When there was no reply, she answered for him. "I think that pool's pretty clean."

Against the back wall was a large glass case, like the snake cages I remembered from the Bronx Zoo. When I was very young—probably Libby's age—my mother would stay home with the babies and my father would take me to the Botanical Gardens or the zoo for what he called father-daughter days.

Here the glass case held a chicken. Or perhaps it was a rooster—a hideous creature with matted, dirty feathers and a growth of tumorous red skin hanging underneath his beak. The bird stalked around the cage with exaggerated movements, one scaly talon in front of the other as if he were a mime. "You girls want to see Hector dance?" the woman asked the girls. On the side of the cage was a sign that said SEE HECTOR DANCE ONLY 25¢; a metal coin slot was connected to a plastic bin of pale yellow feed.

Sensing he was the object of our attention, Hector stopped and stared meanly at the children, who had pressed up close to the glass. Libby's face was just inches from his pointed beak; instinctively, I pulled her toward me.

"Just a quarter," the woman went on. "You just put a quarter in the slot and see what Hector does!" Acting as the rooster's agent seemed to animate the woman and she rose from the chair, went over to the cage and clicked her nails along the glass. "Hi, there, Hector. Hi, there, boy!"

In response, Hector alternately scratched each leg along the floor of the cage in a kind of pre-aerobic warm-up.

Barbara had already opened her wallet, looking for change. "Look at him," she said to the children. "He knows we're about to feed him. Isn't he a smart bird?"

Jana touched the glass with one sweaty palm. "Here, chickie. Cock-a-doodle doo."

I felt my face set in a mask of disgust—my mother's face. "Goyisha," she would say about a caged dancing rooster—though why Gentiles would be connected to this particular exhibit wasn't quite clear. "Goyisha" was her catchall description for anything that was tawdry, commercially connected to ritual, nutritionally unsound, or dangerous. Parades, organza party dresses, July Fourth, bologna sandwiches on white bread and traveling carnivals were goyish. Motorcycles and BB guns, both of which my brothers coveted at one time, were goyish. Adventureland would certainly be. And perhaps Girl Scouts.

Barbara gave a quarter to Jana and showed her the slot. When the coin dropped, and, with some effort, Jana turned the knob that tipped the container of feed, Hector's scrawny chest was visibly palpitating in anticipation.

The corn meal slid down a narrow plastic tube but was blocked before it reached the floor of the cage by a thin, metal disk. Hector's trick was to run back and forth in a rhythmic pattern, so that the weight of his movement would set the disk flapping and release the feed. "There you go, boy," the woman said encouragingly as Hector began his frantic tango.

Eventually, the feed was all pumped out in a neat pile in the corner of the cage and Hector pecked away contentedly.

"That's some chicken," Libby said, echoing words of the admiring spider from her favorite bedtime story.

Tackle boxes and colored lures were spread along the picnic table of campsite number eighteen, and fishing rods leaned up against a silver Airstream trailer with a Missouri license. Covering one side were decals from places such as Acapulco and Bemidji, Minnesota, and a sign that said FISHERMAN ON BOARD. There was nobody around.

"I want to go fishing," Jana said, looking at all the equipment.

"First we'll go swimming," Barbara said brightly, as if it were only the beginning of a long list of planned activities. We took down our suitcases and all crowded into the van to change. My mother had bought Libby a ruffled bikini in some swanky New York children's boutique and I was trying to persuade her to wear only the bottom half. "You'll be more comfortable without this silly top," I said, holding up a skimpy bra that tied around the neck.

"It's not a silly top," Libby said. "You're supposed to wear the whole thing together."

"You don't have to. You only need a bathing suit top if you have breasts."

"I have breasts," Libby said indignantly. "Two breasts." She covered each small brown circle with an index finger.

Amanda took off all her clothes and reclined on the seat. At six, she had lost her baby belly, and her buttocks and thighs were voluptuous in a way that suggested how she would look as an adult. She stretched sensuously, arching her back, and casually put her hand between her legs, rubbing herself.

"I told you about Dr. Stuart, didn't I?" I asked Barbara, looking in the suitcase for my suit. "My college lit professor?"

"The one with the kiddie porn?"

"God, could you believe that?"

"What's kiddie corn?" Libby asked.

"I want a snack," Jana said. "Could we get some chips at the machine?"

"Oh, I never saw your scar," Barbara said, peering at the tiny cross of pink skin on my left breast. "It's not bad at all. It looks like a little star."

Last spring, on a rainy Saturday morning, I had discovered a lump. I hardly ever do one of those self-examinations—though I know I should. It's not that I don't think about doing it. But I start and I become dizzy with fear. Really. I practically fall down faint in the shower. Or I start and think about actually *finding* a lump and usually it would be at such an inconvenient time, because that night I'm going out to dinner and finding a lump would mar a good evening. So I feel around a little, but do a lousy job. This is no excuse, I know.

That time I did find a lump, but in a very casual way, as I was reading in bed, my hand resting lightly on my chest. Under my thin nightgown, under the third finger of my right hand, was a lump. It was round and hard as a dried pea. That, I knew, was a sign of a malignancy because that's how a cancerous lump is described. Not squooshy and gelatinous, but round and hard as a dried pea.

I lay there in bed watching the second hand moving on our clock radio and went through the whole scenario—from the lump to the mastectomy, to my hair falling out from chemotherapy, to dying in the hospital with Jesse at my side, to the funeral. My parents would never recover. I pictured them, hollow-eyed and sedated, reeling before my casket. Would Libby be old enough to understand? I thought of Jesse dressing her in the morning for daycare, putting unmatched barrettes in her knotted hair. And not remembering to use the mitten clips.

Sobbing convulsively, I dialed Barbara's number.

"Calm down now, Sharon. Most lumps are *not malignant*, you know. Where is Jesse?"

"He's at the mall with Libby, buying himself some new tennis shoes," I blubbered. Just this winter, we had joined an indoor tennis club and began playing in a mixed doubles league. Now Jesse would have to get a new partner. I thought of him giving her my Prince Pro racket.

"Stay right there," Barbara commanded, and I slunk obediently back under the covers, listening for her car in the driveway.

She was there in minutes. I remember her feeling my lump between her fingers. "Hmmm," she said, furrowing her brow.

"What do you think?" I asked. Because of her job selling hospital equipment, I imagined her having a certain medical expertise.

"Feels like a lump," she said, ushering me out to the car.

Once we were at the clinic, she handled everything. There was something about insurance and needing a referral from a gynecologist and the lab closing at one o'clock on Saturday with two women with lumpy breasts already before me. I heard Barbara wheeling and dealing in that take-charge way of hers that I find sometimes admirable, sometimes abrasive. I heard her mention something to a nurse about my fragile mental health and how I couldn't possibly wait until Monday, while I cowered in a plastic chair, trying to look deranged.

Then I was led to a green cell where a machine flattened my breast like a pancake between two cold, steel blocks. "You have just enough," said the nurse, looking pleased. She went on to explain that large-breasted women have trouble, spilling over beyond the frame of the machine, while some women had "hardly enough to grab a proper hold of." I sucked in my breath, motionless, while she went behind a screen and snapped a picture of my just-right-sized breast.

The doctor thought my lump was a cyst, but he scheduled a biopsy later that week "just in case." So there I ended up, in a hospital gown in a hospital bed—though as an outpatient I was not permitted to stay the night. When I was wheeled back into the room Jesse was sitting there with Barbara, who was holding a bouquet of helium balloons. Later, Jesse went to get the car, and I stood up weakly as Barbara helped me back into my clothes. "I couldn't bear it if anything ever happened to you," Barbara said, holding me to her as the balloons bobbed overhead.

"I'm sorry for being snappy before," I said now as we sat with our feet dangling in the water. The swimming pool was actually crystal-clear and shallow enough in the roped-off end that the girls could stand, though Libby and Jana only on tiptoe. Over on the grass someone had left an innertube. It was huge. As big as a tire on a semi-truck. Barbara rolled it into the pool and all three girls got on, leaning back and sunning themselves like baby mermaids on a big, black rock.

"I'm sorry, too," Barbara said. "I'm so distracted." She leaned back on her elbows so that her stomach looked muscled and taut. She was wearing a red bikini with tiny white squiggles. It reminded me of Campbell's tomato alphabet soup. "You think I should have thought this out more, don't you?"

"I wish you had told me earlier, is all. I didn't know you were that desperately unhappy."

"Sharon, I didn't even tell myself. I think part of me was unconscious through all of this. And then one day I just woke up and said this is what I have to do. I don't know if you can understand that."

"Do you think I weigh everything so carefully?" I asked, wounded. In fact I had been deliberating the effects of Barbara's decision for weeks. Now the constant company of the children awakened me to a different reality. Andrew had never lived with children. I saw the fact that Andrew had never had children as a strike against him. It's a prejudice, I know, but I think people who don't have children are somehow never completely formed. They seem to spend an inordinate amount of time on things such as finding the right wine to go with dinner. David was a good father. Barbara had to say that for him.

"Sharon, you're the best friend I ever had," Barbara said, kicking her feet in the water; as if in slow motion, shimmery droplets hung in the air with each splash. "I value your opinion."

"I know." I looked down at my legs. Delicate silver stretch marks gleamed just where the bathing suit met the bone of each hip.

"Would you tell me something, honestly?" Barbara asked.

"What?"

"Well, supposing David and I were still together but we were all older—like the kids were grown and out of the house—and then Jesse and I died . . ."

"You died together?" I interrupted.

"Well, not necessarily. But all right. We could just say together. We all went out for dinner and Jesse and I were both killed in a car accident. Okay?"

"Okay."

"So, what I want to know is—would you marry David?"

"Would I marry David?"

"I mean, could you marry David? Do you think you could live happily with him?"

I pictured David and me growing old together in some Florida retirement community. David, gray-haired and stooped, tinkering with antique clocks as I redecorated the condominium and improved my tennis. "I don't know," I said truthfully. Then the more I thought about it, the more comfortable the idea seemed. We would be older, so sexual attraction didn't have to be a primary concern. David had a number of attributes. He was a good cook and didn't see the kitchen as foreign terrain, the way Jesse annoyingly did. Also David didn't watch professional sports on television. I imagined quiet Sundays without the background drone of a football game. "I think possibly I could," I told her.

"What about Jack Silver?"

"What about him?"

"Could you live with him, too?" Barbara asked.

"With him and David?"

"Not with the two of them together. I mean, do you think you could be married to Jack Silver and be happy?"

"I haven't seen Jack Silver in five years. I don't even know what he's like anymore."

"Oh, yes you do," Barbara said.

"You're right," I admitted. Though the letters and phone calls were not frequent, I still knew Jack. I thought of him, buoyant and hopeful, brimming with good intentions. Yet there was also something not quite centered about Jack, a characteristic that caused him to fall prey to trends and follow suspicious leadership. When we were in college, this seemed more dangerous. Now he was off drugs, married, successful, "into" only fatherhood, his recent enthusiasm.

"Are you nervous at all about seeing him again?" Barbara asked.

"I don't know. Maybe if a few more years had gone by I'd be a little worried about how I'd held up over time. No, I'm looking forward to seeing Jack," I said.

"Well, I just meant, you know, if the attraction were still there. . . . Do you ever wonder what would have happened if you'd married him?"

"We'd have been divorced," I answered quickly. "Staying with him would have meant going through his drug trips and schlepping around India." Jack and his first wife, Marcy Klupperman, had both become Sikhs; in a drawer somewhere I have a photograph of them, white-robed and beatific, standing in

front of their ashram. I'm sure that one of the reasons Jesse has
never been able to work up a sufficient jealousy toward Jack
Silver is that he never saw him as a serious rival. I think I have
resented Jesse a little for this. Maybe that is why this year I had
purposely left Jack's recent family photo—where he looked
mainstream and capable—on our bedroom dresser for a couple
of days. But I knew even if Jesse had any qualms about my
stopping at Jack's on this trip, he would never admit it.

"I don't think I could ever be married to Jack Silver," I told
Barbara. I saw myself living in the million-dollar house Jack
described in his letter—all glass, and hanging off the side of a
canyon. It seemed a precarious, if glamorous, existence.

Back at the campsite an elderly man in lot number eighteen was
frying fish over a steady fire. "Oh, that smells wonderful!" Barbara said as we approached.

"Walleye," said the man, turning over the sizzling fish with
a spatula.

"Did you just catch that today?" Barbara asked, looking at
him, not at what he was cooking. There is something about the
way that Barbara looks men directly in the eye that unnerves
me sometimes. I knew the man was going to offer us some fish.

A woman emerged from the trailer, stepping down carefully.
"Wayne, you want beer or pop?" she called. When she saw us
heading toward our van she gave a tight little wave, like babies
do when you ask them to go bye-bye.

Barbara and I had an uninspired dinner planned—shaved ham
sandwiches and cut-up vegetables. I brought some of the food
out to the picnic table and began arranging paper plates, swat-
ting away the black flies that proliferate in the Midwest this
time of year.

The children wandered over to the man's fire and circled him
wordlessly. "Why, how'd you girls get all wet?" the man asked,
smiling. "It's not raining." He looked up at the sky as if to
check.

Amanda stepped forward as spokesperson: "We went swimming in the pool. We all went underwater."

The man called his wife to bring the rest of the fish, and she came out with a plate of carefully cleaned fillets. "I'll cook some up for you," he said to us. "We already have a freezer full." The woman went over and stood next to the fire, holding out the plate to her husband. They looked alike, both with soft tufts of gray hair and rimless eyeglasses.

Before we could protest, the man had placed the fish he had cooked for himself at our table. Then he went back to the fire and started the rest. "Try that," he commanded and we all obediently sat down and began eating.

It was delicious, crispy-skinned and all soft and buttery inside. Libby and I shared a plate; I picked off the meat for her, going through it with my fingers to check for bones.

We went to sleep as soon as it was dark. I looked through the screened open roof of the van. There were so many stars, little chinks of light shining in the dark sky. I burrowed deep into my sleeping bag, remembering that the last time it had been used was the camping trip to Shosh-a-pee Falls. Jesse and I had slept in a tent we had pitched on an uneven spot of ground, so that we both kept sliding down toward one end. David cooked steaks over the grill and he was earnest in asking how we wanted them—rare, medium-rare, well-done—even though they all came out exactly the same.

David was excited. He had sent away for a rock-and-mineral-identification kit and had laid out all the stony specimens on the picnic table. "Look at these," he said to the girls. "Let's try to figure out what these are."

I looked, too. Except for the amethyst, obviously purple, and the shiny black mica, they all just looked like rocks to me. Some were sandy and dull, others quartzy and clear. But mostly they looked like rocks, blank and indistinguishable.

"These rocks are as different as we are," David said, as the stones clunked pleasantly in his palm. "You have to get to know them. Look at this." He offered Amanda a chunk of something. "A conglomerate. It's made up of teeny pebbles clinging together. See those baby rocks?" he said as she looked intently into her hand. He gave a white stone to Libby. "And this. Put your tongue on it, Libby."

Tentatively, she gave a lick. Then another. "It's salty!" she exclaimed, passing it to Jana, who also wanted a taste.

"That's halite. You know halite because it's salty," David said, his blue eyes flickering intelligently behind his glasses. "Now what about this, Sharon?" He gave me a narrow sliver of something that felt slippery, almost greasy. It was so soft I could flake off pieces with my fingernail. "It feels kind of powdery," I said.

"Talc," David said, pleased. "Here, girls. Want to feel it? That's what they make baby powder out of." He passed the talc on. "And what about this?" He held a rosy quartz up to the light. "Isn't it beautiful?"

Soon the girls got bored and David took them for a walk over the ridge to see the falls at twilight. He held hands with Amanda and Libby, and Jana clung to him, piggyback, as they made their way up the slope. Now, David's words echoed in my head: Why is she doing this? Do you understand why she is doing this?

Chapter 11

Everyone was still asleep at dawn when I woke with a start, stiff-necked and sweaty from a bad dream. Though the windows were open, the van had a closed, indoor feel, the air heavy with the aura of sleep. I had been dreaming of Dr. Sevidi, a math teacher from my freshman year at college. Dr. Graves Stuart, the English literature teacher who was arrested in California, was also in the dream, a murky figure sitting over to the side in a director's chair, yelling "Cut!" at different intervals. Under the guise of offering special-help sections for their students, the professors had instead set up their classrooms with costumes and cameras in order to make pornography movies. It was like a scene out of Fellini, with huge-breasted women lolling across the desks and naked girls riding other naked girls like horses up and down the aisles. Dr. Sevidi had a hold of my wrist and was taking me into a dark closet. It was one of those dreams where you try to scream and you can't; you can't seem to open your mouth wide enough to get out even a single sound. I signaled with my eyes for the other girls to help me, but they just smiled vaguely and continued riding each other around the room. As Dr. Sevidi dragged me—mute, but struggling fiercely— toward the closet, I saw the names Jesse Burke and Jack Silver printed on a computer sheet: a mailing list of people who had ordered the films. I thought, Oh, my God and Dr. Sevidi nodded evilly, verifying that yes, Jesse and Jack were involved in this, too. "No, no!" I cried, thrashing my head from side to side, trying to escape from his viselike grip. It was like the awful recognition in horror movies, when the innocent one finally makes the connection, that everyone she has ever trusted— friends and family, the police, the kindly neighbor—are all conspiring against her. Are all, in reality, the enemy. I woke, my heart racing, to the frantic twitter of birds, and, in the distance, the growl of farm machinery. The dream hung in the air for a few minutes like a bad smell, then dissipated. I lay back down and closed my eyes, Sevidi's face still swimming before me. I thought how strange it was—how you don't think of anyone for ten or twenty years and then all of a sudden they pop up in a dream, clear as a newspaper headline. How there must be some kind of imprint in the subconscious to account for that kind of recall. In my mind, he was exactly the same, Dr. Sevidi, as familiar as the picture of someone in my old family albums.

He had been a creepy man. I remember his hands, with long, wormy fingers and his teeth, glaringly white and uniformly pointed so that when he smiled he looked like a dog about to attack.

I had the same trouble with math as I later did with physics. We spent a lot of the semester doing something called Venn diagrams where circles overlapped into other circles to show opened and closed sets. Every assignment I did had so many erasures that there were always holes in the papers I handed in.

The extra-help sessions were at night, in a conference room in the math building, directly across from Sevidi's office. Once, right before the final, I came early, to ask about my grade. To beg about my grade, really. At the end of the semester, I had accumulated almost enough points for the lowest C on Sevidi's curve.

"Is there anything I could do to make those extra points?" I asked, as Dr. Sevidi wheeled his chair away from the barrier of the desk. Then, trying to appear interested, I added, "I think I'm really understanding the concepts a lot better now. It just took me awhile to catch on."

I was wearing a print minidress with a blue-and-gold design batiked against a lighter blue background. I remember that dress, the colors, and how short it was, because Dr. Sevidi said, "That light blue matches the blue of your eyes," as he patted my bare leg. He touched me somewhere higher than a knee, but not as serious as a thigh.

I sat for a moment looking down, detached in a way, as if his slightly yellowed, long-fingered hand was patting someone else's leg. My first thought was banal and brazen: "All I want is a C."

I remember that when he leaned toward me, smiling his doggy smile, he smelled like fried food. "And I've really been studying for the final," I said, pulling away as far as I could without tipping over backward in my chair.

There were noises in the hall, shuffling and giggling. Abruptly, his expression changed, became clouded. He looked at me for a little while with cold, flat eyes before he began to collect the papers on his desk. "I'm sure you'll be able to get your C, Miss Roth," he said, suddenly so proper and professorial that I thought maybe I only imagined him touching me. I moved my own hands to my leg, resting them, folded, on the spot where his had been. Out of politeness, I continued to sit there, still as a statue, until he dismissed me, saying, in a supercilious way, that it was time for him to be at the help session, that he hoped I would listen attentively because he was going to cover material that was going to be on the final.

I never told anyone, because really, I didn't know what there was to tell. But now years later, I recalled how embarrassed I had felt then, how afterward I thought that whatever happened that time in his office was probably my fault because my math skills were so weak, my dress was so short, my eyes were so blue.

We tried to get out early, so we'd make it to Boulder by the afternoon. It was hot, but not as humid as the day before, and the early-morning air had a clean, farmy freshness. The children were happy because they got to eat the Froot Loops and strawberries we had bought at a supermarket in Iowa; Barbara and I were happy because the showers at the campground were strong and hot, as was the coffee set out by the woman in the office. When we went to check out, she was sitting in the same place we had found her the day before, under the pale streamers of flypaper. This morning she was wearing a cotton housedress of bright pink and lime-green Popsicle stripes and drinking a bottle of Orange Crush; all the color gave the drab little office a festive air. Hector the rooster fluffed himself up, looking hopeful, when he saw us come in, but none of the little girls requested a repeat performance.

"Is there a mailbox?" I asked, holding out a postcard—"Welcome to Nebraska"—with a picture of a collie and three puppies sitting in a red wagon next to a weathered barn.

The woman pointed to a wire basket on the counter. "Mail don't come 'til after three," she said with a yawn. Despite the bright attire, she was sluggish as ever.

"That's all right." I wrote out the address of my grandmother's nursing home and turned the card over for a quick check. Last night, I had debated writing big so that my grandmother would be able to read the card herself or small so that she would have the pleasure of a longer message. I chose small, describing in some detail the plains, the sky, camping out under the stars, making it seem as if we were traversing a bucolic wilderness untouched by superhighways and truck stops.

Barbara was signing a check when the door to the back room opened and a man came out, wheeling an old stove on a dolly.

"If you're going to the dump now, Verne, take them cans out back," the woman said sharply to him.

"I'm not going to the dump now," the man said quietly,

walking himself backward through the office, carefully guiding the dolly past Hector's cage and around the front desk. He had the clean, good looks of a high school gym teacher.

"You got to get that sink fixed, Verne. The one up by the last unit," the woman said as he moved out the door. "People in here this morning say it's all backed up. You hear me, Verne?" she called through the screen. If he did, he chose not to respond.

On the way out, we saw him piling a bunch of logs into a pickup and whistling something complicated. "'Bye, ladies," he called as we passed, giving a little nod, as if he were tipping his hat.

We went out on Interstate 80, the sun at our back, heading to Ogallala, Nebraska. I was driving and Barbara had the map opened on her lap, tracing a finger along to the place where we dipped down southwest toward Highway 76 into Colorado. "Do you think they're married?" I asked Barbara.

"Who?" Barbara held the map up, moving it farther from her face. "You know, I think I need glasses. I thought that wasn't supposed to happen until you were at least forty. Shit!" She , adjusted the map back and forth squinting against the glare.

"The woman in the office and that man." I added, "Verne."

"Sure. They were married. Didn't you think so?" Barbara put the map back down and looked at me.

"I don't know. She was so awful. And he was kind of attractive. They seemed too mismatched. Maybe he was a handyman or something."

"No, she was too rude to him for him to be a handyman," Barbara said. "They were married."

I took the map from her and read "Ogallala: forty-eight miles." The girls giggled, repeating the name, not able to get it quite straight. Ogllalala. Ooglala. Ahgolalla. Golly-gollyagla. Barbara began a chant. "Ogallala! Ogallala! Sis-boom-bah!" The girls went with it awhile before degenerating into total silliness. Oogle-bugle. Ogle-booger. Ogle-dodo. Oglapooopy. Libby was very good at scatological reference, her current rage.

Amanda held her own. Ogla-tuchis. Ogle-peepee. Ogle-b.m.-lala.

Somewhere they crossed the line into "going too far," that familiar parental boundary. I think it was Amanda calling her sister an ogle-dody-head that brought Jana first to a whine, then to a full-blown wail. It happened so quickly, the fun turning to tears, that I had to check the rearview mirror twice to make sure that Jana wasn't really laughing. In the mirror, I saw Libby's confused face as she looked at crying Jana. Libby was getting a good introduction on this trip to the dynamics of sibling torture.

"I'm going to play a special game with Jana and Libby and Amanda gets to ride up front for a while," Barbara said, making it sound as if that would be a good deal for everyone. Deftly, she unbuckled her seat belt and climbed over the cooler, as Amanda squeezed by and plopped herself into the front seat. I gave Amanda an affectionate, you-should-know-better smile.

"Do you like to be the one to drive, Sharon?" Amanda asked, leaning toward me with an almost collegial interest.

"It's all right," I said. It had taken me awhile to get used to driving the van. I felt propped up and more important than in a regular car, but I still didn't have a good sense of how close I was to the cars in front of me. I tended to leave lots of extra room.

"I drive with Daddy. He lets me steer."

"I used to do that with my father sometimes." I recalled Sunday drives home from my grandmother's. Off one of the service roads of the Long Island Expressway there was a nearly deserted straightaway. By then, the twins would be asleep, but I'd be waiting for the opportunity to climb over the front seat, place myself in my father's lap, and steer all the way to the stop sign. My father pretended it was I who was stopping the car, by calling for it to slow down. My mother never said anything, but her tight, grim hold on the passenger strap by the window revealed her disapproval.

"When Daddy comes to California, he'll drive the red car," Amanda said.

"When he comes to California?" I repeated. Puzzled, I looked over my shoulder, but Barbara was engrossed in a game of picture lotto, having just matched up a set of baby elephants.

"The red car is the one he lets me steer, not the van." Then, "But you know what?" Amanda grinned. When Amanda smiled she still had the little baggy pockets under her eyes that made me remember her as a baby. In the past few years her hair had gotten very dark, almost black, like Barbara's. Now with her blue eyes and fair skin, she was a strikingly pretty child. She had a soft mouth, loose-lipped and sensual.

"No, what?"

"The red car isn't really red."

"It's not?" For the moment I couldn't recall the Glassers' other car, though that was the one Barbara drove every day to work.

"It's *maroon!*" Amanda said triumphantly as I flashed on a picture of their Toyota, Jana's car seat still in the back. "When we got that car, I was too little to know 'maroon.' I just knew red. So we still call it 'the red car.' See?"

"I see," I assured her, still unsettled by her assertion that David was driving to California in that car. That he was coming to California at all. Maybe Barbara and David had already set a plan for a visit. But somehow I doubted it.

We stopped for a picnic lunch by a reservoir where the water was silver-blue and clumps of purple wildflowers dotted the surrounding hills. With our encouragement, the children had exhausted themselves, racing up the hills, rolling down along the smoother, grassy spaces, and hiking with us along a nature trail. We had seen a deer drinking at a stream and then delicately high-stepping from rock to rock as if she didn't want to get her hooves wet. Back in the van, I told the girls a revised version of Bambi. In my story, Bambi was a female. The hunters were still mean, but Bambi's mother didn't die. In the end, Bambi produced a baby fawn, and lived happily as a single mother in a protected national park. Now all three girls were snuggled together, sleeping in the sunny backseat.

"You're not looking forward to seeing your father, are you?" I asked as the mountains came into view.

"I don't know. Maybe it will be easier with you and all the kids." She sighed.

"You mean, talking about leaving David?"

"No, just talking, period. You'll see. If I don't bring up David and me my father won't say anything at all."

"You're kidding!"

"My mother, too. She'd be the same way. Being with my parents is like being with strangers at a church luncheon. You could tell them that you just had an abortion and they'd start talking about how nice the colored marshmallows look in the fruit salad."

I had met Barbara's mother once right after Libby was born. She was well-coiffed and pretty, but had a blinking, confused look, as if she had just gotten on the wrong train. Now I said to Barbara, "If I were seeing my parents for the first time after leaving Jesse, that's all we *would* talk about."

"Nadine and my mother talk. When I was a teenager, I used to listen to them sometimes together. I couldn't understand them. It was like they were speaking another language or something. Sometimes I'd be in another room and I couldn't make out all the words, but both my mother and sister have these little squeaky voices, and even though they never say anything of substance they both talk a lot. From another room, it was like listening to monkey chatter."

I opened the glove compartment and found the chocolate bar I had bought from the candy machine that morning. "Want some?" I asked, unwrapping it slowly, stealthy as a spy. Libby has a sixth sense with chocolate. She can hear someone crinkling a candy wrapper from another room or smell chocolate on my breath even after I've brushed my teeth.

The chocolate had gotten soft. Barbara took an even four

squares and popped it all into her mouth at once. "I've gained almost ten pounds since the beginning of the summer," she said, licking chocolate off her fingers.

I looked at her skeptically. "Come on. You look great," I said. "I just saw you in that bikini. Where's the ten pounds?"

"I'm sitting on it." Barbara lifted one fleshy cheek and gave it a couple of hearty slaps. "Is there any more?" she asked.

We divided the last few squares and I crumpled the wrapper, burying it in the bottom of the garbage sack we had attached to the door handle. "God, look at the sky here." Before the mountains, the sky was a cloudless, piercing blue. The dry weeds beside the road shimmered in the light and the road seemed almost translucent as the mirages appeared in front of us, one inky puddle after another.

"My mother liked you," Barbara said. "She thought you were a good influence, I could tell."

I started laughing. "What do you mean, 'a good influence'?"

"She said after she met you, 'That Sharon is a fine girl.' 'Fine' is my mother's way of describing someone who does her own housework and doesn't whore around. She was relieved. She's never forgiven me for the friends I had in high school."

"I would have been friends with you in high school," I said, thinking of Patsy Parker. The spunky toughness that she had, so much like Barbara's. The way she had of always convincing people to break the rules. "Remember I told you about my friend Patsy?"

"The girl who died when you were in high school?"

"Yes. When we were seniors. She reminded me so much of you, Barb."

Barbara bit the inside of her cheek, looking thoughtful. "Sharon, is there supposed to be a lesson somewhere here for me?"

I closed my eyes and tried to picture Patsy's face before me. It wouldn't come into focus. I got bits of her. The red hair. The gummy smile. The splash of freckles across her shoulders. But I couldn't get it all together.

"How did she die? Did you ever tell me?" Barbara asked.

I was feeling sad all over. "She died in a car accident. It was the night of our senior prom. The boy she was with was drunk."

"I remember," Barbara said solemnly. "Oh, that must have been something terrible."

That was what my mother had said when she woke me that morning. She said something terrible had happened . . . something terrible. Standing by my window as she pulled up the shade, her face was waxy and unnatural-looking. My world was so small then; I thought, How much more terrible could it be? It was the morning after my senior prom and I did not get to go. My dress, strapless, pristine white, a spray of roses along the bodice, hung wrapped in plastic in the closet.

The day before, I had come down with German measles. Our family doctor said it was the worst case he had ever seen in all his years of practice. He was gray-haired and stooped, so he had seen quite a few cases in his time. He *tsk*ed, shaking his head, and advised my mother to soak towels in calamine lotion and wrap them around me. I was burning with fever. The blisters were everywhere, even on the bottoms of my feet, across my scalp, up my nose. "The prom!" I croaked out to him from my sore, blistered throat. I knew by the look he gave my mother that I would not be going.

My parents felt so bad; every time they came into my room seemed like an apology. My mother brought me raspberry sherbet and magazines and my father moved the television set into my room. Even Sam and Marc were extra nice, never once telling me how ugly I was with all my blisters.

The night of the prom, my boyfriend, Rick Naughton, came over to show me how he looked in his tuxedo and to give me the orchid corsage he had bought. "Rick, you shouldn't have done this," I said. He stood by my bed holding open the box. For a second, in my fever, I thought it was an engagement ring. "Denise should have this," I told him. Denise was his cousin from Westbury. I had convinced Rick to ask her to go with him to the prom since the dinner and the tux and everything were paid for anyway and Rick's friend Pete was depending on him for a ride into the city to go to the Copacabana. I had wanted to go with Patsy and Brian to the Village Gate for jazz, but Rick and Pete were football players and they always hung out together, did everything together.

"I got Denise another one," Rick said, as he awkwardly pinned the flower onto my quilted robe. I was touched by this, and feeling so sorry for myself that I started to cry.

"Ah, don't cry, Sharon," Rick said, getting in next to me on the bed. He held me tight in his arms, my orchid flattening against his starched, pleated shirt.

"Don't," I said as he began kissing me. "You'll get sick."

"I already had the German measles," he said, sliding one hand between the buttons of my robe. "You can't get them again."

"I look so ugly." I sniffled into his broad shoulder. It wasn't only the rash. My hair was lank and greasy and I knew my breath had a fevery, metallic smell.

"I don't care," Rick said, opening up my robe to kiss my breasts. I was lying flat down, so it was almost hard to tell my nipples from all the surrounding bumps and blotches.

The door to my bedroom was closed, which my mother usually didn't allow, but that night I knew she would not come in. Even though she didn't totally approve of Rick as a long-term boyfriend (he wasn't Jewish and he was going to a community college), she was happy he had come to cheer me up.

"I'm sorry you can't go, Sharon," he said earnestly. "I'm going to miss you so much." He kissed me again and promised that as soon as I was well, he would take me to the Copacabana. "It doesn't have to be a prom," he said. "It could just be a regular date."

"Oh, Rick," I sighed, kissing him back with increasing ardor. At that moment I thought I loved him, too.

Rick and I started fooling around a little, right there on the bed, his hands going under my robe. I lifted, so he could take down my underpants, and they slid down and looped around one ankle. I was still a virgin, but Rick and I were very experienced petters. In the last few months we had touched and mouthed each other in all sorts of ways: furtively, in backseats of cars; under the afghan on the old sofa down in my parents' den. I had told Patsy that maybe on prom night I would let him go all the way. Patsy had been having regular sex with Brian, and she had been encouraging me to follow her example. She told me that losing your virginity was something that needed to be done before you could say you were an adult—like losing baby fat.

(By the time I did do it—a few weeks later, by an isolated dune at Jones Beach—Patsy was dead and I had no one to talk to about how much it hurt. And how just seconds afterward, as a pool of blood leaked from between my legs, a white Jeep from the beach patrol zoomed across the flat sands by the water's edge.)

But then Rick had gone, and the morning after the prom my mother woke me and spoke so slowly, it was as if by dragging out the words she could put off saying what needed to be said. Then my father came in and sat on my bed, smoothing back my hair, his hand resting on my forehead, to see if I still had a fever. Somehow in the next few seconds, I understood by looking at the two of them that someone had died. I caught my breath, waiting to hear about the death of one of my grandparents. All four were still alive, still healthy. Which one, then? I looked back and forth between my parents, waiting for the opportunity to comfort one of them, but both looked equally devastated. My father, in fact, had been crying; his eyes were all red-rimmed and the end of his nose had a bright, cherry spot. I thought then it must be Grandma Flossie. He would only cry for his mother.

"There was an accident last night on the Expressway," my mother began. She put her hand on my father's shoulder for support. "Kids coming home after the prom. Patsy's brother called us an hour ago. . . ." She broke off, and covered her face with her hands, unable to go on.

"They ran off the road and hit a divider," my father continued. "Brian's in the hospital in critical condition." My father looked as if in some place deep within him, a sharp object had painfully twisted. "Patsy died last night, sweetheart. She never even made it to the hospital."

I felt as if I were out in the ocean and the waves were crashing overhead, sweeping me out against my will until I was sinking, every part of me sinking; a heaviness like a rock upon my chest pulling me down until I lost my breath; my heart sinking. I looked back and forth to my parents to rescue me; let what they said not be true, let this be a joke. Though never, in all the years, had they ever joked like this, I would forgive them in a flash if they were joking now. They should understand that and tell me the truth.

The phone rang all morning and later Rick came over with Pete, who had never had the German measles but said he didn't care. They had come from the hospital, but didn't get to see Brian. Only family was allowed in. Boys all dressed up in tuxedos and girls in formal gowns, wilted, worn-out after a sleepless prom night, were packed into the waiting room of the intensive-care wing. By the afternoon, Patsy's brothers and sisters had driven in with their families from Queens and upstate, and my father went out to La Guardia to pick up a sister who was coming from Chicago. My fever went back up to 103 degrees and I kept picturing Patsy's face, flying through the windshield, glass shattering into a million tiny bits, like stars.

Jana woke and announced that she had to go to the bathroom. "We're almost to Grandpa Hugh's," Barbara told her. "Just hold it. Why don't you wake Libby and Amanda? Gently. Whisper them awake."

We got off the highway and Barbara made a few turns until we ended up on a street of fifties-style ranch houses that looked all the more ordinary set against the grand backdrop of the mountains. "I can't tell," Barbara said, slowing as she scanned one side of the road. "All these houses look alike to me." When she visited, she usually came in from the airport, the other direction. "That's why I'm all thrown off," she explained. "Wait, I think that's his car."

We parked in front of a pale-peach house with gray shutters and a big picture window facing the street. By the side of the driveway was one of those plastic flower markers whose petals spin around in the wind and a rock with the house number painted a fluorescent silver. I climbed down and slid open the back door of the van to let the children out. "Come on, girls," I said, snapping Libby out of her seat belt. "Ahhhwayyy," she whined, still drugged with sleep, brushing me away with her hand as if I were a pesky mosquito. Amanda and Jana crawled over her and raced to the door. "You go," I said to Barbara. "Let me wait here with her for a few minutes or she'll be a real grouch."

"I'm not a grouch!" Libby growled before she stretched out on the seat and fell back asleep.

I saw Barbara's father standing at the door, bending to kiss Amanda and Jana, and then Barbara pressing her cheek to his, a cocktail party kind of kiss. He gave me a little jaunty wave before he swept them all inside and shut the door.

Chapter 12

I said I would go out to pick up something for a salad, grateful for the excuse to get out of the house. We had been sitting in the kitchen drinking diet soda—Barbara, her father and a middle-aged woman named Mary who was wearing a white pants suit and spongy, white nurse's shoes. The children were in the living room watching television. They still felt the strangeness of the house and were on their visiting behavior, sitting quietly on the couch, hands folded in their laps. You knew it wouldn't last.

Barbara's father offered soda and saltine crackers. He didn't seem to differentiate between Libby and his own grandchildren, but patted each haphazardly on the parts of their bodies that came closest to him when they took their crackers. "Fine girls," he said vaguely, touching Libby on the top of her head, Jana on her outstretched hand. You could tell he was once a handsome man, but now his face looked pinched and his skin was a strange shade, the color of manila envelopes.

It was uncomfortable at the small, round kitchen table. I kept bumping knees with someone every time I moved my leg and Mary lit up one cigarette after the other, so that after a while my eyes burned from the smoke.

Barbara and her father were talking about dinner. She kept saying how she wanted to take him out and he kept saying how he had everything planned, how he was going to barbecue the best steaks she'd ever taste in her life. He opened the refrigerator to reveal three tiers of pink meat, each thick as a plank, rimmed by a glistening circle of fat. There was enough steak there to feed a baseball team.

"I don't want you to go to any trouble, Dad. You can freeze those," Barbara said. "We'll go out."

"No. I bought them for you," Mr. Davis said in a small voice. "For you and the girls."

I was beginning to feel bad already. It's always depressing when someone goes to a lot of trouble and the effort won't be properly appreciated. I knew the kids would rather have hot dogs, and Barbara and I could easily share one of those slabs of meat.

"We'll help," I said brightly. "I'll make a salad." I looked over to Mary, who was finishing her sixth or seventh cigarette. She never pressed quite firmly enough when she put it out, so the smoke kept drifting up in a sickly spiral from the dirty ashtray. I still wasn't sure who she was. It wasn't clear if she was Mr. Davis's nurse, or a friend, or if she was going to stay for supper. Perhaps she was even going to cook the supper.

"Oh. Hmmm," Mr. Davis said, opening and closing the crispers as if he had misplaced something. "I don't think I have any of that."

I looked, too. "That" must have referred to some sort of fresh fruit or vegetable. One of the bins was empty and the other contained a package of prunes and a block of Velveeta.

"You have charcoal lighter fluid, Hugh?" Mary said, looking out the back door where the grill sat next to the side of the garage. "I thought you were all out." She had a harsh, staccato voice, like gravel hitting the side of a car.

"I could get some," I said, rising slowly from the chair, the plastic seat peeling away from the backs of my thighs. I reached into Barbara's purse for the keys. "Just tell me how to go to the nearest grocery store."

"Easy," Mary said, getting up and looking out the front window. "You're parked facing north. Okay. So you go to the corner and make a right. Then down to the next corner and make a right at the stop sign. There's a Safeway after the light. Your first right. Can't miss it." She sat back down and lit up another cigarette.

Barbara took money out of her purse at the same time her father reached into his wallet. I said no to both of them, but ended up with bills stuck deep into each pocket of my hiking shorts. "Maybe the kids would like to go," I said, walking into the living room. It was a small room, neat, with three pieces of matching wood-trimmed furniture upholstered in some itchy-looking orange tweed. Above the couch was a picture of snow-capped mountains surrounding a glassy lake. On one end table was a green ginger-jar lamp, on the other nothing, just a clear square of varnished wood. It was like a motel room, without any sense of personal history. I looked around, but there wasn't a single photograph or even an antique-style clock. The children sat, blank-faced, staring at the television screen. An old-fashioned cartoon was on, where black-and-white mice, thousands of them, streamed from the water faucet when the farmer turned on the spigot. The farmer's wife was so angry that she grabbed a rolling pin, randomly smashing the mice. They flattened like pancakes on the kitchen counter, then peeled themselves off and puffed back into their natural mouse shapes. Boom! Boom! She hit another, then another. The mice kept pouring out in a never-ending stream. "I used to watch these cartoons," I said to nobody in particular. "I didn't think they still showed them."

"They're sort of dumb," Amanda said, her face never leaving the screen.

"Does anyone want to come with me to the grocery store?"

I asked, the sentence not even completed before all three girls hopped from the couch and ran to the door, so eager to get to the van that it was as if we had not all just spent the better part of the day riding in it.

Outside in the bright sun I felt faint. Light shimmered along the edges of things and the concrete path up to the van seemed to pulse under my feet. "Wait a minute," I said to the girls, trying to catch my breath. We were higher up. The air was thinner here in the mountains. There were all those alternative directions on packages for baking a cake if you lived in a high-altitude area, so of course this difference would affect someone who was used to normal, thick air. I took a few more breaths, pausing in between as if I were sampling a wine. It must have been sitting around in all that smoke, too, that made me dizzy.

"Right, right, right," I said as I started the van. "Are you girls hungry?"

"Uh-uh. No. I'm not," they all chorused. "I'm so bloated," Jana said, holding her stomach. "Bloated" was one of the surprising grown-up words she used. For a child just turning four, Jana really had an excellent vocabulary. I liked her better when we were alone together. With Barbara, Jana's voice always took on a sniveling quality so that all the charm of her mature speech was lost in her needy tone.

I said I was sorry she was bloated, that I imagined how saltines and soda could really fill you up.

"Are you hungry, Sharon?" Amanda asked.

"Not very." I hadn't been hungry at all for most of the time we had been traveling and, except for the fresh walleye that we'd had the night before, nothing had tasted good to me. For the past few days, everything I ate had an aftertaste, like the inside of a can. Now the thought of that pile of raw meat in the refrigerator made me gag. "I feel a little bit nauseated, actually," I said to Jana. Aside from bloating, that was her other frequent complaint.

I pushed the cart up and down the aisles of Safeway and the

children scattered, running off for milk, cold cereal, a head of lettuce. I felt like Barbara when I told them that they could each pick one "special" thing and then left them in the cookie–snack–soft drink–candy aisle.

A hippie family who looked like they were caught in a time warp—the woman with long, straight hair parted down the middle, wearing something made from an Indian print bedspread; the ponytailed man in patched jeans; their wild children, all barefoot and tie-dyed—was walking dreamily through produce. The woman leaned over the purple eggplants, a newborn baby in a sling across her chest. I smiled at her as I reached for a plastic bag. Maybe it was the baby. Or maybe it was just seeing that people like this were still around. They were buying lots of vegetables and other healthy food. It made me feel good to see them, like knowing an endangered species still existed despite the hostile environment.

"How old is your baby?" I asked. Under the fluorescent lights, the baby's skin was a milky white-blue; the tiny mouth sucked the air.

"He's two weeks," said the woman, shifting one hip so I could get a better look.

Amanda, Jana and Libby skipped toward us, each clutching the junk-food item of choice. "Ohhh, a newborn," Amanda said, standing on her toes to look inside the bunting.

Obligingly, the woman leaned over, holding the baby out to the girls as if she were presenting an award. Then her other children, one tall boy and two children of indeterminate gender, gathered around. A shopper wanted to get through, but the aisle was clogged with children, so she, too, stopped to look at the baby.

"I would like a baby!" Libby said loudly, her clear voice rising above the crowd.

I felt my face grow hot, my mouth set in a tight, zippered-on smile. The hippie woman smiled back, moving one arm slowly over the zucchini.

Jesse and I had been trying to have another child for over a year. It seemed with each baby it was getting harder and harder to conceive. With Carlie I had become pregnant only a few months after going off the pill. With Libby, it was almost a year. Now I had the sense that as I grew older my eggs were drying up, losing their density and floating along like dustballs under the bed.

I thought of all the months before when I felt the first cramp, then the thin, mucusy stream of blood that signaled the beginning of another period. The last two periods had been late and their arrival had made me weep. I had started to look longingly at babies in supermarkets and malls.

Jesse was not nearly as upset as I was—in fact, it was hard to tell that he was upset at all. Dutifully, he performed when my chart indicated I was ovulating. On some level, I resented him for looking at this time as an excuse to have a lot of sex, while I had become a serious scholar of all aspects of infertility.

The deeper rift evolved because as I became obsessed with the need to have another child, Jesse started getting comfortable with the idea that the three of us—me, himself, Libby—were quite a nice little family and if we didn't have a baby, that would be all right with him.

"You know, if I get a leave next year, we could all go to Europe," Jesse had begun innocently enough. I was snuggled in the crook of his arm after we had made love. It was sometime at the beginning of the summer, a few weeks before Barbara had told me she was leaving David. I had just stopped work and turned all my attention to becoming pregnant. I remember that it was the first night we had the air conditioner on, and how thankful I was later that all the windows were closed. Mrs. Wilcox from next door thinks we are "the most wonderful young couple." That's what she once told Barbara. I would never be able to face Mrs. Wilcox again if I thought she'd heard all the things we said that night.

I guess I was upset with Jesse even before he came home from work that day. Early that afternoon I had called him to let him know my temperature was up, that the time was right. It was around noon and Libby had been invited to a friend's house for lunch.

"I can't come home now, Sharon. I have to meet Hassan in twenty minutes," Jesse told me. Hassan was an eternal graduate student from some Middle Eastern country that he didn't want to go back to. Jesse was always helping Hassan extend his visa.

"It's time now," I said, licking peanut butter off my fingers. I had made a sandwich and was eating it, standing up, at the kitchen counter. "How about if I come into the office for a quickie? Belinda can tell Hassan you're still in conference." I was joking. But only sort of.

"No," Jesse said seriously. "Listen, I'll see you tonight. I have to finish reading Hassan's paper before I see him."

"Tonight might be too late."

"Too late for what?"

"Too late for me to get pregnant. I think this is the last day this month I'll be ovulating."

"Sharon, it won't be too late in just a few hours. Listen. I really have to go." Jesse kissed a few times into the phone and hung up, not even waiting for my good-bye. The peanut butter stuck, making a lump in my throat.

One thing led to another and I didn't take my temperature again that day. Libby didn't get to bed until after nine. Then Jesse wanted to watch the end of the Chicago Cubs game. He was hooting and hollering as someone tied it up in the ninth inning. "It's a squibbler. It's a little squibbler right between first and second. And he beat it out! Goddamn!" Jesse slapped his thigh. "The ball had eyes! Come watch the end of this with me, Sharon." He pulled me down on the bed and started rubbing the back of my neck, kissing my shoulders. These were placating, wait-until-the-game-is-over gestures. Jesse massaged me through the commercial where three Neanderthal types argued about the merits of light beer.

I went downstairs and watered the plants, picking the dried ends off the Boston ferns hanging in the dining room window. Out of boredom, I opened the refrigerator, took out a jar of black olives and fished out a couple with my fingers. Tomorrow morning I'd go grocery shopping, so I looked to see what was missing. I added "eggs" to the shopping list by the phone. Then I ran a damp cloth around each plastic pocket in the empty egg compartment. I threw out a soft clump of cauliflower with browned edges and a piece of stale lemon pie whose meringue had slid off onto the side of the plate. Going back up the stairs, I heard Jesse whistle softly under his breath. "Way to hustle, baby. Way to hustle."

"The game's still on?" I hung back in the doorway as if the bedroom were contaminated by the rays from the television set. "I want to go to bed." I yawned, indicating that going to bed now meant going to sleep.

"Sharon, it's tied, three-three. This is a great game. Come watch the end of it with me."

"I don't care," I said, sounding sour. There are times when I think that Jesse's desire that we should share his interest in sports despite my refusal is a sign of some deeper, more essential incompatability. "Why don't you go downstairs and watch the game?" We have a second television tucked into a corner of the living room, but Jesse always likes to watch in bed. He was eating red licorice and finishing off a beer, belching when he squeezed the can. Then he shot it across the room into the wastebasket.

"Do you have to do that?" I asked.

"What? Burping or throwing the can?"

"Both," I said disgustedly.

"I got it in, didn't I? Think you could do that? From over here. From my side of the bed?" He was playful, trying to tease me out of my bad temper. He got up and retrieved the can from the trash. "Come on, Sharon, try it. Bet you can't. I'll give you three tries. I bet you can't even do it in three."

"What do you want to bet?" I asked, eyeing the distance across the room. It wasn't that far, but the angle was odd.

"A week's worth of dishes," Jesse said slyly—in the summer, the weekends were his, Friday night to Sunday, while I did the dishes during the week. "Or perhaps some exotic sexual treat?"

"Dishes," I said without pause. I crunched the ends of the beer can, making it more compact.

"Hey . . . ," Jesse began.

"Hey yourself, you didn't say anything," I said, tossing the can across the room. It fell short by almost a foot. "Two more." I got up, retrieved the can and went back to the bed. I took longer this time, moving my arm back and forth in practice. When I let it go, the can bounced off the wall and dropped right into the wastebasket. "Two points. And dishes all week starting tomorrow morning," I said, triumphant. Jesse congratulated me. I have to say that he's always a good sport.

We watched the end of the game. Jesse was happy that the Cubs won. I was feeling affectionate again, reaching for him under the covers when he turned off the light.

"You know, every time we make love, you don't have to think about having a baby," Jesse said, above me. "We can do this just for fun sometimes."

"I know," I said, moving slowly against him, his face outlined in the green glow of the clock radio.

I was about to tell him that I wasn't going to come, to go ahead without me, when something just switched on inside me and I felt all opened, lit up.

"Now?" he asked, continuing a steady rhythm.

"Wait." I caught my breath. "Yes. Now." My eyes closed tight, I had the image of thousands of tiny sperm, *rat-a-tat-tat*, heading into me, aiming for that one bull's-eye egg.

Afterward, we started talking in a desultory way. We talked about planting melons in the garden. And about whether he'd have to work this weekend. He told me that he was almost finished getting together the data for the new grant. This was an important one. That's when he mentioned going to Europe.

"What about my job?" I asked. Actually, I didn't care about my job. The best thing about it was that I didn't have to work three months of the year. I knew there was something wrong if the best thing about a job was when you weren't working at it.

"Maybe you can get a leave."

"I can't get a leave from extension service, Jess. It's not like a tenured university job."

"Ah, so quit, then. You can get something better when we come back. They don't pay what you're worth and you're not going to go anywhere with them, Sharon. It's a shit job, anyway."

"Well, it's *my* job," I said tightly. Though I had said those things myself, I was offended. It was like someone criticizing your parents—even if what they say is true, saying it is something only *you* should be able to do. "I didn't get to go to graduate school, or travel around the country for a post-doc," I added.

"Sharon, if you wanted to go to graduate school, you could have gone," Jesse said calmly. "Don't make it sound like you were following me from state to state like I was in a rock band or something."

I just sniffed. "Where would we go in Europe?"

"Well, probably Germany. I'd want to study with Frierhoff in Munich. He's there with the other physicist who was on the Nobel committee."

"Germany! You think I'd want to live in Germany?!"

Jesse blinked in surprise. "Well, why not? We could stay there, but that doesn't mean we wouldn't get to travel around . . ."

"Because I'm Jewish, Jesse, in case you've forgotten. Because my grandparents' families on both sides were gassed by the Germans. You think I want to hang out for a year in that kind of company?"

"Those were Nazis, Sharon. All Germans weren't Nazis. And there's a whole new generation of people now."

"And plenty left over who used to be *Hitler Jungend*. I'd look at every person over fifty as a potential murderer." I shook my head. "It would ruin my time."

"The German people don't have a franchise on this kind of behavior, for Christ's sake. You know that. You look at what we did to the Indians in this country! What happened to the Armenians; what the Nigerians did to the Ibos; look at Cambodia, for crying out loud. . . ."

"Don't start, please." I interrupted what I knew was a long list of genocidal atrocities. We had been through this before. Jesse refused to see the Holocaust as a special, terrible example among history's other terrible examples. Intellectually, I sometimes agreed with him, but there was always something that made me wary; it's a look that non-Jews get sometimes when the subject of the Holocaust comes up—like, "Uh-oh, there they go again." "Listen," I said evenly. "I'm a Jew and if I have a choice, I don't want to go to Germany. If I were Iranian, I wouldn't want to spend a year in Iraq. Isn't that understandable?"

"Well, I've been meaning to talk to you about this anyway, Sharon," Jesse said, concerned, his eyebrows coming together in a severe line across his forehead. "Sometimes I think you're really prejudiced. And I don't want Libby to hear this kind of talk."

"Me? *I'm* prejudiced?!" The accusation made me gasp. "You think I'm a prejudiced person?" I sat up in bed and turned on the light by the night table.

"I do," Jesse continued. "And I think you don't even realize it. It's not only this German thing. You make cracks all the time about Hassan. You're very anti-Arab."

"God, Jesse. Hassan is sneaky and manipulative and he uses you."

"You think that because he's an Arab."

"Come on. I wouldn't like Hassan if he were a rabbi. You complain yourself. You're always saying what a lousy grad student he is."

"It's different. I know him as a person. You don't really. You never see Hassan as a person."

I got up to go to the bathroom. Then Jesse got up to go to the bathroom. In the hallway we moved by each other silently like strangers passing in the aisle of a plane. By that time we were both all riled up and the fight started to escalate. Back in bed, I opened by saying that Germany or no Germany, by next year, we might have another baby and going to Europe with two very young children would be difficult for me. While he would be off in the pubs drinking steins of beer and eating Wiener schnitzel with Nobel laureates, I'd be shlepping around the city with two children, looking for Pampers.

"Well, maybe this is telling us something. Maybe it's not a good time to have another baby if you're feeling so put upon," Jesse said in a patronizing tone. "I've been thinking about it for a while, and I'm not sure that having another baby is the absolutely right thing for us to do. We're so much more free this year with Libby getting older. And she'll be in school pretty soon." He added, "My work's going so well this year. You know that. And if I get that grant . . ."

I looked at him in disbelief. Did he really mean what he just said? For that moment he looked different to me. He had just had a haircut last week and there must have been a new barber at his regular shop, because instead of just Jesse's hair made shorter, this cut was definitely styled, with close-cropped sides and a tight crunch of curl at the top. Jesse didn't pay it too much attention, but when he first came home, I said that he looked terrific, like a model out of *GQ*. I meant it, too. Then, in that moment when he said maybe we shouldn't have any more children, I looked at him as if for the first time, hating what I saw. Suddenly, he looked slick and selfish to me. "I hate that haircut," I said, my upper lip curling in contempt.

Off guard, Jesse touched his hand to his head. "I thought you liked it."

"I don't," I said meanly. "You look like every other stupid yuppie."

"Sharon, what are you talking about? I'm trying to have a logical discussion about maybe going to Europe and whether or not we should have another child and you go off the deep end talking about Nazis and bad haircuts. You're not making sense."

"You don't know what I'm talking about? You don't think I'm making sense?" I started spluttering, but anger sharpened and controlled my response until I felt the viciousness of its thrust. When Jesse portrays us in this way—he is calm, logical and sane; I am emotional, premenstrual, irrational—I literally feel like going berserk. When Jesse intimates I am an hysteric, I become hysterical. "I'll tell you what I'm talking about, you selfish prick! You think only of yourself, your ridiculous work, which is so goddamned esoteric that only two other people in the entire country can ever understand what the hell you're talking about"—at this point, I flung one of his journals across the room; it hit the wall with a muffled *thwap*—"and you think what you do is so important that heaven forbid, another human might take up some more of your precious time. The time that you could use to devote to your work. Shit, let's send Libby off to private school. Why take her to Europe at all? You can get more work done without her. You think your work is so fucking important? Well, I have news for you, buddy. More people read what *I* write than will *ever* read the obscure bullshit science you produce. Big deal—a quantum theory of particles. At least when I write about removing a stain there's a concrete result!" I rose up from the bed, my fists clenched.

"Are you quite finished?" Jesse asked coldly. He started talking in this really detached, clinical voice, as if I were an escaped mental patient he was trying to lure back to the hospital. He said that perhaps *I* was really the selfish one, if I needed this baby to feel complete; that he took parenting seriously and to do it *unselfishly*—which was, in his opinion, the only way he thought it could be done—one needed a realistic view of the situation, rather than yielding to some romantic yearning, some immature baby-love.

We went on and on, throwing all the old baggage at each other with a violence that we couldn't seem to stop. Jesse lost it, too, telling me that he blamed my mother for creating the bigoted, neurotic Jewish princess that I was. "You think the world is designed to please only you?!" he bellowed. "Go ahead and cry. Go call your parents. Maybe they'll buy you something to make you feel better. You want them to try to buy you a baby?"

I moved on the bed, curling my leg and kicking out at him. "Stop it," he growled, grabbing my ankle until I twisted away from him and bolted across the room to pick up the journal from the floor. I ripped apart the pages, throwing them like confetti into the air. I told him with a stabbing venom how remarkable it was that he had been able to go back to work so soon after Carlie's death; how lucky that he was so quickly able to pull himself together and apply for yet another grant so he could make himself a famous scientist after the loss of his only son!

Almost reflexively, he reached his hand back and slapped me, a stinging slap that numbed the whole side of my face. He threw on a shirt and jeans and stormed out of the room, doors slamming in his wake, and I stood by the side of the bed until I heard our car screech meanly out into the night. I stripped the bed, took everything into the study, and lay on the couch, crying myself to sleep.

The next morning, the three of us sat at the kitchen table as Libby chattered away about a stuffed bunny pictured on the back of the box of Honey Nut Cheerios. All filled up by such an enthusiasm, she seemed particularly beautiful that morning, glowing and innocent. I knew Jesse sensed it, too. We drank black coffee beside her, feeling worn out and shamed. Jesse was stubbled and smelled like stale smoke and booze. I felt like the worn-out wife someone was coming home to in a country-and-western song. Afterward, we hugged by the sink, Jesse sobbing as I held him. For days afterward, we felt sick with each other, with ourselves, with what we had done and said. Even after we had talked and made up, we both felt weakened and fragile, as if we had just come out of a fever.

The woman, Mary, was not there when we got back to Barbara's father's house, and her name was not mentioned again. We went out to the backyard to eat, and Jana and Libby got up on their knees on the picnic bench. I cut up Libby's steak into pellet-sized portions and handed her back the fork. With the other hand, she picked up a piece of meat and popped it into her mouth, nodding approvingly with the air of a connoisseur. "Good steak," she said, smiling as she chewed. Her baby teeth looked perfect, even and white, with hardly any space between them. It was just a few weeks ago that the dentist, on our very first visit, surprised me by saying that this was not necessarily a good thing, this lack of space. Holding Libby's delicate chin, the dentist's hand looked massive. "Crowding," he said ominously. Later, when I told Jesse what the dentist said, he had the same reaction as I did. "She has a beautiful mouth," Jesse had said defensively.

"Is the steak too rare for you, Sharon?" Mr. Davis asked, seeing I had taken just a small slice for myself.

"No, it's fine. Delicious!" Briskly, I cut into the soft, pink center. I chewed and chewed until the meat was just a watery paste in my mouth. I passed the platter down to Barbara. The meat smelled strong to me, like cows.

"I got this plate at the 1964 World's Fair in New York," Mr.

Davis said as he lifted off a slab of meat for himself. Around the border of the plate were illustrations of children all in different native dress. By now the plate was worn, so parts of the children were rubbed off and you could only see outlines of faces and costumes. "Living in New York then, your family must have gone all the time, I'll bet," Mr. Davis said. It seemed more a rhetorical observation than a real question. I just nodded. I wasn't able to recall if my family had gone at all.

Amanda plucked the pieces of radish and cucumber out of her salad, setting them on the side of the plate.

"You like cucumber, sweetie," Barbara said.

"Not this cucumber," Amanda replied. "There's slime on the pits."

"*Eeeeouy!*" Jana made a face and picked through her salad with a spoon, removing the offending bits of cucumber as if they were dead bugs.

I threw Libby a don't-you-dare look and moved her glass of milk away from the edge of the table.

True to Barbara's word, her father made nothing but the smallest of small talk. After the children left the table, he discussed in great length how he came to a decision about which VCR to buy. Then he switched to an account of his dietary restrictions following the last liver attack. I must have seemed interested because he proceeded to list all the ingredients for delicious, nonalcoholic piña coladas and daiquiris. "You'd never know the difference," he assured me. "Not in a hundred years."

After dinner I took the girls for a walk while Barbara and her father went back to the kitchen to do the dishes. We circled the block and the second time around a posse of small boys followed on bicycles and Big Wheels. "Hey you girls," one of them called. "Comeer!"

We stopped in our tracks. The girls looked at me and giggled. They thought it was funny that he had included me, a mother, with the rest of the group.

"Hello," I called back. The girls positioned themselves behind me, lined up like baby ducks.

"Where you girls going?" the same boy said as he got closer to us. He had the authoritative tone of a playground bully.

"We're just taking a little walk. What's your name?" I asked pleasantly, trying to set a good example.

"Hey, better not cut through our property," said another boy. He stood up, straddling his small bicycle as if it were a Harley.

"Come on," I said, slowly walking away with the girls. I half expected to feel the thud of a rock against my back.

"Who are those mean boys?" Libby asked, taking my hand. Amanda had taken the other hand and Jana clung on to a pocket of my shorts, looking worriedly over her shoulder.

"Oh, just some little boys trying to act tough," I said casually, though my teeth were clenched in anger.

"I can do karate," Amanda said, feeling braver when the boys were out of view. She made quick chops in the air, accompanying them with short explosions of breath. "At school, if a boy hits me, I karate him back."

"Yes," I said. "You shouldn't let a boy hit you."

"Or you could walk away and tell the teacher," Libby said practically.

It was strange to be strolling in a regular neighborhood and see mountains. There were two asymmetrical, conical peaks dotted occasionally by houses and a groove of road circling about halfway up; the rest of the mountain was dense and green except for two nipples of white at the very top. I realized that I had always lived in places where the land was flat and undramatic.

Later, I gave the children baths, scrubbing them down as if they had been out backpacking for weeks on a dusty trail. Barbara's father left out clean, fluffy towels that had the April freshness of a strong fabric softener. Tonight I was looking forward to sleeping indoors. Sleeping in a real bed. It seemed impossible that we had only been gone for three days. I couldn't

Chapter 13

"How come you're so quiet today?" Barbara said as we rode through the desert. In the distance were unusual rock formations, stony knobs polished to a dull smoothness like a crowd of bald-headed men.

More and more I was thinking that what Barbara was doing was wrong. Not impetuous. Or reckless. Or romantic. But wrong. "I'm just tired," I lied. "I didn't sleep very well last night."

"It's uncomfortable being with my father, isn't it? It's wearing just to listen to him talk," Barbara said, so misreading my mood that I felt all of our past intimacy was suddenly suspect. Tension gathered in the air between us like a swarm of gnats.

We had folded down the seat in the back and the children had made a nest of pillows, blankets, dolls and stuffed toys. Jana was sucking a finger contentedly and Libby and Amanda were dancing their Care Bears around the edge of the blanket. "He doesn't *connect*," Barbara continued. "He doesn't ever ask you anything because he's afraid to find out about someone else. And my mother is just the same. They really were a perfect couple." Barbara shook her head. "Now they're getting back say that I really liked camping all that much. There was always an effort to do the simplest thing, like brush your teeth in the morning or make something to eat. And we were hardly roughing it with the van. Still, there was a lot about the general outdoors that I found annoying—the damp nights, the bugs, the dirt.

Mentally, I organized the rest of the trip. If we left early, we'd make it to Dinosaur National Monument by the afternoon. Then two more outside nights before a Hyatt Regency in Reno. Then Barbara's new place in San Francisco. The next day Libby and I would fly to San Diego for two days. Jack had a swimming pool and a hot tub overlooking La Jolla Canyon. Why I didn't tell Jesse that, I don't know. Maybe I didn't want him to think we would have too good a time without him.

The girls were going to sleep downstairs in what Mr. Davis referred to as the "rumpus room," while Barbara and I were going to have the twin single beds in the spare bedroom. After we got the girls settled, I went to bed, too, though it wasn't even ten o'clock. On the table next to the bed was a detective magazine. I read a story about a former movie stuntman who hired himself out as a chauffeur to rich women and stole all their jewelry before killing them by plunging their cars off a cliff. Through his previous employment, he knew how to jump out and roll safely away. Finally, he was caught by the California Motor Vehicle Bureau for his bad driving record.

I turned out the light and listened for the sounds of Barbara and her father talking, but there was only the drone of the television in the living room. Later, as if in a dream, I saw Barbara's silhouette in the doorway. Slowly, she pulled down the covers and got into bed. She sighed and sighed. Still drugged by sleep, I felt as if her sighs were filling up the room like helium.

together. I would bet without once talking about why he ever left, or her remarriage, or why anything."

"Do you think she's coming because he's sick or because she wants to be married to him again?"

"Who knows!" Barbara said, throwing up her hands. The van stayed on course because the highway was laid out straight and clean in front of us, like a runway for a jumbo jet. "Nobody says anything. My mother mentioned that she'd be packing some things and going to Colorado as if it were a summer vacation. And she hasn't seen him in—how many years? Well, since my sister's wedding. Almost ten years ago."

"Who was that woman Mary?"

"A friend. That's what my father called her. 'A friend.' "

"A girlfriend?"

Barbara shrugged. "Your guess is as good as mine." She added, "You know what the really ironic thing is?"

"What?"

"How one of the things that I thought I was going to get being married to David was warmth and intensity, not all the polite Waspy shit that I grew up with. And then David turns out to be just like my father."

"I don't think David is like your father," I said quietly.

The cloudless sky was like a big, blue canopy. We were close to Jensen, Utah, the headquarters of the Dinosaur National Monument. The view from both sides looked like the backdrop to a cowboy movie and I half expected to see a dusty trail of horses' hooves up ahead. "This is fabulous," I said. "Look out the window, girls. Look at that scene." A river cut its way deep into a jagged canyon and along the steepest part were craggy caves that looked secret and mysterious.

The children looked quickly out at the landscape. "Uh-huh." Amanda nodded before going back to her Care Bears.

"David is scarred," Barbara went on. "You can't come out of a toxic environment like that and not have scars."

I thought of David in his neat, pressed pants, the habit he had of taking off his glasses and cleaning them before he answered a question. There was something tidy and careful about him. "I don't think he's so scarred," I said.

"Well, come on, Sharon." Barbara's voice started to rise. "The way he can't emote. The way everything has to be pried out of him. And half the time I didn't know if it was worth the effort."

"He's reserved," I said.

"He's hollow," Barbara said bitterly.

"Oh, Barbara stop it. That's not true. He's not hollow. It just makes you feel better to paint him as some kind of emotional zombie, that's all." There! I felt better.

Barbara let out a long sigh, like the air going out of a tire. "Look, I'm not asking for sympathy. Just a little of the liberal open-mindedness you people are so famous for."

"What does that mean, exactly?" I asked archly. "*You* people?"

"Sharon, I was kidding around. Can you lighten up a bit?"

"Okay," I said grimly.

"Okay," Barbara repeated.

We both remained silent, waiting for the other to speak. "Look, I'm sorry," I began. "This is hard for me. To listen and not be able to respond honestly."

"I don't want you to be dishonest, Sharon. I just want you to—well, to be more understanding."

"I am trying," I said.

"Well, okay, then."

"Okay."

Just then Libby tapped me on the shoulder and asked why people have spit in their mouths.

"Why what?" I asked, though I had heard the first time.

"Why do people have this spit in their mouths?"

I told her that saliva was used to soften our food, so it was easier to eat certain foods.

"Like graham crackers?" she asked.

"Yes."

"But not like orange juice. You don't need spit for orange juice."

"Right. Not for drinks."

"But like peanut butter sandwiches?"

"Yes."

"But not like applesauce?"

I said I guessed not. Not applesauce.

"What about french fries?"

"Yes."

"And hamburgers?"

"Libby, I don't think I want to do this anymore."

A few minutes passed while she stood behind me, her warm breath along my neck. "Mommy?" she asked softly, her voice tight.

"What, baby?" I petted the hand she had resting on my shoulder.

"I think I have too much spit."

As I turned to look at her, she opened up her mouth and I saw her small, pink tongue and what seemed to be a normal wetness. "What do you mean, Lib?"

"I have spit even when I'm not even eating anything. It's just there in my mouth," she said worriedly. "Sitting there."

"Saliva is there in everybody's mouth, sweetheart."

"Everybody has spit," Barbara added. "Me. Your mommy. Amanda. Jana."

"What do you do with it?" Libby asked.

"Well," Barbara said casually, "you just swallow what you're not using. You don't even have to think about it. You just swallow automatically."

"Okay," Libby said, settling back down on the blanket.

"What do you think goes on in their heads?" Barbara said to me.

✦

"THE MIGHTY BRONTOSAURUS, OR THUNDER LIZARD, WEIGHED MORE THAN FORTY TONS AND MEASURED EIGHTY FEET IN LENGTH," Barbara read from a plaque next to a thighbone as big as a semitrailer.

We followed a solemn row of tourist families. In front of us a whole side of a cliff was cut through to reveal pieces of bone, chunks and bits of what had once been dinosaurs, preserved for thousands of years and splashed randomly throughout the rock. It reminded me of fruit floating in a Jell-O mold. "These are called fossils," Barbara explained.

The children did not seem particularly impressed. It was hard to imagine these white bones actually being part of a live animal. I looked out at the quarry, picturing dinosaurs ambling through the canyons, bending to drink at the river's edge, nibbling the leaves off cottonwood and chokecherry trees.

"Where are the dinosaurs?" Jana asked, looking over toward a clot of people. There were two or three families up ahead, the parents diligently reading aloud every word on every sign.

"Here, sweetheart. These are fossils. The bones of dinosaurs who lived here a long time ago," Barbara explained. "This next one here is a stegosaurus." She pointed to a picture of a dragony beast with armor plating and yard-long spines on its tail.

"But where are the *real* dinosaurs?" Libby asked.

"*Real* dinosaurs?" Barbara and I chorused. Soon we learned that all three of the girls—even Amanda—had expected to see dinosaurs. Live ones. What else would there be in a dinosaur park except dinosaurs? They had all been to natural habitat zoos. To animal safaris. It seemed none of them had quite gotten a handle on the word "extinct." You mean we came all this way to look at bones?

Barbara stayed with the girls in the gift shop while I wrote out a postcard for Grandma Lela. It had a picture of an allosaurus, a fierce, carnivorous creature whose long, sharp teeth had serrated edges like a bread knife. On the front I drew a little bubble coming from his mouth and the words, "And these are my own teeth, 100%." It's a statement my grandmother uses quite frequently when she is complimented on her smile.

The sun made it too hot to picnic, so we ate in the van and drove on to the Great Salt Lake. A billboard on the side of the road said YOU BOB LIKE A CORK! and you really do, though nobody but tourists would ever go in the Great Salt Lake. Any cut or opening in the skin and the salt burns like crazy. Amanda cried about a scratch on her arm and Jana cried about a mosquito bite on her shoulder. Libby, standing waist-high next to an old man who was wading out with a plastic float, exclaimed, "Why, my vagina feels all tingly!" and the man looked away, embarrassed.

After a few minutes we came out covered with a film of salt, feeling dried out and scratchy as tissue paper. One, two, three, we passed the girls, shrieking, under the cold-water showers right on the beach. Libby dropped the last clean towel we had onto a cement platform coated with gray muck. "Oh, goddamn it, Libby!" I said through clenched teeth. There was another family lined up, waiting—a young, pug-nosed blond mother and three blond children with the same face, as if they had all been stamped out with a cookie cutter.

"Don't say that, Mom," Libby said primly. She walked away and started brushing the excess water off her shoulders as if she had just gotten a haircut. The blond mother herded her brood into the shower and smiled. I felt self-conscious about being blasphemous in Mormon country.

We had wine in the cooler, and the kids were already asleep as we spread out a blanket under the stars. "That was a great dinner," I said, putting up the hood of my sweatshirt and tying the cords tightly under my chin. The temperature must have fallen twenty degrees in the last hour.

"It was," Barbara agreed. We had made chicken on the grill, new potatoes and onions wrapped in foil, a green salad with fresh snow peas. And for dessert, s'mores over the campfire. One bite brought me back to cookouts in upstate New York at Camp Kendall where I had spent the summers of my childhood. With the sticky, sweet marshmallow and the melted chocolate, I could almost smell the pines, hear the loons call across the lake.

Then the second bite made me gag. I ended up leaving the s'more on a paper plate, and throwing it away.

"I don't think I should drink," I said to Barbara as she passed me a cup of Chablis. In the background, an eerie light, like something burning, hung behind the cliffs in the distance. It seemed as if it would never get truly dark here in the desert.

"Why not?" she asked.

I didn't want to say it. Even thinking it and wanting to believe it felt like a jinx. Let alone saying it aloud. Barbara waited, holding the paper cup aloft as if she were about to make a toast. I held my breath, almost whispering: "I think I could be pregnant."

Barbara was ecstatic. "Oh, Sharon! That would be *wonderful!*" Then, "Well, how late are you?"

"Just a week. I've been late before, but I've been feeling a little nauseated the last few days." Hurriedly, I added, "Probably it's just the traveling."

Barbara began to sip her wine, looking thoughtful. "You want to take a test? It's probably too early for one of those do-it-yourself jobs, but in Reno, we could go to a clinic or something."

"I don't know," I said dully.

"I'm sure they'd be able to find out in one day in Reno," Barbara pressed on. "Wouldn't you like to set your mind at ease, just to know?"

"I don't know," I repeated, wondering if I should have brought it up at all.

Barbara's tone was matter-of-fact. "You've been wanting this for over a year, hon."

"I know. But I'm late a lot. There've been so many disappointments. . . ." My voice trailed off as I fingered the rim of an empty cup.

"I know," Barbara said kindly, reaching to pet my arm. "I'm sorry. We don't even have to talk about it yet if that makes you nervous. Don't even think about it yet."

"The end of May," I said longingly.

"What?"

"The baby would be born the end of May. That would be wonderful. I'd be off then."

Barbara smiled. "What are your names now?" She knew these changed frequently.

"Sophia if it's a girl. Or maybe Emily. Jacob for a boy."

"They'll call her 'Sophie.' "

"I like that, too," I said emphatically.

"David has two great aunts, Sophie and Zelda. Like two little birds. They each weigh about eighty pounds."

Just then we heard the crunch of gravel and saw someone walking up the trail to the outhouse. "Ladies, hello!" He waved heartily and paused, as if waiting for an invitation to join us.

"Hi!" Barbara and I chorused and hurriedly turned back to our own conversation. His name was Fred and he was an earth-science teacher from Provo, camping with his two sons in a tent-trailer a few sites down. A few hours before, his boys, hard up for youthful companionship, had lured our girls to play while Fred had held forth in an officious way about fossils and sedimentary rock formation. "Where are you girls from?" he asked, his eyes searching. We were used to people taking an interest. We had gotten a lot of looks, the five of us females camping together. Most of it friendly—winks from a park ranger, polite smiles from a gas station attendant. It was clear—what with all the luggage piled on the rack atop the van—that this was a long trip, and we were not the usual type of family. "You ladies go camping together often?" he asked, fishing around to try our true identities.

"Yes, we do," I replied mysteriously. Obviously Barbara and

I were not sisters. Maybe he thought we were lovers, outdoorsy lesbians who brought the kids along.

"I'm moving to California," Barbara said. "She's helping me drive."

I frowned. It made me sound like something rented from U-Haul.

"Oh, really?" he said, moving on quickly to introduce himself. Eventually he told us that he was divorced with shared custody and this was his week to have the children. "Yes, it's the best arrangement," Fred said, rubbing his hands together like sticks. "If you can work it out and stay friends with your ex, then it's really great."

I said that if you were able to stay friends with your ex, then you might as well stay married. Then I smiled to show that I was just kidding around. Fred flashed me a patronizing look before he went on to give Barbara his full attention. I noticed that the bald spot in the back of his head was perfectly round and quite sunburned, so that it looked as if he was wearing a little pink yarmulke. He told her she had a great tan, looking all the while at the space between her tube top and her neck. Then he asked if we had eaten dinner yet. Really, he had asked Barbara, the "you" directed only toward her. For a minute I thought she would go off with him and there I'd be, stuck baby-sitting for five kids in the desert.

I watched the flirtatious way Barbara threw her head back when she smiled. Fred was pleased and puffed his chest out a little bit, like Hector the rooster strutting back and forth in his cage. "Well, the reason I asked," Fred said, referring to his inquiry about dinner, "is that I've got my charcoals already going. If you want, you're welcome to share our grill."

When Barbara wavered, I thanked him, but said firmly that *our* charcoals, too, were going. That, in fact, they were pretty near ready.

When his boys came back to claim him, Fred regretfully said

good night, throwing one last over-the-shoulder look at Barbara as he walked away.

"Maybe there aren't a lot of single women in Provo," Barbara said as we walked back to our picnic table.

"Well, you *were* coming on to him," I said.

"Sharon, I wasn't!" Barbara exclaimed, sounding hurt.

"But you do. You do it unconsciously. You never talk to men the way you talk to women."

"Oh, who does!" Barbara said, clapping her hands to get the girls' attention. They were out in the scrub, hitting back the bushes with sticks, the way Fred's sons had done.

Now we waved back to Fred when he passed but did not give him further encouragement. We watched as he walked over to the wooden shed behind a thatch of tangled bush. When he emerged, scarcely minutes later, it had gotten darker. I saw that he was leading the way with the beam from a flashlight.

"Are you cold? Do you want to go back to the van and sleep?" Barbara asked solicitously.

"Just a little longer," I said, rubbing my cold toes. I had been too lazy to take down the suitcase and get socks.

Barbara poured herself another cup of wine. "You know, I remember thinking when I got pregnant with Jana, 'Good, because then when I divorce David, Amanda will have some company. She won't be an only child with just me.' So I knew even then. I felt sorry for David, but I knew I couldn't spend the rest of my life with him."

That made me so sad, her saying that. I tried to think of David as he was with Barbara, before he was the one being left. I started to think of him as someone people would feel sorry for. As if she knew what I was thinking, Barbara went on. "You don't have to feel so bad for David. He'll meet someone, Sharon."

My mind was already churning with possibilities. There were a number of female graduate students in Jesse's department, though most of the American ones seemed brainy and odd. I thought of planning a party. I might feel better about things if I knew that David could be recoupled.

Barbara started talking about who David was. Or who he was not. It was like a eulogy in some ways. There was not overt bad behavior on his part as much as deficiencies. His preoccupation with work. How he never really listened to anything she said. "I mean, Jesse's a workaholic, too, and not exactly the warmest guy," Barbara said, "but at least he always knows you're there."

"Do you think Jesse is cold?" I asked, surprised.

"Well, sort of. Standoffish sometimes. Don't you?"

"Yes, I guess he is." I remembered when we first started going together, the most startling difference between Jesse and Jack Silver seemed to be Jesse's need for privacy. And it was true that one of the things I liked best about Jack Silver was that he was an unconscious toucher. That we never walked anywhere together without his taking my hand. When we slept together, Jack would always hang on to a piece of me, effortlessly turning with me in the night so that we could fit. With Jesse, it seemed *I* was the one reaching out, touching him.

"Does that bother you?" Barbara asked.

"Maybe sometimes," I said. "But what I can't stand about Jesse . . ." I began, feeling an immediate pang of guilt. Right before we left, Jesse had made an offhanded remark about how Barbara would most likely be criticizing David to me all during the trip. "I can just hear her, ripping the poor bastard to shreds, pieces of him strewn along the highway like garbage," Jesse said. I replied that she was going through a difficult time and needed to justify herself.

"And you'll have a lot to contribute, I guess?" Jesse had asked.

"About you? Not a whole lot."

"But you'll think of something, right?"

"Jesse," I had said. "You're not perfect!"

Now, sitting with Barbara in the cool, calm desert night, I

thought of Jesse's sometimes cool, calm detachment. How it seemed that the stronger I felt about something—having another baby, for example—the less emotionally involved Jesse became. "What I really don't like is when he gets analytic on me, and when he feels cornered in an argument, he starts sounding all professorial and pedantic." I tightened my jaw and began to imitate him: " 'Well, Sharon, you're obviously missing the whole point. . . .' " I reached over to take a sip of Barbara's wine. Just a sip couldn't hurt. "You know, he really can be a prick sometimes," I said. "Maybe I shouldn't be saying that . . ."

"A woman who doesn't sometimes speak badly of her husband is not to be trusted," Barbara said decisively.

"I love him most of the time. . . ."

"Oh, you'd always stand by Jesse," Barbara said, laughing. "You would never, ever do what I'm doing."

I started to sing "Stand By Your Man" in a serviceable country twang.

My voice echoed through the canyons, the night air so still and clear it was like singing in the inside of a bubble. When I finished the song, Barbara began to applaud. "God, you are *so* good. I mean it, Sharon. You could sing professionally. I really mean it. You could get discovered."

"I used to think about that," I said, taking another small sip of wine. "But it takes a lot of effort to make it. You have to really want it."

"Don't you ever regret not trying?"

I told her that I didn't think I did, that I was pretty sure I could never make it.

We stood up together to shake off the blanket. "Who could ever be sure?" she said, meeting me halfway as we folded, meeting each other corner to corner.

Chapter 14

It took two more days to get to Reno. Two days of sandy scrub and the peculiar gray-green of desert vegetation. Occasionally we would pass a town—a blur of houses, a gas station, a post office—off the highway. Some of the places were like ghost towns with boarded-up shacks leaning into the wind and scraggles of tumbleweed caught up against rusted fence posts. Whenever we saw a restaurant, we stopped, just to break the monotony. The women who served us had the lined, dusty faces of those who had been battered by the elements. I wondered how they survived living out here in winter.

The combination of sun, silence and the relentless road was stunning in its isolation and the children were so bored that they stopped being cranky and eventually either slept or assumed the blank stares that you see in photos of undernourished children in Third World countries.

We pulled into Reno about three o'clock in the afternoon and coming into a city after those hours in the desert made me feel like I did when I used to drive back home with my family after a day at the beach, the salty beach smells still in the car and the sand gritty between my toes.

We had reservations at a hotel that had advertised suites with Jacuzzis and complimentary continental breakfasts; it was also

the first place we called that promised baby-sitting arrangements
for the evening. The hourly wage was a little more than I make
at my job. Barbara had insisted, "We'll need to get away from
the kids for a while. And you want to feel at ease knowing you
have a responsible person."

I said that at that price we should be getting Mary Poppins.

In the lobby of the hotel, we signed in and a teenage bellhop
took our bags, whisking us through an over-air-conditioned
corridor at a fast clip, the little girls running at our heels. Expertly, he slid the metal disk in the computer lock and paused
for us to enter. We watched as he drew the heavy drapes and
flipped up a panel to show how to regulate the temperature.
Everything smelled new. Like wallpaper paste and the acrylic
fluff of just-laid carpet. It was one large room rather than an
actual suite, but one side jutted off into an L-shaped portion
with two love seats and a coffee table. "Those open up," he
instructed, "and there's more blankets and sheets in the closet."

"Thank you," Barbara and I said at the same time, each
producing a bill. She was closer and put hers in the boy's hand.
"Thank you," I repeated to Barbara.

The room was mauve with accents of silver gray, though on
one table there was an orange lamp, a refugee left behind from
another color scheme. "I love this room!" Amanda was enthusiastic, going from bathroom to closet to mauve-and-silver sofa.
After the confines of the van, the room seemed as big as a
gymnasium and the kids jumped from double bed to double
bed, up and down, back and forth, until they were giddy with
dizzy delight.

"Let's see the view," Barbara said, walking over to the window. Against my wishes we were on the fourth floor, the closest
we could get to the ground, but still too far to jump from the
balcony in case of fire without doing damage to internal organs.
It was that or ground level facing the parking lot and Barbara
thought we'd hear drunks coming and going at all hours of the
night. "Look, there's the pool," she said. "Let's go in for a dip."

I was still standing at the window as the girls stripped off their clothes and continued to jump on the beds. Below was a grassy courtyard bordered with purple flowers and in the middle was a swimming pool with the irregular contour of a malignant cell. From this height the water was a brilliant turquoise, a mirror image of the sky. Suddenly, I became so tired that I could have fallen asleep standing up, leaning my head against the cool glass of the window. "I think I really need a nap, Barb. I can hardly keep my eyes open."

"Go to sleep," she said quickly. "I'll take them down."

"You're sure?" I looked longingly at the flat double beds.

"Sure, it's fine."

I barely managed to stay awake to go through our suitcase to find Libby's bathing suit and help her into it before I pulled the covers back on the bed and sank down, exhausted. "Good night, dear Mommy," Libby said, kissing me passionately on the lips. She smelled sweet and a little stale, like spilled milk out in the sun. I floated to sleep, hearing off in the distance the heavy closing of the hotel room door, the happy chatter of the girls as they ran down the hall.

Dreams came one after the other, vivid, Technicolor dreams. I woke once hearing a man's deep laughter outside the door and felt disoriented but too tired to care. The dreams followed each other like commercials on television. There was Patsy trying on clothes in my old bedroom, unable to get anything to fit around her waist. "Patsy, I thought you were dead," I said to her, hanging up all the items she discarded. She was older and a little chubby, but her red hair still flew out from her face, electric. For some reason, we were going to get in trouble if the clothes were not put away and, glad as I was to see her, I was annoyed at her slovenliness. "We'll pick it up later," Patsy said, throwing one of my dresses across the room.

In the next dream I was in a strange kitchen in a beach house and my parents were playing Scrabble; my mother was complaining about being stuck with no vowels for the second turn in a row. The woman, Mary, Barbara's father's friend, was at the stove, making jam in her white nurse's uniform. She asked, "Does anyone around here know how to get grape stains out of white nylon?"

Later I was with Jesse at a picnic barbecue with the physics department. We were all around a table filling our plates and everybody was commenting exuberantly about the food. Ron Simone had Jesse's secretary, Belinda, up against a tree and was kissing her, but no one seemed to see them but me. Her hands were on his back, pressing him to her, her pink nails flashing. I ate charcoaled hamburgers and baked beans, embarrassed to feel myself grow excited watching the rhythm of Ron Simone's ass as he humped Belinda against the rough tree bark.

The baby-sitter introduced herself as Grandma Pearl. She was about seventy years old, but miniskirted and made up, so that at first glance she looked not like an old woman, but a young woman who perhaps had some incurable disease. In five minutes we received decades of history: a stint as a showgirl, a dealer in the casinos, a munitions assembly worker; operations for female problems; a husband dead of lung cancer; a son named Billy who was a policeman in San Jose. As she talked, she used her hands for emphasis and about a dozen plastic bracelets clacked up and down both arms. "You ask why I stay here in Reno?" said Grandma Pearl. Actually we had not. "I don't know myself, except it's hard to teach an old dog new tricks."

I asked Pearl how long she had been baby-sitting for the hotel.

"I can't even count the years," she said casually. "Hey, look, can I hang up my wrap someplace?" She extricated herself from a homemade mohair sweater made of pastel blues and pinks that looked like a baby blanket.

Jana was coloring happily, sitting on the floor in between the beds, but Libby and Amanda stood across the room, watchful and guarded. Libby flashed me a look: You are going to leave me with this strange lady?! Barbara gave instructions for bedtime routines as if Grandma Pearl were a regular baby-sitter from down the block.

"Let's go back," I said to Barbara when we were barely to the elevator.

"Sharon! Don't be ridiculous." Inside, Barbara pressed the lobby button about a half dozen times. "They'll be perfectly fine. This is a woman the hotel uses all the time. You think a hotel like this is going to take a chance and hire a screwball?"

"Barbara, she clearly *is* a screwball!"

"You know what I mean. A *dangerous* screwball. She's nice. Did you see all that stuff that she brought for the kids to play with?" Grandma Pearl had brought in a satchel filled with toys and games.

"She looks like a bag lady," I said. "And those bracelets!"

"You are such a snob. You'd feel better if she were wearing a Rolex?"

We got off the elevator and walked through the lobby underneath a dome of frosted glass out into the brightly lit night. "I'd feel better if she were a teenager and wearing Esprit."

The street was so lit up with glowing neon you couldn't tell that it was really night. Then, too, there weren't doors on any of the casinos, just wide-open entrances, so there was no clear differentiation, inside from outside. The effect of being unrooted in time and place was disquieting, as if we were in one of those sensory deprivation tanks.

"I wish we had just left on our shorts and sneakers," I said. I had on a bright, summer dress with a cutout back and Barbara was wearing a black skirt and a red silk blouse. We were both wearing heels. We looked good but overdressed for this crowd. Most of the people in the street were more casual. And some even had the grizzled look of the urban homeless, though they, too, were busy playing the slot machines. "I thought gambling casinos would have women in long gowns and pearls, men in dinner jackets. . . ." We stepped around a little old lady in a flowered housedress who was headed for the blackjack tables, dragging a tank of oxygen behind her. She had a dark, wrinkled face with so many tiny, fine lines that she looked like a brown, cracked egg. Barbara and I walked up the block toward one of the more elegant casinos. In the front was a fountain with dancing waters and statues of nymphs circling a row of gleaming slot machines. "What do you want to do? You want to try these?" I asked, trying to get into the spirit of the place.

"You do it," Barbara said. "Do it all, quickly." We had a free roll of quarters, given to us when we registered at the hotel. It seemed like throwaway money and that's exactly what I did with it. I started putting one quarter in after another, waiting a few seconds for the pictures to line up. There were cherries, oranges and a clump of something that I think was supposed to be grapes, though they were colored a pale orange. Nothing ever matched straight across. There was an anticipatory tingle each time I swung the silver arm of the machine, followed by a dull disappointment as the new images appeared. "We lost," I said, apologetic, after the last spin. Afterward, I felt used. Ten dollars worth of quarters thrown away in a couple of minutes.

We went to the bar and ordered drinks, using the coupons that the hotel had given us. I got a diet pop and Barbara had a scotch and soda. We still had three coupons left. "The idea is, they want you to drink, so you'll gamble more," Barbara said, bringing the glass to her lips. "They make it seem as if everything is on the house, but it's all a money-making proposition." We started walking around the casino and paused at a roulette table which was surrounded by a group of middle-aged couples who clapped each time the wheel rolled to a stop. The women were all tightly permed and dressed in pastels; the men had on new summer shirts, open collared.

Barbara went to an open spot on the other side of the table and one of the men edged over to make room for me. "Here you go, we'll get you in here," he said, smiling. He was broad faced and jolly. "Don't you move away from me, now, Ralph," said a woman in a nubby pink sweater. She gave his muscled arm a squeeze. "You're my lucky charm."

"We've been lucky with the odd numbers tonight," Ralph said, doling out a few small chips to the woman in pink. The other couples began to clap encouragingly even before the wheel started to spin.

Barbara placed two bets, pointing decisively with one manicured finger. I looked across the table at her, strikingly beautiful in red silk with her dark hair falling over one eye. "Comeoncomeoncomeoncomeon," urged one of the women. Leaning into the table and standing on the very tips of her toes, she seemed about to jump bodily onto the spinning wheel.

"Ohhhhh!" Barbara pursed her lips in disappointment as the wheel slowly clicked to a stop. "I lost."

"You know what they say," said the woman in pink as she piled her winnings in front of her on the green felt table. "Unlucky in cards, lucky in love!"

"This is roulette," Barbara noted.

"It's all a gamble," the woman said generously. "Same difference!"

I learned early on how to make things go smoothly, how to avoid a fuss. When I was young, it was expected not only that I be agreeable, but also that I be able to detect the first sign of disagreeability in others and soothe them before a fuss began. My mother used to send me into my brothers' room if she heard an argument start: "Go Sharon, sweetheart, please. You know how to handle them. Stop their bickering." Marc and Sam would be on the floor, arguing over baseball cards or Monopoly property or who should get last licks and I would peek in, "Listen guys," I said, trying to turn them around, to find a compromise which would please them both and keep the peace.

For the first few years of marriage, I did that with Jesse, too. I was watchful, aware of any subtle change of mood. I knew when he came home how his day had gone, whether or not he was annoyed at traffic, at someone in the lab, at himself for not getting enough work done. Sometimes he was more quiet than usual and sunk into a sulk. I sensed when it was coming by the perfunctory nature of his kiss, or by the way he immersed himself in the newspaper. Then I brought him a beer, massaged his neck, held in check any news of debts or broken appliances.

I stopped doing this after a while. Or at least I made the effort to. Somehow, after Carlie died I had a stronger clarity about what I wanted and was no longer so eager to please, to suppress my own desires. Jesse and I fought more, but I knew he loved me just the same.

Now with Barbara there were times when we talked and laughed together that I felt like a fraud.

"Tomorrow I get to see him," Barbara said as we started on the way back to the hotel. She was a little drunk and beginning to weave. "I know it's going to be hard. Don't think I don't know it's going to be hard, Sharon."

I said nothing, just took her arm as we crossed the street. Soon she started talking about Andrew and got this moony, lovesick expression on her face. Her enthusiasm had a disquieting effect on me. "I didn't really get to know Andrew," I said.

"He's very special. You'll see. Wait until tomorrow when you get to talk with him. You'll see."

"Well, we shouldn't both be in love with him," I said crisply.

"No, I suppose not," Barbara said, too foggy with drink and desire to see I meant it as a joke.

We walked by an outdoor courtyard cafe with white starched cloths and flowers on every table. The ever-present bank of slot machines stood against the wall. "Don't you think it would be horrible to live in a city with gambling around you all the time?" I asked.

"Maybe you'd get used to it," Barbara said.

"I wouldn't *want* to ever get used to it."

"The whole world can't be one safe little college town," Barbara said pointedly. I was about to say something in defense when a group of conventioneers, some still with white stickum tags on their lapels, spilled out of the lounge next to the cafe. They were all red faced and boisterous, as if they had just come from a stag party. Walking up behind us they wolf-whistled and called out. "Hey, beautiful girls! Come have a drink with us!" When we didn't answer, but continued walking, another voice yelled, "Hey, stuck-up! Hey, you two women's-libbers?"

We walked past an ornate arched doorway next to another hotel. "Oh, this looks nice," Barbara said. "Let's go in. I still have one drink coupon left." She stumbled, giggling, as she caught herself.

"I think you've really had enough, Barbara," I said, hearing myself rolling out the *r*'s in her name, so that I sounded schoolmarmish. Still, I followed her, finding two seats at the end of the bar next to a man who stared, hang-dog, into his beer.

Barbara ordered another scotch and soda and I asked for a tomato juice, which was served to me with a stalk of celery with all the leaves still on it. I ate it, leaning over the counter so I wouldn't drip tomato juice all over myself (though just a simple cold water soak with any liquid cleaning agent will prevent tomato juice from causing permanent damage).

In the next room there was a man singing a highly embellished version of "Somewhere My Love." The man was overmiked, trilling in a strained falsetto. It was awful.

"God, I love this song," Barbara said, closing her eyes.

"Did you see the movie?" I asked.

"What movie?"

"*Dr. Zhivago.*" I nodded in the direction of the music. "That's 'Lara's theme.' That's the real name of the song."

In the smoky glass behind the bar Barbara looked sophisticated and sure of herself. "Wasn't that a wonderful movie? I wish they made more movies like that now. You know, those real old-fashioned love stories?"

I started telling her then how much I hated *Dr. Zhivago*. "I mean, all that ice. Who cared?"

"I thought it was beautiful," Barbara said, staring at her reflection in the glass. "It was a very moving love story."

"I wasn't moved." I bit noisily into my celery, remembering that when I had seen the movie years ago, I had felt bad for Geraldine Chaplin, the wife left in Moscow while Zhivago romped across the tundra with blond Julie Christie. (It is true that Geraldine Chaplin could be a little annoying, but still, she didn't deserve to be treated that way.)

Abruptly, Barbara turned to me, her drunken good spirit turned sour. "You really got a bug up your ass, you know that? What's the matter with you?" She placed her drink down with such force that it waved over the top, wetting her fingers.

"Nothing," I said tightly. "I just didn't like the movie and you did."

"Bullshit!" Barbara said loudly. The hang-dog man next to us looked up from his beer.

"Can you lower your voice, please?" I said, looking down at my drink.

"You know, I am really sick of this!" Barbara said even more loudly.

"*Please* lower your voice," I said through clenched teeth. "You're sick of what?"

"Of your self-righteousness. Of your prissy, goddamned self-righteousness!" Barbara bellowed.

"Because I said you already had enough to drink? Because I didn't like a movie you liked? Please, Barb."

Barbara pointed her chin aggressively in my direction. "Because you're always telling me how much I should drink and how fast I should drive and how I should live my life!"

"It's not only your life," I said tightly.

"Sure. It's David's life. And the girls. Well, do you want to know something about Prince David? Father of the year? Do you want to know something about how much he wants those girls?" Barbara's eyes blazed, tears balancing on the pencil-darkened rims.

"What do you mean?" I asked.

"I mean that not *once* did he say he wanted them. Not once did he say that he wanted the children to live with him."

"He told me you talked about leaving the girls with him while you got settled," I began.

Barbara scowled. "That was temporary. But even that he really didn't want. I mean, think about it, Sharon. Would Jesse let you do that without a fight—pack up and take Libby a thousand miles away?" She answered immediately. "You bet he wouldn't!"

"But that's not why you're leaving him. I mean, just because he didn't fight you for the girls, doesn't mean he wasn't a good father when he was with them," I said.

Barbara made a sour face. "Oh, shit. Why am I on trial here? Why do I have to keep *justifying* this to you?" She shook her head, moaning. "Do you think this is easy for me? God, Sharon. You're my best friend. You should be sticking up for me. Sharon, Sharon. . . ." Despairing, she shook her head from side to side and slurred her words. I thought of Brando doing his "Charley, Charley," speech in *On the Waterfront*. "Hey! I want another scotch and soda here!" Barbara yelled to the bartender, slapping her hand on the counter.

"Barbara, really. No." I stood up from the stool and touched her elbow. "Let's go, now. It's late."

Belligerently, she pulled her arm away. "Leggo. Lemmee alone." The bartender gave her the change for her drink. "Keep it!" she said grandly, pushing the silver across the counter.

"I'm going now," I said, starting to walk slowly away. In truth, it was an empty threat. Like when you say you're going to walk off and leave your crying child in a store.

"Don't walk away from me when I'm talking to you!" Barbara rose shakily from the stool.

"Come with me, then."

"I'm staying!"

"Come on now. You're drunk." I grasped, somewhat firmly, the underside of her arm. "Let's go back now."

"Goddamn it, Sharon!" Barbara wrenched herself free, swinging her purse at the side of my head. I leaned backward and she followed through the empty air, throwing herself off balance so that she fell across the bar. We must have looked ridiculous. The hang-dog man looked on, stunned.

I reached for her again but she wriggled free, like a child in a tantrum. "Barbara, shhh."

"Don't shh me." She pulled back, her chest heaving.

"All right."

"Don't *ever* shh me," Barbara said, taking another angry jab at the air. When she brought her arm back, her elbow caught my glass and spilled the tomato juice across the counter. I grabbed her wrist as the hand with the purse swung out again. Someone yelled from the other side of the room, "Go for it, baby. Let her have it!"

Barbara turned her fury on him, her shoulder bag still dangling from her hand. "Fuck you!" she screamed, focusing in the general direction of the voice from the end of the bar. "Why don't you just go take a flying fuck yourself!"

"Lady," said the bartender, gently to me. He was a big bearded man, soft-looking, like a honey bear. "Lady. You better go now with your friend there. Get her out of here."

In an alley between two hotels, Barbara put her head in her hands and cried. "Tell me that you don't hate me. Tell me that I'm not a bad person."

"You're not a bad person," I said, tenderly brushing back her hair. "I just don't know if this is the best thing for you to do."

"Do you see this as some kind of threat?" Barbara asked thickly. "My leaving?"

"It would be hard not to." The words practically choked me.

"You know, you think you have life planned out a certain way and then suddenly everything falls apart."

"It wasn't a terrible marriage. You're right about that. But I need to start over with someone else. Can you understand that?" Her dark eyes looked bruised and desperate.

I thought of Amanda and Jana and David standing on the ridge at Shosh-a-pee Falls, holding hands, looking out at the sun going down beyond the green hills. "No," I said truthfully. "No, I don't think I can."

We were back in the hotel room a little before twelve. The scene was peaceful. The girls were all sleeping soundly in one of the beds and Grandma Pearl was watching television and crocheting what looked like one of those covers that people use along the backs of toilet tanks. "How'd you make out?" Pearl wanted to know.

"We lost right at the beginning and then just walked around," I said. "We didn't really gamble much," I said as Barbara stumbled, fully clothed, into the other bed and curled herself into a fetal position. I went into my wallet and took out a twenty dollar bill.

"I knew you two didn't look the type," Pearl said, as she put on her fuzzy sweater. "Not like real gamblers. Those that look the type, I ask to pay me in advance."

"How were the girls?" I asked.

"Fine. Fine," Pearl said quickly. "What'd you play? Play any blackjack?" She was more interested in hearing about our gambling than she was in telling us about her night with the children. Suddenly, I wanted her out of there more than anything. I touched the small of her back, leading her to the door. "Thank you," I whispered. "Thank you so much."

Chapter 15

I had the night crazies. At home, when they come, I go downstairs and make myself a cup of hot milk and do a crossword puzzle. I do that rather than lie in bed to feel the gnawing pain in my hip and think of cancer. Or envision the wiring in our old house like coiled snakes in the walls, waiting to set themselves ablaze. I go downstairs rather than lie next to Jesse in bed, imagining how it would be to live without him. Or blink back the tears, and think of Carlie and who he would have been. The walls creak and my ears prick up listening for someone on the stairs. He is armed and vicious. In the morning Libby could find our nude bodies on blood-soaked sheets and be traumatized into a life of silence. In the lonely night I can make myself crazy listening for the wail of sirens. I know then how what we have is held together as tenuously as the fluff around the head of a dandelion.

Here in the hotel there was no place to go, so I tried to bully my way through, but the night crazies were coming. They started when Barbara turned off the light and pitched the room into a velvety blackness. She had the double bed by the door and I was on the open-up sofa in the alcove. "Good night," she whispered across our sleeping children. "Good night," I whispered back, not the least bit tired, feeling instead as if I could do an hour of aerobics. "Go to sleep," I said to myself, thinking of the drive tomorrow to San Francisco, finding the apartment, helping Barbara unpack. Three trunks had been sent and were supposed to be waiting. So was Andrew, who was meeting us at the real estate office at three o'clock. I thought how odd it was to drive halfway across a continent to meet someone at such a precise time. Like planes that are supposed to come from all around the country and arrive at four-eleven or two-forty-seven. Of course they never really do.

Libby coughed a couple of times, the same sharp, barky cough that she had had the night before. I shouldn't have let her go swimming. I couldn't remember if she had been coughing that afternoon. Silently, I crept across the room to feel her head, bumping up my knee against the corner of the bed. I reached across and touched a face, following it out to the little hand connected to it; the mouth made gentle, pulsing motions. Jana sucking her thumb. I moved my hand across to Libby in the middle. I could tell from the hair, the long, soft tendrils along the side of her face. I reached over Jana, feeling Libby's forehead to test for fever. She was cool. Just to be sure I felt Amanda and Jana. Both seemed warmer than Libby. Instead of reassuring me, this difference gave me pause. Why was Libby so cool? Awkwardly, I worked myself around the bed, testing all three foreheads with my lips. Maybe Libby wasn't that much cooler than Jana, but Amanda was definitely warm. Or *was* that Amanda on the end? Her hair was the same texture as Jana's, with a tight, wiry curl, but was it that much longer? I retested the child in the middle. The soft skin on her cheek was like the inside of a satin slipper.

"Sharon?" A voice hissed in the darkness. "What are you doing?"

I made my way over to Barbara's bed. "Was Libby coughing today?"

"I don't remember. Why, is she sick?"

"She was coughing just now. I just wanted to see if she was feverish."

"Is she?"

"I don't think so."

"Go to sleep," Barbara said.

"Could I turn on the light in the bathroom? I'll shut the door, so it will only be a shadow."

"Are you afraid of the dark?" Barbara asked.

"It's *too* dark. It makes me feel loony."

"Go ahead, put the light on if you want." Barbara sighed. "I'm just exhausted."

In the fluorescent shadow I made my way back to the couch and slipped between the sheets. Across the room, the children appeared ghostly in the semi-dark. It was after one. I added up the hours of sleep I would have if we got up for breakfast as planned. Six hours if I fell asleep right there on the spot. The pressure of it made my heart suddenly start to race. Think of something else, I willed myself. I imagined going to Barbara's apartment, lifting something heavy up the winding staircase (though as far as I knew, Barbara's apartment did not have a winding staircase); then I would find out I was pregnant for sure because I would miscarry and have to be hospitalized in San Francisco. There could be complications and Jesse would have to fly out, missing the deadline on his grant. He would stay with Barbara and Andrew, hating them both, blaming me all the while for making this trip and losing the baby that by now he realized he wanted with all his heart. It was a boy. Hard to tell so early, but the doctor somehow knew. Then I begin to bleed again. In order to stop the flow there has to be emergency surgery, probably a hysterectomy. Jesse waits in agony, though bravely I forbid him to call my parents.

Something moved across the pillow and along my cheek, fine as spider web. I bolted upright, brushing myself vigorously, before I turned the pillow over, put my head down, and steered myself toward thoughts of chubby, white sheep jumping over wooden fences. I counted only a dozen or so when I saw the sheep, with a will of their own, run off through the meadow that then became a meandering mountain road that Barbara, in her haste to get to her lover, drove off the side of. The girls tumbled around the van like broken toys.

I willed myself to stop thinking. On the side of the bed was a watercolor print of what looked like an antique quilt, though now I could only make out a wash of pale color under the glass. I closed my eyes, remembering the patchwork quilts we had on the beds out on Jack Silver's farm. Well, we called it a farm. There were no animals there except for an old dog with terrible halitosis and no one ever grew anything except for a couple of marijuana plants back behind the garage. All the people were just like me, suburban kids who went upstate to go to college. Jack and his friends rented an old farmhouse a few miles from the school and I came out every weekend. It was like playing house. We'd go to auctions and shop in the farmers' market. There was a fabric factory outlet in the next town and we bought remnants and I made curtains with all different floral prints for the windows and glassed doors. The farmhouse was uninsulated and so leaky that in the middle of winter the wind would blow through the house and all the curtains would sway. The waltz of the flowers, we used to say. Sunday mornings, Jack would put on music, and I'd type my papers in a tiny back room that used to be a pantry, so cold I wore gloves with the tips of the fingers cut off. Then I'd go to Jack in the living room to drink my tea in the white shaft of sunlight that came through the southeast windows.

I wasn't happy then, but I wasn't unhappy either. Everything was just kind of stopped for a while and no one had plans about what to do with their lives or even plans about how to get through the rest of the semester. At one time, I think I was the only one from the house who was still enrolled full-time in school. There was Tim Fray, a fifth-year poli sci major who worked as a janitor in the dorms, and his girlfriend, Reba, who waitressed at The Grill and only took dance classes at the university; Jeff, a kid from Farmingdale who started on a basketball scholarship, but hurt his knee first semester and never went to another class. There were transients, too, in and out of the house all the time. You could walk out at any hour in the middle of the night and find someone sleeping on the living room couch or a couple rolled together in a sleeping bag in the upstairs hall. On weekends, we'd all chip in for food. Everyone would throw in a couple of dollars and Jack and I would take a ride to the supermarket and get fixings for tacos or spaghetti and salad. Jack and I were domestic, so we did the cooking and cleaning up. I never cared, coming down the next morning and emptying coffee cans of old butts and roaches and doing a sinkful of dishes. The other men were all slobs. I don't know why I didn't care. Maybe my consciousness was not sufficiently raised at that point. Or maybe I just never saw that way of life as a permanent condition.

Jack was the first boy with whom I was ever totally comfortable. The first time we went out together, I got sick on him, and then anything after that seemed acceptable. I had known Jack for a while before we went out because he was in the crowd I hung around with at school. But then, everybody knew Jack— the jocks, the politicos, the dopers. He'd come into the school newspaper office where I worked because Tim Fray wrote a weekly column; it was one part movie review, one part editorial about the state of the world. The movie review part was terrible. Tim loved phony-baloney French films and put down anything from Hollywood that made money, even if it was really good.

One night, Jack came in looking for Tim just as I was locking up the office to go back to the dorm. Jack asked me out for a beer. I would go, I told him, but I really didn't feel well. Around dinner time, someone had come to the office with sandwiches and distractedly, I gobbled one down, before someone else said that he thought the pastrami "tasted a little funny." Sometimes, all I need to make me go over the edge is the *suggestion* that the food might be tainted. We opened another sandwich and saw that indeed the meat had a shiny, gray tinge.

"Just keep me company for a while, then," Jack urged. "Have a Coke, it'll settle your stomach." He said he was celebrating. I don't recall what. Finishing a term paper or something like that. He was so cute looking, with a stocky wrestler body and a thin-lipped, rubbery kind of grin. I remember later, the first time I saw Robin Williams on television, I thought for a minute that it was Jack Silver.

So we went out. Just downtown to The Grill. Jack had a beer and a double cheeseburger with a pyramid of onion rings. I could hardly bear to watch him eat, and excused myself to walk out into the cold night air. After a few minutes, Jack came out to see me holding on to a street lamp and throwing up over the curb. He touched my arm and as I whirled away from him, I turned too far, coming full circle to vomit on his shoes, brown leather work boots held together with knotted laces.

We started going together after that. I slept with him the next week.

The first time I had an orgasm was with Jack. I was twenty years old and, besides Rick Naughton, had had sex only once with a boy whose name I cannot even recall. He was a lifeguard at a summer camp where I was a counselor. The last weekend the staff had a party on the beach and we sat around a campfire, smoking grass. When you are stoned your sense of time is distorted so that you think something takes a really *long* time, but then you look at the clock, surprised to find that only a few minutes have actually passed. But with the lifeguard it was the other way around. We started to walk to the dunes and it seemed I was just turning to kiss him when—poof—it was over. We had intercourse, but it was antiseptic and startling, like a stranger on a bus suddenly sticking a finger in your nose.

Even with Jack, I don't think I was ready. It was a time when girls had no excuse to say no. Not wanting to was not reason enough. Jack was uninhibited and spontaneous in bed and teased me out of my self-consciousness. I'd wake sometimes to find him nibbling my ass or kissing my underarm. He was such an enthusiastic admirer of all my body parts that after a while I felt free to be naked around him. I liked making love with Jack, but what I wanted was the cuddling and the stroking. Even though I got excited, there was something in me that wouldn't let go.

Then one night Jack and I were fooling around as we were watching television in the living room with Tim and a bunch of other people who were passing around a bong. Jack and I were on a lumpy, old couch whose springs curled right into our ribs, and we were snuggling under one of the quilts. I had just taken a hot bath and had on a long terrycloth robe with nothing underneath. Jack ran his hands down my body, massaging my legs, my belly, stopping occasionally between my thighs. Then he took my hand down to feel his erection under his jeans, rubbing my palm along the material until he unzipped himself and sprang free against my hip. "Squeeze me," he whispered in my ear.

In the kitchen, Reba was making brownies and brought out the bowl and spoon for us to lick. Jack and I, our hands busy under the covers, picked our heads up, opening our mouths. Reba was still wearing her waitress uniform from The Grill, a brown miniskirt and a fluffy orange apron. "Mmmmm," Jack said, licking his lips of chocolate batter, his fingers slippery between my legs.

After a while, I put my hand on his wrist for him to stop, embarrassed that the others in the room would know what we were doing, that they could sense the rhythm of our movement or hear the sucking sounds muffled under the quilt. "Relax," Jack whispered into my neck. "They're smashed." When Jack kissed me, I always felt his teeth. His lips were so thin that there was no cushiony backup. "Touch me," he urged, licking my hand so that it would slide along his penis, which was hard and slick as polished wood. When Jack came with a slight tremble, a groan muffled in his throat, I held him, every muscle in my body taut. "Don't stop," I whispered in his ear, after he had used the edge of his workshirt to wipe my hand. There was the smell of baking brownies and the soapy scent of semen.

Jack put his head under the covers and found my breast, taking it into his mouth, at the same time his hand never stopping, flicking and stroking with his glistening fingers, and sometimes, pressing up against me with the whole palm of his hand. I arched against him, my body opening to him like a flower in one of those slow-motion photographic sequences.

On television there was a car chase across a desert landscape. One police car careened into a gulch as another took up the slack. In the car being chased were drug dealers who were shooting out from the glassless windows. "Get those fuckers," yelled Tim Fray. "Put them away!" He meant the cops, not the drug dealers.

The whole time Jack's hand didn't stop. One finger, then two, moved inside me as the pad of his thumb rubbed along the outside and I found myself totally free, not caring if anyone knew what we were doing. I saw the place I usually got to in sex, the relaxed and pleasurable plateau; then saw myself, as if in a dream, go past that, beyond to a place where I was not a body made up of legs and arms and lips and vagina, but something organic and whole. So this is what they're talking about, I thought, shuddering against him, locking my legs tight together to hold his hand still because at the very peak the sensation was unbearable in its intensity.

I almost married Jack. The next year we were at the planning stage, though at that time, planning meant setting aside a weekend to elope, to go off to someplace like Niagara Falls and do the wax museums. Tim Fray went with Reba (although they didn't get married) and came back with photographs of the two of them passing joints to JFK and Jackie.

Jack and I had plans to go into the Peace Corps to teach the natives what we learned from our years at a liberal arts university. But first we were going to hitchhike around South America or India or someplace. I could write and Jack was going to take pictures. We talked about putting together a book, though neither of us was clear about a unifying theme.

Jack's parents were from Kings Point and very rich. His father had patented a stretch material that was used to make ski pants and dancewear. (I still have about half a dozen unworn leotards tucked away in a suitcase somewhere in my house in Urbana.) The Silvers thought that I would be good for Jack. That a nice Jewish girl like me would encourage him to do something sensible, like cut his hair and go to law school. I sensed that there was a part of Jack that rebelled only to get their attention.

I don't know why I broke up with Jack. I said I needed more time, more space. I told him that I loved him, but didn't want to be tied down. I made it seem as if I were a wild, free spirit, that it was only commitment, not Jack from which I withdrew. I said those words even though that summer Jesse and I became engaged. It is to Jack's credit that he would still talk to me. Though, if the facts be known, he *did* run off to India with Marcy Klupperman, even before Jesse and I were married.

At dawn, after what I calculated to be only a few hours of sleep, I threw on a big shirt, quietly left the room and made my way down to the lobby to call Jesse. At home it would be after seven. Jesse would be just getting out of the shower. I pictured him shaving at the sink, a towel wrapped around his waist. Or maybe he would be naked. It is only in the past year that he has worn the towel, following Libby's interest in his genitalia. "How do you get it to grow, Daddy?" she asked once, seeing him get out of bed with a morning erection. "Just luck, I guess," he said, opening a drawer for his shorts. But after that he wore the towel.

The elevator stopped on the floor below and a disheveled man, reeking of whiskey, got on, smashing his whole palm flat against the buttons. Like the polite midwesterner I'd become, I smiled and said, "Hi." The man made a flapping sound with his lips, like a horse, but when the elevator came to a stop, he waited chivalrously for me to exit before him.

I was disappointed that the pay phones were not tucked away in a cozy booth, but hung against a wall at the far end of the lobby. By the time Jesse answered on the fifth ring, I was breathless with anticipation, and his deep hello sent a shiver through me. "I took you out of the shower," I said.

"Hi, honey!" He told me that he was finishing a shave and didn't hear the phone because of the running water. "What the hell time is it there?" he asked.

I said that I had trouble sleeping. That today we were leaving for San Francisco. Jesse and I spoke about the most mundane things. The weather in the Midwest, still blistering hot; his progress on the grant; Libby's sudden refusal to eat meat. "She says now she wants to become a *vegenarian*."

"She's missing me, is all," Jesse said.

"I am, too." I wanted to say something else, something bold and provocative.

"You know, Sharon, you didn't *have* to go on this trip."

"Jess . . ."

"I'm sorry. I didn't have to say that."

"So what else is happening?" I asked. A barefoot woman in a black dress tiptoed across the lobby, holding her shoes, as if she were afraid of waking someone.

"I saw David," Jesse said. "We went out for pizza last night."

"How's he doing?"

"Okay, I guess." There was something protective in his tone.

"Well, what'd you talk about?"

"You know David and I can make conversation without you and Barbara around," Jesse said.

"I know that," I said too quickly. Then, "How's he really doing?"

There was a long sigh at the other end. "He blames himself, in a way. He keeps looking for reasons, something to explain everything that happened." Jesse added, low and menacing, "She's really a bitch. I'd feel like killing her if she did this to me."

"She's not, Jess," I said softly. "She has reasons."

"Yeah," he said bitterly.

I wanted to tell him that my period was late, that maybe I was pregnant. I put my hand along the side of my belly. Now wasn't the time to say anything. "I lost everything gambling," I said lightly. "The house, the car . . ."

"Not the mortgage on the ranch?" I knew he was smiling. "What did you play?"

"The slots. Roulette. Cards. A little of everything. We didn't know what we were doing."

"Well, how is it there? Is Reno exciting?"

"It's kind of depressing, actually. Too many people who look as if they can't afford to be here."

"Including you. Come home," Jesse said plaintively.

"Soon. I'm going to stay over just one night with Barbara and take a late morning flight out to San Diego. Should I call you from Jack and Ellen's?" I always said Jack and Ellen as if they were both equally connected to me.

"If you want." Now Jesse was casual. "I have all the flight information, right? About when you're coming home?"

"On the kitchen bulletin board. Also Jack and Ellen's phone number. It's unlisted."

"Why is it unlisted?" Jesse asked, suspicious.

"I don't know. Jack's a big-shot lawyer. Maybe he's afraid his old guru will track him down and ask for a handout. How do you think new ashrams get built?"

"Oh, Belinda got braces," Jesse said, changing the subject. "She went to a doctor who said that her migraines were caused by a bad bite. She looks about thirteen now." He added, "A kind of trampy thirteen."

I thought how this might pique Ron Simone's interest. "Do you think she's attractive?" I asked.

"Belinda?"

"Yes, Belinda."

"Belinda is a right-wing nut," Jesse said, as if that dismissed anyone from serious esthetic consideration.

"I meant to tell you," I said, "the insulation people are coming at the end of the week to give an estimate. I won't be home yet." We had been thinking about making our old house energy-efficient.

"I don't know. I don't think we should do it if it's going to be more than a thousand dollars," Jesse said. "What do you think?"

"Well, what if it's like eleven hundred?"

"It depends on how much we'd be saving on the heating bills," Jesse said.

"Still, we have to draw the line someplace," I said. "I don't really want to spend more than a thousand."

"Fine," Jesse said agreeably. "I'll tell him to go ahead if it's less than a thousand."

"Okay," I said. "Good." I felt as if we had just completed an important tricky negotiation.

"Is Libby there with you?" He sounded expectant.

"She's up in the room. Still sleeping."

"Awww." Then, "Do you think she's having a good time?"

I told him about how Dinosaur National Monument was a flop and what Libby said to the old man who waded next to us in the Great Salt Lake. I told him how good the children had been.

"Jana, too?"

"I'm liking her more now. Actually, Amanda can be a tease. Jana just doesn't deal with it well. So she whines a lot. I think the move is going to be a hard adjustment for her."

"He doesn't know what he's getting himself in for," Jesse said.

"Who?"

"The boyfriend. The guy Barbara's running off to."

"Andrew?"

"That poor, dumb sap," Jesse said, refusing to use his name.

An older couple walked briskly by as if on an early-morning constitutional. The man moved with a long, loping stride while the woman added extra steps to keep up next to him. When they got out the door, he looked at her, stopping for a split second, to brush something—a smudge, an eyelash—off her cheek, while she trustingly turned her face up to him. "I should let you get ready for work," I said, watching the couple disappear down the street. Outside, the neon still shone brightly against the dawn, the lights on the hotel marquee like low-hung stars.

"Don't hang up yet," Jesse said, his voice thickening.

"Are you lonesome?" I asked.

"I'm lonesome for you," Jesse answered, his voice catching.

Was it the miles between that made us want each other so? I thought of all the nights we spent together, reading or watching television, talking to each other through the bathroom door, lying next to each other in bed and chatting like we were friends over each other's houses on a sleep-over. Sometimes we would ask each other "Do you want to have sex?" in the same way we might ask "Do you want a bowl of ice cream?" or "Do you want to watch the news?" Sometimes I think of making love as an effort, though when we do, it is always good. Sometimes it is comfort sex, companionable and chummy, the kind where I can keep my socks on. Sometimes it is passionate sex, and we are lost in such a heat of tongues and touching that all the clichés about colored lights and the earth moving become personal and new. Afterward I think, why don't we do this all the time?

"I'll see you soon," I promised. I said I loved him—feeling an ache in the words and a longing across the wires.

Chapter 16

We parked down the block from the real estate office on a street so steep that Barbara paused after pulling the emergency brake, holding her breath to see if the van would stay still. "That's something I'll have to get used to," she said. "These hills."

"You really know how to park," I said admiringly. The space, between two foreign cars, was small—one I would not have attempted. All added up, there have been hours of my life spent driving around to avoid certain parallel parking situations.

One time when Jesse and I were living in Rochester I tried to park on a downtown street in front of the post office. I was sending out the newsletters for the Chamber of Commerce. The space was not big enough to be able to come in from behind as I prefer. I pulled up to the car in front of me to what I thought was the appropriate distance and began to turn the wheel. Halfway in, I realized that I was hitting the curb. I know if you screw it up, it's always easier to pull out and start over, but I was determined to straighten out the car with sheer force of will. I turned the wheel of that old Chevy so hard I thought it would break off in my hand. Eventually, I ended up perpendicular to the curb, the nose of the car edged dangerously out into the traffic lane. I began to pull out and start over, when I saw a group of construction workers on the sidewalk. One was digging with a shovel, but two others were just sort of leaning on their drills, watching to see what I'd do next. The car waiting in back of me honked. I tried again, backing in enough so that the other car was able to slide by, but I ended up a good three feet from the curb. The workers began to laugh, slapping their thighs. "Honey, you need some help?" one of them called. Humiliated, I drove away and went to a post office in one of the suburbs, parking in one of the spacious blacktopped lots.

"I've let a lot of spaces go, because I'm always afraid I can't make it," I said to Barbara as she got the children out of the car. "But you would never think of not trying it." I saw by her face that she wasn't interested in how this perception symbolized something about the way we led our lives. She popped a Tic-Tac into her mouth and looked in the side mirror of the van, giving her hair a quick fluff. "We're in San Francisco now!" she said to nobody in particular.

Andrew was waiting, sitting cross-legged in a chair, reading a newspaper when the five of us all poured into the front room of the real estate office. He was wearing sneakers and a beige linen jacket with the sleeves pushed up. He looked much different from the conservative businessman I had met two summers ago at Medi-core. He looked up, blinking and surprised for a moment, as if he didn't expect quite so many of us.

Barbara went to him, looking strained, and gave him a peck on the cheek. Briefly, they touched hands. "This is my friend, Andrew," she said to Amanda and Jana. "Remember I told you I had a friend in San Francisco who was going to help us get all set up in our new house?" Occasionally, Andrew's name had been mentioned on the trip, always prefaced by the words "Mommy's friend."

Amanda and Jana hung back warily. "Hi, Andrew!" I chirped, shaking his hand. I started talking about being late because of traffic—which wasn't true at all—and how Barbara was such a terrific parker. I felt it was important for the girls to remember the initial encounter as ordinary. But it was peculiar for all of us, Andrew, tall and male, in the midst of our female throng. Suddenly all of us—even Barbara—became almost shy in Andrew's presence.

Barbara signed some papers and wrote out a check while the receptionist went looking for an extra set of keys. "I'll follow you over," Barbara said to Andrew, after everything was taken care of.

We were only a few blocks away. The apartment was in the middle of a block of brick townhouses and on the corner were a French bakery, a florist, a nouveau ice cream place. It was a neighborhood so gentrified that I couldn't imagine how Barbara would ever be able to get a baby-sitter. We walked up the path to the door, single file, Andrew, then Barbara, me, Amanda, Jana, Libby. Size places. We waited silently as Andrew fiddled with the lock, bending to check, yes, this key with this lock, before he put it in again. "Tricky," he said under his breath. When he got it, he flung open the door with a flourish, and stood tall. There was something military in his posture. I noticed that he had a heavy beard, that this late in the afternoon his cheek was already shadowed. But, God, he was handsome!

Barbara brushed by him to get in, her hand lingering briefly on his shoulder. "Very nice," she said, walking into the living room. There was a large bay window and lots of light. A dining room connected to the end of the L-shaped kitchen. All the walls were freshly painted a plain off-white and there was a pale green carpet in acceptable condition. "Really," she turned to Andrew with a dazzling smile. "It's just what I would have wanted."

The upstairs felt disappointingly like an attic and the bedrooms were small, but Barbara didn't say anything. Though both the bedrooms looked identical to me, Barbara used her special voice to tell Amanda and Jana that they could pick the room they wanted for their own. "You don't have to decide right now," Barbara said, touching the walls as if secret treasure might lie behind. "Let's sleep in them both before you see which room you like best."

"The beds are going to be delivered tomorrow, hon," Andrew said. Downstairs, there was rental furniture—a copper-colored couch, and some end tables and chairs of Scandinavian design, as clean and as welcoming as a dentist's office. Barbara wouldn't care about this. Except for the antique clocks, she was never very much into homey touches. Even her beautiful old house in Urbana with the oak woodwork and stained-glass had bare walls and plantless windows.

As for myself, I was, quite unexpectedly, overwhelmed by depression. I didn't know if it was because of the bland contemporary furniture or seeing Barbara here adrift, this man her only connection in a strange city of dangerous tilting streets.

Andrew had to duck his head going down the narrow stairs. Barbara followed. Then the children and I brought up the rear. The girls had said barely a word in this, their new home.

Andrew took us to one of his favorite restaurants in Chinatown, a place where the flowered chintz booths were separated by bamboo partitions. The waiters, all of whom appeared to understand not a word of English, moved slowly, passing on cushioned feet back and forth to the kitchen with steaming platters of food. Amanda walked twice to the bathroom, both times nearly careening into the tray tables that were set up. After about a half hour, Andrew said that it was unusual that the place was so busy, he was sorry we had to wait. Barbara and I assured him we didn't mind, but Jana started crying that her stomach hurt and Barbara had to stop her from pouring sugar into her open palm.

When the food finally arrived, all three of the girls started talking at once with comments and questions about every dish, with lots of pointing and suspicious looks. There were requests for shrimp without vegetables and vegetables without shrimp, rice on the side or rice underneath, sauce and no sauce. In just the few seconds after the plates were uncovered it seemed, in fact, that there were more demands than Barbara and I could handle efficiently. "Just hush up a minute," I said, annoyed at all of them. Over at a table behind us, a Chinese family sat with two serious, silent children. Our girls all seemed noisily American and impossibly bratty.

Andrew ate expertly with chopsticks and was already finished by the time Amanda had picked all the scallions out of the moo-shoo pork and was set to begin. Jana complained that the milk tasted funny. "It tastes like the inside of my lunchbox," she said loudly. Barbara ordered her a Coke, but then Jana said that the bubbles tickled her nose and she couldn't drink it. "Here," Barbara said, vigorously stirring the soda with a spoon. "Now the bubbles will be all gone."

Amanda said that she wanted a Coke, too. That she didn't think that Chinese food "went" with milk.

"How would you know?" Barbara asked. "You haven't eaten any."

Libby had a noodle go down the wrong pipe and coughed until her nose began to run. She spit the chewed noodle into her napkin, holding it open in front of her for inspection.

Jana said that just looking at that chewed noodle made her want to throw up.

Andrew, finishing the last of the plum wine, looked detached from the scene. "Is it always this wild?" he asked Barbara.

Barbara began to protest that really, the trip had been fun. She made excuses, saying the children were overtired and not used to sitting for long periods in restaurants. I didn't rise to their defense, though later, thinking about it, I realized that the girls behaved worse during that meal than they had the entire time on the road. Maybe it was an unconscious response to Andrew's intrusion into our group.

Maybe I felt it, too, which was why I didn't say anything.

There was a part of me that may have even been glad. What did Andrew think? That this was going to be easy? That Barbara came to him without history . . . strings . . . baggage . . . all the stuff that had been her life?

When Andrew was paying the check—against my protest he insisted on treating us all—I saw Barbara's face and felt guilty. It broke my heart to see Barbara, so brave and reckless most of the time, wanting everything to work in an orderly fashion. "When we get the kids to bed, why don't you go back to Andrew's for a while, so you can have some time alone together?" I whispered in her ear.

Barbara was immediately grateful. "Oh, Sharon, you wouldn't mind? You really wouldn't care if I left you our last night together?"

"I'm tired anyway. I was just going to read a little and go right to sleep." I yawned, open-mouthed, to show that this was true.

"You know, this means so much to me . . . ," Barbara began, her face shiny with happiness as she turned to Andrew coming back to the table, his jacket flung over his shoulder at a jaunty angle and a toothpick in his mouth.

In the doorway of the restaurant stood a tiny Chinese woman who smiled at us, revealing a set of odd-shaped teeth that looked as though they were all loose in her head. "Happy memories," she said, bowing, as we walked into the cool San Francisco night.

Alone in Barbara's new living room, I lay back on the copper-colored sofa, so exhausted I could barely lift my arm, which was dangling at an uncomfortable angle off the cushions. It was the same Jell-O–bodied weariness I used to feel when Libby was a baby, up at dawn, fresh-faced and ready to start the day. I would pluck her from the crib so her squeals would not wake Jesse, make her a bottle in the cold kitchen, and go into the living room. Then I'd throw a bunch of toys on the floor and lie on the couch as she drank her bottle and played, occasionally dotting milk along the edge of the upholstery.

Now I listened again for footsteps on the stairs. It wasn't until after eleven that the girls had finally stopped coming down. They said they needed drinks of water, more blankets, a light on in the hall. What they were really doing was checking up on Barbara. An hour before, when there had been ten minutes of quiet, she and Andrew had sneaked out. It was Jana who discovered it first. She came down crying because Amanda kept putting her feet on Jana's sleeping bag. When she looked around the room and saw Barbara was not there, she suddenly composed herself. "Where's my mom?" she asked, scanning the room.

"She just went out for a walk," I said casually. "She'll be back pretty soon."

"With Andrew?" Jana asked, her eyes narrowing.

"Uh-huh." I offered to come up and help settle the dispute. "Is Libby sleeping?" I asked, heading up the stairs.

"No one is," Jana said ominously.

Eventually, all three of them tiptoed down the stairs with various complaints. The last was Amanda, looking overgrown in her pink, footed pajamas. The top and bottom were too small to snap together properly so her stomach protruded over the elastic waistband. "My mom isn't back yet?" she said, about to cry.

"Sweetie, come here," I said, taking her, all fleshy and soft, on my lap. "What's the matter, hon? Are you having a hard time falling asleep?" I held her to me and swayed gently, as if I were rocking a baby.

"I just want my mom, is all," Amanda said, snuggling against me. "I don't like it when she goes out at night."

"Well, I'm here. Your mom would never go out and leave you girls alone. Is that what you're worried about?" Amanda shrugged and buried her face in my chest. "Well, it is scary to move to a new house and go to a new school and . . ."

Amanda interrupted me: "I don't like this house. The toilet doesn't have a soft seat like in our real bathroom. It's a dumb house." She added, "I like my own room the way it is at home."

I didn't argue. "Maybe sometime this week you and Mom could go buy some new ballet posters to hang on the walls," I said. "You know the one that Libby likes? With the ballet shoe balancing on the egg?"

Amanda nodded. "A girl, Julie Jensen, in my dancing class has that one. They have them at the Lincoln Square Mall."

"When I go back to Urbana, I'll send you one. Okay?" I touched her quivering chin in my hands, searching for a smile, not realizing I had said exactly the wrong thing.

"I want to go back to Urbana, too. I want to go home," Amanda said, the last distinguishable words I heard before she broke into despairing, hiccoughing sobs.

"Oh, sweetheart, don't," I said, and started to cry along with her. I had an image of Barbara and Andrew fucking away in his bed, her black hair spread like a fan along the pillow, his rough-bearded face making its scratchy way down her body. Her face, as I imagined it in passion, was greedy with delight. Smoothing Amanda's hair back from her tear-stained face, I couldn't help thinking, "This for that."

Barbara maintained that children were adaptable and could survive a lot worse than the breakup of a marriage. Look how many do, she said. She said that it was unhealthy for the girls to grow up in a house with parents who no longer loved each other. She pointed out that if *she* were happy—and she would be with Andrew—then the girls would be happy.

This is what my father calls "selling yourself a bill of goods."

At midnight, I was sitting on the air mattress in the other bedroom, leaning against a laundry bag full of dirty clothes. I had a book open in my lap, but what I was doing was writing a letter to Barbara in my head. I had been thinking about our friendship, how Barbara and I fit together. I realized that just as there are women who are drawn to certain men who fill their lives with a sense of danger, so I have always chosen women friends who were different from me, reckless women.

Recalling all the things we had done together, I was teary, awash with sentiment. Remember, Barbara (the letter went), visiting each other in the hospital, after each baby's birth? (You sneaked in after visiting hours when I had Libby, with a pint of Häagen-Dazs, chocolate chocolate-chip.) The aerobics class where the instructor reprimanded us for talking so much (and you said, "Isn't talking aerobic?"). The stolen minutes of phone time as we made supper, drinking a glass of wine after we plugged the kids in front of the TV, the theme from "Sesame Street" echoing in the background?

Remember, Barbara, the night of the Sears Midnight Madness Sale? We had come from a party where the host passed around a joint that looked like the bloated finger of a fat person. (It had been years since we had all smoked grass at a party and I haven't done it since. Remember, I looked across the room at you, surprised?) On the way home from the party, Jesse and David decided to stop at Sears to look at snowblowers. The store was open until twelve and everything was 20 percent off.

Sears was mobbed. You kept saying how everyone who was *anyone* was at the store that night, but nobody *we* personally knew. It was one of those stoned comments you think is hysterically funny at the time, so you keep repeating it.

Jesse and David went off by themselves and we ended up in the men's department. You said you were cold and I said—it was a dare, actually, but how could I have doubted that you would not follow through—"Well, why don't you just put on some of this stuff?" So, of course, you did. Men's chambray workshirts and flannel shirts and hooded sweatshirts, all on top of each other until you looked like one of those top-heavy, roly-poly toys. You added a pair of canvas, heavy-duty work gloves.

"Come on, let's go for it," you said. And before I knew what was happening you were walking away, past the salesgirls in Cheryl Tiegs sportswear, the cashiers in small appliances. You walked confidently, plump and padded with layers of clothing, the sales tags hanging at your wrist and along your neck. You passed through an aisle of children's bicycles and walked out the main exit of Sears. I stood there, open-mouthed, until it clicked somewhere in my distorted consciousness that you were not going to be coming back. That, in fact, you had just shoplifted about a hundred dollars of men's work clothing from Sears. I went looking for Jesse and David, my heart thumping against my chest.

In the car, you split the spoils. David knew, but Jesse was confused. He kept saying, "These were all on sale, right? Well, why'd you buy all this?" Stolen goods.

Did you know I wore that green, hooded sweatshirt in the cold desert just the other night? It's with me now in this pile of dirty laundry I'm leaning against.

What I want to say is that this trip has been hard for me. I fear I've been tested and found wanting. That, despite my iconoclastic leanings, I am smaller than I wish to be and unforgiving. Soon, I hope, I will only want you to be happy. But now, oh, I guess I'm feeling sorry for myself. This is a breakup of another kind, isn't it? Good-bye to our girl duo. Like Lucy and Ethel, Mary and Rhoda. Betty and Veronica. (You, dark and devious. Me, that dumb, blond, trusting pal.) No more.

Oh, Barbara, I miss you already.

In the morning, Andrew came over with bagels, fresh croissants, warm blueberry muffins. Barbara had unpacked the dishes and set up the Mr. Coffee. I went upstairs to finish my packing and to comb Libby's hair. The plane to San Diego was at ten-forty and Andrew was going to take Libby and me to the airport before going to work.

In the night, my period had started. I had gone to sleep with cramps and woke in the fuzzy dawn, hunting through my duffel bag for Tampax. On the way to the bathroom, I peeked over the banister and saw Barbara, still in her clothes, asleep on the living room couch.

I took off my underpants, put them in the sink, and watched the blood swirl under the cold rush of water. I thought, almost simultaneously, three things: that I was painfully sorry I was— once again—not pregnant; that I was glad I hadn't told Jesse I thought I was; that I wouldn't say anything to Barbara.

Then I realized, this is what it's like to be a truly independent person, to keep certain recesses of your emotional life private and inaccessible even to those closest to you. I felt like someone traveling alone for the first time, finding my own way. The knowledge of this made me feel that I had finally grown in a way that even Carlie's death had not revealed to me. It also made me feel more alone than ever before.

Chapter 17

Jack was late. Libby and I had already claimed our bags and dragged them over to a corner where she proceeded to line up her animals and dolls against the wall. She had Woo-baby, a ballet Barbie and a half dozen small, stuffed things including the purple horse we had bought in Peoria. "Don't take them all out, Lib," I said. "Jack will be here any minute."

"You don't *know,*" Libby said, her dark eyes challenging me. Almost as soon as we had crossed the state line into California, she had been difficult. Perhaps there was something in the air that she sensed, an intuitive danger. Barbara came to California to be with another man. Now a strange man was picking us up at the airport. What was to prevent me from staying here, too?

"Jack said that his little boy is excited to meet you. And tomorrow we can all go to the zoo or to Sea World to see Shamoo, the white whale . . ."

"What's his name again?" Libby said grudgingly.

"Shamoo."

"No, that little boy."

"Daniel," I said. "I think everyone calls him Danny."

Libby thrust her chin out defiantly. "I might call him just 'Dan.' "

Daniel was one year older than Libby. I had seen him only

as an infant when Jack and Ellen were in New York. I had come in to visit my family and Jack's mother had invited me for dinner. It was the last year Jesse and I were in Rochester when I was working at Kodak. It was an awkward time, too long after Carlie's death for me to still mourn in a public way, but too soon for me to see a new baby and feel anything but pain. Awkward, too, because the place at the table set for Ellen remained empty. Sometime, early in the evening, she had called saying that she would be staying over in the city with her sister who was flat on her back with a herniated disk. I thought then that she didn't want to meet me, but Jack said that wasn't so. That the disk thing had really just happened.

That was the last time we were all in New York together. I remember that I could hardly look at each of the Silvers cooing at baby Daniel across the table. After dinner, Jack's father went to watch "Wall Street Week" and Mrs. Silver was in the kitchen, warming a baby bottle. "Are you all right, Sharon?" Jack asked, kissing me on the top of my head. I nodded mutely, afraid that if I spoke at all, I would end up with one of those messy cries where you can't get your chest to stop heaving. That would have been permissible if I had only been with Jack, but Mrs. Silver was about to bring out the chocolate mousse.

"I'm sorry I didn't get to meet Ellen," I said after a while, fingering a cut-glass bowl filled with grapes and walnuts. I meant that, too. Part of what made me sad was seeing this baby without a mother and there I was, a mother without a baby.

After I moved to Illinois Jack and I were in touch occasionally. I sent him an announcement after Libby was born; he wrote to say his father had had open-heart surgery but that everything was fine. I called one brilliant morning, the first of May, remembering Jack's birthday because in the Midwest all the neighborhood children leave baskets of candy and flowers to celebrate May Day. Then, most recently, there'd been my call about Graves Stuart, professor and pornographer.

♦

Now I smiled seeing Jack Silver, frantic and boyish, sprinting down the long corridor toward the baggage claim. From this distance, it seemed the last five years had not changed him. He was still muscled and stocky, his short, sandy hair swept cleanly over to one side—though even in his hippie days, when his hair was down to his shoulders, Jack wore it tied neatly back in a ponytail, so that he always had a smooth, sleek appearance. Now he also looked like he belonged here in California—the golden tan, the baggy pants, the shirt open at the neck. Suddenly, I felt all pasty and midwestern.

I waved as Jack headed toward us, not seeming to slow down so that I nervously did a quick two-step to the side of the luggage in case he ran into everything. "Sharon!!" He was exuberant, lifting me off my feet with a big bear hug and twirling me around. The feel of his body, his smell, was familiar and comforting. Libby pressed herself against the wall and looked wary. "I couldn't get out of the damned office," Jack was explaining breathlessly. "I had one foot out the door and three people pushed me back, shit, I shouldn't have gone in at all, I knew that was going to happen. But we could eat at the wharf if you like, or just go home, relax, get in the hot tub and we'll take something there, whatever you want to do. How was the flight? Are you tired?"

"It's only a forty-minute flight, Jack." I found myself talking in a slow, measured way, my old response toward his manic patter. "And we both ate before we left."

"God, you look great, the same, really," Jack said touching my hair. "Those cheeks, I miss those cheeks!" He pinched me along the side of my face the way my grandmother always does. "And you must be—" Jack squatted down next to Libby and snapped his fingers together as if he were trying to recall.

"Libby Burke," she said helpfully.

"I like that name. Libby Burke. It's a very good name."

"Do you know how to spell it?" Libby asked coyly. Then, not waiting for a response, she began, "*L-i-b-b* . . ."

"That's how I thought you were going to spell it," Jack said as she finished up. He was still on his knees, so I could see the top of his head, the hair just thinning slightly in the back. He looked up to me. "She looks just like Jesse, doesn't she?" he said, gazing into her coffee-colored eyes.

"You know my dad?" Libby asked.

"Yes, we went to the same school together. Your mom and dad and me." The way he said it made it sound as if we were all together like the Three Musketeers, as if we were friends. In truth, I don't think Jesse and Jack ever had a single conversation.

Jack led us out to the parking lot and into a white Mercedes that smelled like the inside of an expensive department store. Danny was in day camp, Jack explained to Libby, but the bus would bring him home in the afternoon. We cruised down the highway, Jack going too fast as he always did, but the ride was so smooth it felt as if the car were baffled in cotton. "So, I've become my father," Jack said to me, patting the dash. Everything was lights and buttons surrounded by burgundy leather.

"I always liked your father," I said. "He's a nice man."

"You don't think anymore that it's a character flaw to be rich?" Jack gave a little staccato laugh.

"Oh, I probably still do," I said, smiling. We streamed by clumps of magenta and yellow flowers growing along the island that separated the traffic. "But I never used to feel as strongly about that as you did. And now look at you."

"And now look at me," Jack repeated. "From mantras to Mercedes."

"From gurus to Gucci," I said.

"Do you know there are more lawyers than children in southern California?"

"Jack, is that true?" I asked.

"Well, some of the children *are* lawyers in southern California. They do their parents' divorces. Make out like bandits here."

I said, "Marriage is in now. People are going to stay together."

As I said it I wanted to spit three times as my grandmother did, to ward off the evil eye. Would Jesse ever leave me? Couldn't he come home one day and announce that he had fallen in love with a graduate student? That she made him feel alive and light in a way that I do not, what with my constant attention about whose turn it is to go grocery shopping?

"Staying together? Not in southern California," Jack sniffed. "Sounds like one of those flashy midwestern trends to me."

"How do those houses stay up there?" Libby asked from the backseat, pointing a finger between us toward a cliff off the side of the road. At the top, huge houses of glass and wood hung off the side of the rock.

"Balloons," Jack said. "Inside the house they always keep a couple of rooms filled with balloons. It makes the whole house very light."

"He's kidding, sweetheart," I said, turning back to Libby.

Libby gave me an exasperated look indicating that she already knew that.

"I think," I said to her, "the people who build the houses just dig very deep and put in all sorts of cement to hold the house into the side of the hills . . ."

"Now *she's* kidding," Jack interrupted. "One good rain. Whoosh!" He made an arc with one hand to show a rapid decline and started to sing: "The party's over . . ."

"Jack . . . ," I said warningly.

"I'm kidding," Jack said, turning around to Libby.

Jack drove up to La Jolla Cove because he said he wanted us to see the ocean before we saw his house. "We'll build toward the more impressive view," he said as we parked the car and walked along a path overlooking a beach where waves crashed upon jagged rock. Everywhere there were people strolling, jogging, riding bikes. "It's like this practically all year round," Jack said, pointing around to the sun and sky. "Cool in the mornings, sometimes a little foggy, then by noon—paradise!"

"It is beautiful," I admitted. I thought of the long winter that stretched ahead of us in Urbana. The snow and the wind. Rochester had been worse, though. Because of the lake, there was that bone-chilling damp. "Do you ever take it for granted?"

"No. I love it every day. But I think you lose your resistance or something when you get used to the sun. Now when I go back to New York, I'm cold all the time."

"Well, we were cold all the time when we lived at the farmhouse," I said. I looked away because right after I said that, I had an image of Jack and me together in bed under a pile of quilts.

Libby asked to go see the water so Jack helped her down the rocky steps and I followed. On the beach were shining, black-green vines all tangled up together like a bunch of chains thrown into a jewelry box. "Look at this, girls!" Jack squatted next to a pond of water where a part of a tree had fallen into a depression. Dead branches lay sogging in the water, and the air smelled sharp and fishy.

Libby peered curiously over the water's edge. "What is that?" she asked, her eyebrows arched in concentration.

"Sea anemones," Jack said. "Watch what they do." Jack put one of his hands into the clear, shallow water and slowly moved to touch the knoblike center of the plant. In response, the leaves curled shut along his finger.

"It bites you," Libby said, pulling back.

"It doesn't hurt at all," Jack said. "Go ahead and try it."

Libby looked tentatively at the water, then at me. "No thank you," she said politely.

We took off our shoes and left them on a flat plane of rock that jutted out like a shelf from the cliff. "That's the special place for shoes," Jack said to Libby, lining up the three pairs of sneakers—Papa, Mama and Baby Bear sizes. That morning I had thought of wearing a dress and pink, strappy sandals, then decided that the plane could be cold or we'd have to walk a long way at the terminal so, opting for comfort over glamour, chose instead jeans, a cotton T-shirt and my old Nikes. When

I came down to breakfast Barbara had said, "You're going to see an old boyfriend dressed like *that?*"

Jack raced Libby up and down the beach, letting her have enough head starts so that she felt her wins were legitimate. This buoyed her spirits and they walked up ahead, chatting companionably. Soon she was charmed by him. Jack did all his tricks—plucking quarters out from behind her ears, turning one-handed cartwheels, making babies-in-the-cradle out of the stiff white handkerchief he had in his pocket. She warmed to each one, clapping greedily for more.

Yet, there was something frenzied in Jack's determination to win Libby over. I thought of how Jesse would behave with someone else's child. He might ask a few of the usual questions about school and such, but otherwise he wouldn't be too interested. Then I remembered how Barbara had called Jesse "cold," and thought how perhaps that was what I had grown used to, that more reserved response.

The three of us walked up the beach, Libby in the middle swinging from each of our arms as each frothy wave came in. A gray-haired woman, bent over searching for shells, paused as we came into view. She straightened up, smiling warmly as she watched us pass, thinking, most likely, what a happy and attractive family we were.

Jack's house was deceiving. From the outside, in the front at least, it looked almost modest, a meandering ranch-style house painted a rusty red, the color of old barns in the Midwest. There was a country mailbox on a post, but the house was set close to the road without any front lawn, just flowers and ground covering running along a thin strip of land. Other houses were placed at odd angles up and down the hills with no sidewalk to make connections, so that even though the houses were fairly close together, they didn't seem like a neighborhood exactly.

We went in the front door, Jack carrying both suitcases. I could only gasp. "Room with a view," Jack said, following my gaze. We stood facing a two-story glass window—well, really a glass wall—and looked out over a hot tub, a swimming pool as long as a track field, and a white gazebo beside a wooden deck, which wrapped itself between two huge, twisted banyon trees. All of this seemed to hang over a valley of flowers, hot pinks and purples of such startling color that you had to blink looking out. In the distance there were mountains—far away, with smoky gray tops and fuzzy perimeters, but mountains, nonetheless. Mountains right in your own backyard.

"La Jolla Canyon," Jack said, dropping our bags on the flagstone entryway. A chubby, dark-skinned woman came out of a side hall, carrying a load of folded clothing in a basket. "Mrs. Silver called," she said, standing close enough so that the fragrance of clean wash wafted through the hall.

I thought I saw Jack's jaw tighten. "Did she leave a message?"

"She didn't, Mr. Silver." The woman stood in front of Jack holding the basket of wash as if waiting to be dismissed. I noticed that the shirt on top of the pile had what looked like a tea stain right below the collar. (Spills from coffee and tea should be sponged immediately with cool water. Then the material can be soaked in a solution of one quart lukewarm water, one-half teaspoon of liquid dishwashing detergent and one teaspoon of white vinegar. Here the stain had been baked in with the heat of the dryer and it was probably too late, even with an additional enzyme presoak.)

"Connie, this is Sharon and Libby. They're going to stay with us a couple of days," Jack said.

The woman nodded briefly. "Do you want me to take the suitcases to unpack in the guest room?" she asked Jack, not looking in my direction.

"Oh, no, I'll do that," I said too quickly, as if I had dope or guns hidden away. I added, "Thanks anyway though," and gave a tinny, inappropriate laugh. The truth is, I always feel uncomfortable with servants—not that in my own life I have had all that much experience, but even in restaurants I tend to start helping the waitress by piling the dishes and passing them over instead of just sitting there while she clears around me.

The guest suite ran along one side of the house, two spacious rooms connected by a bathroom with a bidet and a bath "environment," an enclosure with a high-tech instrument panel that looked like the cockpit of an airplane. Embedded in a clear, Plexiglas wall were dials for shower, sauna, steam and sun. "This really is something, Jack," I said, looking at our reflection on one of the mirrored walls, remembering our faces, the ones we wore at nineteen and twenty. For Jack, the years had added a bit of fleshiness around the jaw and laugh lines in the corners of his eyes. For me, I was right on the edge. I could feel the lines mapping themselves out on the surface of my face, but they were visible only in a strong light when I hadn't enough sleep. Two or three good years left. Five at the outside. I have the kind of perishable thin skin that never gave me a pimple in adolescence but will assure me an early middle age.

Ten minutes later I was in my bathing suit, sitting poolside beside Jack, sipping papaya juice from an icy tumbler. Libby was practicing her ducking in the shallow end. Sensing my divided attention, she called to me frequently after every surfacing. "How was that, Mom? Did you see that one, Mom?" After a while I called back with a firm tone, "I don't want to watch anymore, Lib. You just swim by yourself now." She said nothing, but sent me a dark scowl before she went under again. One good thing: Libby can be depended upon rarely to make a scene in public because she is sufficiently socialized not to embarrass herself. This consciousness started when she was quite young. Even as a toddler, she was contemptuous of children who would lose themselves in a rage of temper in shopping malls or grocery stores.

Jack leaned back on a white wicker chaise with a plumped-up cushion and put his already tanned face up to the sun. With a drink in one hand and his other resting lightly on a table that held a cordless telephone and a mini TV, he looked like someone you would see in a photograph in *People* magazine with the caption "Young movie mogul takes five at his vacation villa."

Libby's head rose out of the water, just from the nose up, her wet hair matted down her face. She continued across the width of the pool, bobbing up and down, leaving a trail.

"Tell me about your trip," Jack said, turning toward me. He reached over and stroked the length of my arm as if I were a cat sitting beside him.

I began with geography, but ended up talking about Barbara and David and Andrew. "I don't know," I concluded. "I think David's really a nice man. . . ."

"Nice," Jack interrupted. "That's the word people use when they're setting you up on a blind date with someone who's boring and homely as sin."

"David is neither," I said, defensive. "He's very pleasant look-ing and practically brilliant." Picturing David standing at the door in the glare of the porch light of some anonymous blind date made me feel a sudden sorrow.

"Sharon, people break up for all sorts of reasons nobody can really understand. I guess the reason people stay together is because they *want* to stay together. What else does it have to do with?"

"So you don't really know why you and Marcy Klupperman broke up?"

"More properly, the question is—why did Marcy and I ever get married? I don't know," Jack said, twirling the ice in his glass. "That didn't seem like much of a marriage as I recall. It was more like a long date."

"You were too young."

"It's like I was a different person," Jack said soberly. "The drugs were very bad. It seemed all right then. It didn't seem as if there would be consequences."

"What were the consequences?" I asked.

"The acid messed me up. You were with Jesse already, so

maybe you don't remember. Right before Marcy and I left for India, my parents tried to institutionalize me."

"Jack, I didn't know that!"

"It probably would have been more damaging if they had succeeded. God, I was so paranoid then. I might not have come back together from that." Jack poured himself more juice and reached across to refill my glass, leaning his warm, brown shoulder against my arm. "You never did acid with me, did you?" Jack asked. "Why not?"

"I guess I was afraid. Also, I thought that there was supposed to be someone who stayed straight in case anything happened." The acid had names like Orange Sunshine and Blue Cheer. Still, I was afraid. I recalled that one of the things I liked about Jesse when we first started going together was that he was always the one who stayed straight.

"Listen," Jack said, looking at his watch. "Danny's going to be home soon and there's something I should tell you. Uh . . . it's about me and Ellen. Uh . . . well, the shit kind of hit the fan around here the other night . . ." Jack trailed off, looking uncomfortable. He ran his hand through his hair. "Oh, boy!"

"Because of me?" I asked softly. "Because I'm here?" I drew back my foot, which had been touching Jack's chaise lounge.

"No, not at all," Jack was quick to reply. "Honey, no. This has nothing to do with you." He moved closer to pat my shoulder.

"Well, what does it have to do with?" I imagined Ellen working into a jealous snit over my visit. Plenty of women would.

"Really, Ellen was happy about your coming here," Jack insisted. "She's not like that."

"Well, what is she *not* happy about?" I asked tightly. In some way, I felt tricked. Jack with all his talk about oceans and beautiful views and the great San Diego Zoo, what a fine time we'd all have together.

"Well, she's not happy about me," Jack said, looking miserable. "God, I really made a bit of a mess."

"What kind of mess?" After all this time with Barbara, what first came to mind was another-woman kind of mess. One of Jack's attractions to women was that he always seemed so accessible, that if he was with you, he always made you feel that that was just the place he wanted to be. So I was surprised when Jack answered, "It's about money."

We sat silently for a few moments, watching the way the sun reflected off the water of the pool, the dancing, quick light off the cool aqua. "In the last few days, I lost a lot of money," Jack said. "A *lot* of money," he added.

I wanted to know how much money was a lot to a person in Jack's circumstances, but I didn't ask.

Jack turned his face up to me. "Almost two hundred thousand dollars," he said.

I swallowed hard, repeating Jack's phrase: "Oh, boy." I whistled low under my breath.

"Ellen just found out last night. She found out because she started up a new business of her own and one of the loans didn't go through because of what happened."

"What happened exactly?"

"It's complicated," Jack said, licking his lips. "Commodities. Bad tips. I was listening to this sleazebag who really took me to the cleaners. One of the things was I bought a racehorse who got bursitis or something like that."

"So now what are you going to do?" I looked at the back of the house whose solar panels mirrored the sky. One cloud hung like a giant puff of smoke. "Are you going to have to sell your house?"

"Oh, no. Nothing like that," Jack said quickly. "Look, it's not really as bad as it sounds. It's over two hundred thousand but . . ." Jack paused. "Well, a lot of it is just on paper. I mean, our life-style isn't going to change because I lost this money."

I nodded. It was hard to imagine a life-style that wouldn't be changed by losing two hundred thousand dollars.

"The problem is," Jack continued, "that I kind of, well, I lied to Ellen. I was getting deeper and deeper and . . . well, I thought we could get out. Ellen says she feels betrayed."

"I could understand that," I said, finally.

"And she's, well . . ." Jack's smile was devilish, disarming in a way. Of course, I was not the one on the other end of the betrayal. "I guess I should warn you, Sharon. She's pretty pissed."

Libby came out of the pool, shivering. I wrapped her in a towel and she sat cuddled in my lap, feeling against my skin warm and cold at the same time. "Does that boy Dan know how to ride a two-wheeler?" she whispered into my ear.

Chapter 18

Before I met Ellen, I heard her. I was in the hall bathroom when she came in from the garage listening to her and Jack in the entryway. It was almost seven and we had been waiting for dinner. "All right. That's okay," I heard Jack say. His voice was low, soothing; Ellen's was a venomous hiss, like gas seeping under the door. I felt a sweet ache rise up in the back of my throat. Poor Jack. A closet door opened and slammed and then they started again. I couldn't hear what they were saying, but every once in a while Ellen's voice would rise and Jack would use her name over and over—"Ellen . . . da da dada . . . Ellen . . . da da . . . dada . . . Ellen." Then Jack talked for a while and I thought I heard her say, "Oh, my God, Jack!"

In the bathroom everything was color-coordinated and there was a marble-topped counter with a picture of Jack and Ellen in a silver frame. They were on a boat and they both had their arms around each other and were squinting into the sun. There was also a picture of a blond boy on a rocking horse.

I coughed noisily and flushed before coming out. Jack took my hand and introduced us, at the same time calling out to Libby and Danny, who were playing somewhere in the house. I had the feeling that Jack wanted to surround himself with as many people as possible.

Ellen was a pretty brunette with a heart-shaped face. She was wearing a tank-top dress of tie-dyed pastels and had the long, bony arms of a ballet dancer. She managed a smile, but I could see by the puffiness under her eyes that she had been crying.

At dinner, Ellen's fury was like a crackling, angry aura. Even Connie, who made appearances from the kitchen to put out a platter of lemon sole, a salad, a cheese soufflé teased into browned peaks, made a wide arc around Ellen.

We sat in a formal dining room whose glass wall faced the canyon. The other walls were covered with earth-toned pottery and Mexican Indian string paintings done in lurid, fluorescent colors. As if determined to ignore Jack's presence across the long oak table, Ellen kept her head cocked in my direction, asking me about the trip. She liked the idea of women and children going across the country together. "You and Barbara must be very close," Ellen said, pouring a neat shot of vodka into her empty Bloody Mary glass where red flecks collected in the clear liquid. "I mean, it's not everyone who can vacation like that together with their children."

Jack refilled my glass with a white wine that had more grape, more importance than the Chablis I usually drank. I asked Jack the name of it but forgot it as soon as he told me. The fish was slightly dry and slow to go down, so I kept sipping the wine and by the third glass I was pretty sloshed.

"We were very close," I agreed. "I mean, we are. Though, it wasn't exactly a vacation in that sense. I mean, we weren't going just to have a good time." I felt myself stammering out a number of qualifications.

"Jana always throws up," Libby said decisively, as if to affirm that the trip was, in many ways, a trial. The night before, after Barbara had gone off with Andrew, Jana had christened the new apartment by throwing up her entire Chinese food dinner into the toilet.

"Oh, yuk," Danny said, plopping his fork back into the soufflé. Danny looked like Jack, with ash-blond hair and a sturdy, compact body. He had a low, hoarse voice that sounded almost like a mechanical toy. Libby, from first glance, was completely taken, and she was in good humor, trying to please.

"It's disgusting! You should see . . .," Libby began before I interrupted: "Lib, why don't you tell Danny about the Dinosaur National Monument? All the things we saw in the rocks?"

"I have dinosaurs in my room," Danny said, already pushing himself away from the table.

"*Real* ones?" Libby asked, wide-eyed.

"Gol, not *real* ones," Danny said, laughing, turning to Jack with a look of masculine camaraderie, as if—do you believe this kid? "*Real* dinosaurs? There are no real dinosaurs anymore! They're extinct."

"I *know* they're distinct," Libby sniffed. "I thought you had fossils. Some *real* fossils from dinosaurs." I beamed at her across the table.

"Danny, eat a little salad, please," Ellen said, though most of her own food lay untouched on the plate.

There was a desultory quality to the grown-up conversation, with Jack starting stories he didn't finish and Ellen asking questions that didn't seem to need answers. The issue at large stood between them, crowding us at the table, pushing off all ordinary conversation. I wished that I were somewhere else. Anywhere else. It was like driving bumper-to-bumper in rush-hour traffic. You know you have not caused the problem. You know it will go on the same whether you are there or not. But you wish you were not there.

After a while, Danny asked Libby if she wanted to see the dinosaurs he had in his room. "The *models* of dinosaurs," he said, smiling at Jack.

Libby carefully folded her napkin and put it down by the side of her plate. "May I please be excused?" she said to no one in particular.

"Would you like ice cream later, then?" Ellen asked.

"Yes, please," Libby answered, rising from her chair.

"She's very polite," Ellen said to me when both the kids had gone off down the hall. "Sometimes I think I'm too casual with Danny. About manners and all that. I don't really know how he would behave in someone else's house for dinner." It struck me that Ellen said "I'm too casual" rather than "We're too casual," even with Jack sitting right there. Ellen still had her neck crimped and she looked only in my direction.

"I don't think so," Jack said, clearing his throat. "At school the teachers have always said how polite Danny is, remember at nursery . . ."

"When did you ever go to a school conference, Jack? As I recall, you were always off making deals." Ellen's dark brown eyes, hard as enameled beads, flashed at him. "Big, important deals."

I curled the end of my napkin and took another swallow of wine.

"Ellen, please don't start," Jack said quietly.

A phone rang several times, but nobody got up. Connie stuck her head out of the kitchen, calling, "For you, Mr. Silver, Michael Rakosi on the phone." Jack pushed away from the table with a loud scrape of his chair. "Thanks, Connie. I'll take it in the study."

Ellen concentrated on picking a Greek olive out of the salad. "Shit," she whispered under her breath.

"I'm sorry," I said, finishing the last of the wine. "I've come at a bad time for both of you." I worked to speak with clarity and precision, but was drunk enough so that my lips felt rubbery and numb, as if they'd been shot with Novocain.

It didn't matter. Ellen was drunk, too, and so disgusted with Jack that she seemed relieved when he left the room. "Why do *I* always feel like the villain?" she said, depositing the olive pit in her wineglass with an angry clink. "In everything, I'm always the heavy. The last housekeeper we had, Jack let her have her own phone number and paid for it. So she calls her boyfriend in Texas, and they speak every night for hours. They'd stay up and watch television together on the phone! Of course, I'm the one who has to fire her. Then Jack gets suckered into this race-horse business and loses a quarter of a million dollars and I'm the bitch because I'm not being the supporting wife when he's down. . . ." Ellen interrupted herself. "He told you about this, didn't he?"

"Yes. Right before you came home," I said. I wanted to ask if the loss was really a quarter million and not closer to two hundred thousand. Maybe in their bracket, fifty thousand here or there didn't matter.

"Michael Rakosi's some real estate tycoon who Jack knew from high school in New York. He's supposed to help bail us out of all this. Of course, you know Jack," Ellen said, sighing. "He's still the man who buys drinks for everyone in the house and keeps in touch with all the old buddies." She squeezed a fist until her knuckles whitened. "All that money for racehorses. He makes me so angry."

I nodded. There was something tough-minded and honest about her, and she seemed grounded in a way that Jack was not. "Once he put all our money into grapes," I confided.

Ellen looked puzzled. "A vineyard?"

"No. Just grapes. It was when we were at school. At the farmhouse. Everybody chipped in five dollars for food for the weekend. That was what—fifteen years ago—and five dollars apiece could feed us all for a couple of days." Ellen nodded, interested. I wondered what stories Jack had ever told her about my life with him. "Anyway," I continued, "Jack went grocery shopping by himself—I don't know why I didn't go—and he was supposed to buy, you know, the usual stuff, meat, eggs, vegetables, like that. Enough for the whole weekend. It was in the fall and in upstate New York, the grapes were out. Those big purple ones that burst in your mouth."

"Concord grapes."

"Yes, that's it. So Jack passes a farmstand on the way to the store and stops and gets into this conversation with the farmer's daughter and what does he do but spend about twenty dollars on grapes. Twenty dollars was most of the grocery money! He bought a whole bushelful of grapes." I smiled, remembering Jack, flushed and happy, coming in the door, one paper bag balanced on top of a whole bushel of inky-blue grapes! Tim Fray and Reba were home and Tim looked at the grapes and said, "Oh, wow. Where'd you get all these, man?" He didn't know that Jack had spent nearly all the grocery money on grapes. Jack, pleased, started washing bunches of grapes, putting them in bowls, saying how these were the best grapes he'd ever tasted. Then Tim started unpacking the one grocery bag from the IGA, looking for cold cuts to make himself a sandwich. There was only a half gallon of milk, and a couple of cans of chili beans.

As I told all this to Ellen, she nodded sympathetically. "And I bet Jack was hurt when everybody got mad at him."

"He was. He felt terrible."

"He usually does," Ellen said, something in her tone revealing that she was beginning to soften. "Then did you have to eat just grapes all weekend?"

"No. Reba got the idea that we would take the bushel, drive out to one of the dorms, and sell the grapes to the students. We all went and sold off each bunch for about a dollar. We ended up making money over the original twenty."

Ellen looked thoughtful. "Maybe Jack can make some money selling these horses for gourmet dog food."

Things eased up after that. Jack came back to the table, pleased with whatever it was that Michael Rakosi had suggested. He started to explain to Ellen, but she stopped him: "Let's forget about this for a while, Jack. Let's just have a good time."

The children played together in Danny's room and we changed into bathing suits and went out to the hot tub. Ellen said that she and Jack hardly ever used the hot tub anymore, that it was something that they just didn't think of. "It's fun to have a guest and do this again," Ellen said, dropping a terry-cloth robe over the chaise lounge. I looked at her in her bathing suit as she eased herself into the water. She was straight-hipped, with small, high breasts. We were probably just the same size. The night air felt cool around our faces and steam from the tub rose around our shoulders. Jack sat on the ledge between us with his legs crossed, like a happy Buddha. "Isn't this the life!" he said grandly. "A beautiful night and beautiful women and . . ." He let out a yell. Ellen, I think, had reached under the bubbling water and grabbed him between the legs.

Friends stopped over, a couple named Mickey and Bill. Bill had a hearty handshake and a loud laugh that echoed through the canyon. He was in his late thirties, but he seemed more like someone from my parents' generation. Mickey had opened a sportswear boutique in partnership with Ellen. They sold warm-up suits and tie-dyed T-shirt dresses. Mickey knew all about what had happened with the racehorses, too. "You still on her list?" she said, bending over Jack in the tub, ruffling his hair. She was wearing the same kind of dress I had seen first on Ellen. After we came out of the hot tub, Ellen gave me a dress, too. Mine was all purples and blues. Later Ellen, Mickey and I sat around the kitchen table eating raspberry sorbet, all three of us in our tie-dyed dresses. We looked like a backup group for a sixties band.

Mickey told me that she had five children—two from Bill, two from a second husband, one from a high school marriage that had lasted only a few months. "I get pregnant if I watch TV with a man," Mickey said, licking her spoon.

I thought about going home to Jesse, starting again with temperature charts. After another month, Jesse was supposed to go in to have his sperm tested for motility. He had a sufficient number, the doctor had said, but it might be a question of whether or not the sperm knew where it was going. "Some of those little fellas get confused sometimes," the doctor had said on our last visit. Jesse had been grim. I knew he didn't like it that the doctor talked about sperm as if they were tiny pets that one could control.

"Can you imagine—five children!" Ellen said to me.

I shook my head, envying Mickey's casual fecundity.

"After our business gets settled, I'd like to have another baby," Ellen said. "Maybe next year."

Libby and Danny came into the kitchen wanting something to drink. Libby was in a sweat, pink-faced and out of breath. "What have you been doing, pumpkin?" I asked her.

"Games," she replied, settling herself on my lap and chugging down the apple juice that Ellen set before her.

"Galactic invaders and prehistoric monsters," Danny said. "It's a game I made up."

"It's fun, Mom," Libby said, assuringly.

"I'll bet," I said, kissing her neck. "But I think you should calm down a little. Will you be ready for a story soon?"

"Let's go," Danny said, wiping his mouth with the back of a hand.

I started to say something to Libby about starting to get ready for bed, but she whipped right out of the kitchen and down the hall after him. "Libby's in love," I said to Ellen and Mickey.

Bill and Jack came in through the glass doors of the dining room, talking about stocks. "A small growth investment," Bill was saying. "Slow, but a sure thing. A real sure thing."

I slept with Libby between cool, striped sheets, both of us cuddled together in the middle of the bed. Sometime in the night she woke, talking in her sleep. "Is anybody out there?" she said, her voice clear as a ringing phone in the night.

"Where, sweetie?" I said. "Are you dreaming?"

"There," she said, impatiently. "Out there."

"I don't think so. Go back to sleep, Lib," I said, stroking her head.

"Tomorrow we're going to the zoo?" she said, suddenly awake. "And then home?" A night light glowed on the wall to the bathroom. The whites of Libby's eyes had a bluish tinge.

"Yes. We'll be home tomorrow night, late. Daddy will pick us up at the airport."

"Good," Libby said, snuggling back down under the covers.

"You've had a nice time, haven't you, Lib?"

"Yes," she said, yawning. "But I've had enough."

We were at the zoo when it opened, Ellen, Danny, Libby and I hotfooting it after Jack as he raced around, wanting us to see everything. No cages here, the lions and tigers no longer pacing ominously, the way I remembered from my childhood visits to the Bronx Zoo. Here the big cats lounged in the sun on big rocks, stretching and looking bored. Moats and cliffs surrounded their grassy tract of land. "This is the best zoo in the world," Jack said, "because the animals are in their natural habitat. This is what zoos should be." He maintained his enthusiasm until we were in the open-air aviary and a bird shit on his shoulder. Mucusy gray slime covered dark turds that looked like chocolate chips. When we found a men's room, I told Jack not to use very hot water at first, because the smear could "cook" into the fabric permanently. The children thought the whole thing was uproariously funny.

We whizzed past the monkeys and the elephants before eating lunch in a restaurant with an outdoor piazza. The french fries tasted like peanuts to me. As soon as we finished, Jack clapped the children to attention and raced them toward the reptile house.

In the afternoon, we dropped Ellen at her shop, which was on the way to the airport. Through the glass door, I saw Mickey at the counter amid dozens of tie-dyed T-shirt dresses of every imaginable hue. "I'm glad you came," Ellen said, taking me in her arms after I got out of the car. It was like hugging myself.

Although we weren't late, Jack drove too fast to the airport, weaving his car in and out of traffic in a dizzying design. "She's better," Jack said to me, grinning. It took me a moment to realize that he meant Ellen.

"You're impossible," I said, leaning back against the buttery leather of the seat. Danny and Libby were quiet in the back. "If I were married to you, you would make me crazy."

"No, I wouldn't," Jack said tenderly. "If I were married to you, we would be fine together."

We were waiting for our seat numbers to be called. Jack squatted down next to Libby. "Plant one right here," he said, pointing to his cheek. She stepped forward and gave him a loud smacking. "What about Danny?" Jack said, but, suddenly shy, Danny had pulled away and shook his head.

"And what about me?" I said, reaching for Jack, feeling a welling up of affection and sympathy just at that moment.

"I love you," Jack said simply before he kissed me on the lips. The kiss was friendly and intense at the same time. I pulled back first, flushed and guilty. Jack laughed. "Oh, my sweet Sharon. You were always such a good girl."

Chapter 19

On the plane, Libby colored while I listened to the woman sitting in back of me explaining how the eighties lacked affect. "I mean, when you think about it, this is a decade that has no consciousness, no soul," she said to the man next to her. The man said something, but he was directly behind me so the back of the chair muffled his reply. The woman went on. She was using phrases like "an emotional ledger of the times" and "the geography of the heart."

I peeked between the crack in the seats, trying not to be obvious. She looked ordinary and middle-aged, even a trifle schoolmarmish. "The eighties have depressed the shit out of me," the woman sighed.

Somewhere over Colorado, I fell into one of those sleeps where your mouth falls slack and saliva pools in the hollow of one cheek. I dreamed I was on a show similar to "The Dating Game," but instead of just going out together, the contestants had to get married. Then they would be sent on a honeymoon to some fabulous, exotic place.

I suspected that Jesse would be behind the curtain, but the voices were all disguised, so I couldn't tell whether he was bachelor number one, two or three. They introduced themselves:

"Hello, Sharon! Hi there, Sharon! How you doing, Sharon?!" After the last one spoke, I looked down at my blank notecards, realizing that I hadn't prepared any questions. Stammering, I began asking the bachelors where they went to school and what they did for a living. I was reprimanded by the host. "We like to ask fun questions on this show," he said, sternly.

"What do you think keeps people together in relationships?" I asked bachelor number one. The host frowned.

Bachelor number one was stymied. He fished around, his voice going up after each answer as if to check it out with me. "Maybe because you grow accustomed to each other's ways? Because love grows with the passage of time? Because you made a promise to be together . . .?"

"Thank you, bachelor number one," I said, sensing he could go on. "What about you, bachelor number two?"

Bachelor number two made a joke about Krazy Glue. "That *really* keeps 'em together," he said. Then he laughed this kind of hee-haw laugh that made him seem demented. I immediately eliminated him as a possibility.

"Bachelor number three?" I asked brightly, sure that Jesse would be the last one.

"What is it?" an unfamiliar voice growled. He sounded bearish and uncivilized.

"Same question. Why do you think people stay together in relationships?" Although I was shaken by bachelor number three's tone, I remained smiling and composed for the media viewers.

"What do *you* think?" he asked, still belligerent. "What the hell kind of question is that?"

I decided to go back to bachelor number one when the host signaled that it was time for me to choose. I started to protest that I had only had a single question, but the audience started to chant and stomp on the floor, drowning me out. "Better make your selection now," said the host, looking scornful.

It occurred to me that I could say no. I didn't *have* to pick anyone. After all, this was only a television show. And in some other part of my consciousness, I also knew that the whole thing was only a dream. The audience was growing restless, though. The room was filling up with their energy.

Off to the side there was a stage door and, throwing off the microphone clipped to my dress, I decided to make a run for it. "Wait a minute!" yelled the host after me. The audience rose from their seats like ugly drunks at a football game.

I read Libby three books and played the guessing game, "I see something . . ." You had to name a color. "I see something red," I said, starting off. Libby got up on her knees to get a better perspective. Looking at the fleshy skin on the head of the man in front of us she asked, "Mom, what color do you say is 'bald'?"

My mind wasn't on the game. I kept picturing a lineup of men. Jesse. David. Jack Silver. Andrew. They were on the dating game of my dream. Wouldn't they all be acceptable? Jack was adorable and fun to be with. He was generous to a fault. He loved children. He was also exhausting and somewhat undependable.

Jesse was the tallest and the sexiest (I believed) and had the driest sense of humor. He was loyal and unpretentious. He was very smart. He did not do his share of housework.

David was gentle and easygoing. He had a wonderful smile. He was practically a world-famous scientist. True, he had a slightly distracted quality when it came to personal relations, but he made an effort. He could talk about feelings, if you asked. When he told a story, he took too long to get to the point.

Andrew was abnormally handsome. Barbara told me that he listened to everything she ever said with incredible empathy. She said he was a terrific lover. He was sophisticated without being stuffy. Well, maybe he seemed a little stuffy to me.

Jesse. David. Jack. Andrew. Jesse. David. Jack. Andrew . . .

I thought of living with Jack in his house in La Jolla, swimming laps in the heated pool, planning dinner for the week with the housekeeper. Jack and I could go into Mexico to buy pottery and leather goods. (Jack loves to shop, something Jesse and I have never done together.) I would have to handle all the money, though.

I thought of David, sitting at his computer, rubbing his tired eyes. I would bring him a cup of tea and massage the back of his neck. David is very clean and always smells like lemons.

I thought of sitting across from Andrew at a table lit with candles. Of him looking into my eyes and hanging on to my every word. Of making love, slowly, in a room where there is Vivaldi playing.

I thought of going home to Jesse.

The entrée was a chicken breast stuffed with spinach and cheese. As airplane food went, it was better than average, which meant it was edible. "Try it, Lib," I coaxed, scraping off everything green until there was a forkful of pure white meat. I looked at her, straining for objectivity, trying to decide if she was too thin. On her fourth-year checkup, she was at the bottom twentieth percentile for weight. The pediatrician patted me and said, "She'll probably be pretty and petite like her mommy." He was only a few years older than I was, but he had prematurely gray hair and a patronizing manner.

Libby wouldn't touch the chicken. After a few minutes, she ate an olive and a breadstick dipped in cheese food. Watching as Libby sucked the end of the breadstick, I wondered if there would ever be a time when I would tire of looking at her, if just the sight of her wouldn't fill me up. I remembered my father had once written me my first year away at college that he missed seeing my face. Not that he missed me—which I suppose he did—but that he missed seeing my face.

After the stewardess took our trays, I went with Libby to the bathroom. The woman who hated the eighties was flipping through a *New Yorker,* reading the cartoons.

It was night when we started the descent, the lights of the city sparkling in the night.

"Daddy will be here to get us," Libby said.

"Yes."

"It looks like diamonds down there, Mom."

"It really does," I said and started to search my pockets for gum. "Do your ears feel plugged, Lib?"

Libby shrugged. "I don't know."

I took out a pack of gum and offered her a piece. "It's good to chew gum as we land."

Libby eyed the pack carefully. "Is that sugarless?"

It was Wrigley's Doublemint. "No, but that's okay. You could have a piece of this if you want."

"Daddy only lets me chew sugarless," Libby said softly. She turned her head, searching the darkened runway.

Jesse stood out above the crowd and Libby, spotting him, darted between the people in front of us and ran on ahead. Jesse scooped her up, covering her face with kisses. In his arms, Libby suddenly looked like she did when she was a toddler, though during the trip I had thought of her as more of a traveling companion.

"Hi," he said, as I came toward him, a crooked smile on his face. It was a funny expression, a little abashed for being so full of joy and pride in public. We kissed with Libby squashed in the middle and I grabbed the back of his hair, which had grown curly over the collar of his shirt.

"We missed you," I said as we made our way toward baggage.

"We did, Dad," Libby said.

I stood off to the side with all the carry-ons from the plane and Libby and Jesse went to the carousel as the suitcases rolled out. They were both quiet and watchful. In the car, though, she was all wound up, kicking her legs along the back of the seat and talking nonstop. It was as if she had to get everything in before she forgot. Ordinarily, we would have eventually hushed her, but then her voice, piping and sweet from the backseat, seemed pleasant.

Libby talked about Danny Silver's bedroom, which was designed to resemble a space module, his bed a rocket ship. She told Jesse about Hector the dancing rooster. About the sun-bleached bones we found in the desert. About the time Jana threw up in the sink at Adventureland.

It wasn't until we were driving up our own block that she began to nod off. Then she said, "I want only Daddy to put me to bed."

It seemed as if we had been gone for such a long time that I was surprised to see everything exactly the same as we'd left it. "How does the house look?" Jesse asked, turning on the light in the hall.

"Nice."

"I cleaned, you know," he said, carrying Libby up the stairs.

There were only a few pieces of mail—some bills, a *Newsweek*. Even some of the same foods were in the refrigerator from before we left—a piece of Brie, an unopened bottle of raspberry seltzer, the leftover taco sauce from the dinner with David and Barbara.

I threw a duffel bag full of dirty wash down the basement steps when Jesse came into the kitchen. "She's off already. God, did she talk that much on the trip? She must have driven you crazy."

"The kids were really good," I said. "I don't know. I think after a while, if you're with children all the time you get into a rhythm. They don't seem to need you so much if they know you're there all the time. Maybe I just got used to it."

Jesse went into the refrigerator for a beer. "Do you want a cup of tea?" he asked, as if I were a guest in my own kitchen.

"That would be good."

"And how was Jack?" Jesse asked, filling the kettle.

I told the story about Jack and the money, the first meeting with Ellen and how I wanted to die just being there at first. I described the house and meeting Mickey and Bill. "Imagine, Jack lost almost a quarter of a million dollars!" I said. "And still, it won't change how they live."

Jesse let out a low whistle and shook his head. "I didn't know he was that loaded."

I smelled the milk container before I added some to my tea. "Did this turn?" I asked. Jesse bent his head, sniffed, and wrinkled his nose. "It's on the way out," he said. "I guess I didn't drink enough all by myself."

"Oh, poor Jess. All by yourself. Were you feeling bad that we were gone?"

"What, that you were drinking champagne in hot tubs and I was home putting sour milk on my cereal?"

"Were you jealous that I was at Jack's?"

Absently, Jesse rinsed out a sponge and wiped down an already clean counter. Then a few moments later: "No, I really don't think so."

"It's after twelve already," I said, looking at the clock on the stove. "Do you want to go up to bed?"

Jesse put away the sponge and wiped his hands on a towel.

"Come over here," he said across the kitchen, looking at me in a way that drew me in like an undertow.

I'll say one thing for getting away—it makes the sex so fantastic when you get home that for a while afterward, I wished Jesse had a job as a traveling salesman, on the road for days at a time. For both of us, in every kiss, every caress, there was such a hunger. We started kissing in the kitchen, worked our way up the stairs and, as we reached the first landing, Jesse cupped my ass in his hands as he pressed against me. "We've been in this house for over five years and we never kissed in this spot," I whispered in his ear. Somehow that aroused me.

"Take these off," Jesse said, opening the buttons of my shorts.

"I should take a shower. I'm a little funky from the trip."

"I like you funky," Jesse said, pulling off my shorts, slipping one finger inside me, then two, as I sank, heavy against the wall, and opened myself to him.

I was already naked when we got to the bedroom and I watched Jesse undress with such an urgency that I thought he would rip his clothes. When he slid into bed beside me, I reached to take him in my hand. "Don't," he said. "I'm too excited." He loomed over me, kissing my breasts, my belly, so by the time he moved down to put his mouth on me, I was moaning out loud.

The times when Jesse goes down on me I wish could last forever. Then I always think of that scene in *Annie Hall,* where they're making love and Woody Allen comes up, adjusting his stiff jaw. "Go into me," I said after what seemed a long enough interval and not wanting to take advantage. I tasted myself on his lips when we kissed and we came, fiercely and tenderly, within seconds of each other.

The next week was busy. Jesse started teaching and I went back to work and Libby went back to daycare. When I brought her in the first day there was a groundswell from the children who knew her, children who had spent the summer at daycare. "Libby's back! Libby's back!" I heard as we came into the big playroom. It was like showing up someplace with a famous movie star.

There was a dinner party that weekend at the Fitzhughs'. Dr. Fitzhugh, the chairman of the physics department, was a distinguished old gentleman with a mane of silver hair and an erudite manner; his wife, Mrs. Fitzhugh—no one would ever think of calling her by a first name—was equally elegant, the kind of dutiful faculty wife we never see anymore. Mrs. Fitzhugh was from the old school of educated and talented women who so devoted themselves to their husband's careers that they always used the first person plural when referring to any of their husband's accomplishments (as in *"We're* giving a paper in Paris next spring"). Mrs. Fitzhugh was also a fabulous cook.

That night—it was the first Saturday before the new semester began—the Fitzhughs had over some of the physics faculty to meet a visiting professor, a woman from Stanford who had just done some kind of breakthrough work in pulse lasers.

Jesse was looking forward to meeting her. I was looking forward to one of Mrs. Fitzhugh's Grand Marnier soufflés. Other than that, I didn't expect to have a good time. Ron Simone, although lascivious, was the only one who was any fun. The other tenured scientists (all male) were boring and pompous, the kind of men who assume they have all the natural rights in directing the conversation. The Fitzhughs' parties were usually geared to *power talk* and university politics, and I always ended up smiling politely as I listened to stories that made my eyes glaze over.

Jesse and I came in as a student bartender in white gloves came through the living room with a tray of Manhattans. I don't even know what's in a Manhattan, but I always had one at the Fitzhughs'. There was a cluster of people over by the buffet table. The visiting scientist was seated in the middle of a long, black leather sofa and the men surrounding her were holding their glasses, their eyes on her, as if at any moment she would be the object of a toast. She was a woman in her mid-fifties, blond, with a high color in her cheeks and a body that was plump and fleshy in the bosomy, grand way of an opera singer. On this summer night—it was still quite hot and the Fitzhughs weren't much for air conditioning—she was wearing a white beaded sweater, cut low to reveal an ample cleavage, and a lavender skirt made of some gossamerlike material that fanned out around her. Dr. Fitzhugh and Philip Huang—the only Asian male I ever met who gets his hair permed—sat on either side of her and Ron Simone sat on an ottoman in front of her. Seeing them there reminded me of the birthday scene in *Terms of*

Endearment where a gussied-up Shirley MacLaine is surrounded by adoring but inappropriate suitors.

"Jesse!" Dr. Fitzhugh bellowed. "Come here. I want you to meet Anna Carver!" Since my name had not been called, I politely sidestepped over to pick up a Manhattan. Over by the window were Toy Ping Huang, Stephanie and Jay Levitt, and a thin, young man I had never seen before. Stephanie beckoned me over with a crook of one ringed finger and I went slowly over to them. Jay Levitt I actively disliked. He was supposed to be brilliant, but he was abrasive and mean, given to publicly humiliating his graduate students. I sensed, too, that he was jealous of Jesse, who, now the youngest tenured professor, had usurped Jay's place as the department wonder boy. When we first came to Urbana, Stephanie had made friendly overtures, inviting us over for family dinners and potlucks, but I had stopped reciprocating. Now we saw them only at these faculty parties and I always felt a little guilty.

"This is Sandford Carver," Stephanie said chirpily. "He's a writer, too, Sharon."

"Hello," he said, extending his hand. "I'm Anna's husband." He had watery blue eyes and hair the color of whitened honey. I thought he was maybe twenty-five years old. Twenty-eight at the most. "What do you write, Sharon?" he asked.

He was so serious that I answered seriously. I started telling them about the article I was working on. It was interesting, really. Some laundry detergents contain optical brighteners that convert invisible rays into blue light. This causes the wash to appear brighter.

Jay Levitt started explaining, "Fluorescent substances take up the light and radiate it at a different frequency. . . ."

"Tell Sharon about your writing," Stephanie urged Sandford Carver. "It's so interesting."

I reached across the table to sample crab Rangoon, sneaking a look back over at the couch. There had to be more than a twenty-five-year difference in their ages.

"I'm a playwright," he said dramatically. "I'm finishing a trilogy based on the life of the Czar's family before, during and after the Russian revolution."

"That's sounds very ambitious," I told him.

"Well, I've been working on it for five years now," he said.

At dinner there was a lot going on at the table. First, I noticed something in the tone of Stephanie Levitt's frequent interruptions of Jay's monologues that suggested the marriage was changing, that she was going public and affirming she didn't have to put up with him anymore. I had never seen Stephanie so abandoned, so free.

More interesting, though, was the way that Sandford Carver looked at Ron Simone. I wondered if I were reading something into it, but Sandford seemed to soften when Ron spoke, and Sandford's eyes rested too long on Ron's face after he finished speaking.

There was a time just after the salad but before the veal Prince Orloff, a time when everyone had had plenty to drink but not yet enough to eat, that I thought Sandford, staring at Ron, actually had his mouth open and was beginning to drool.

Everyone else seemed oblivious. Philip Huang was talking about the new expensive lab equipment the department had just bought and how building security was so lax. Anybody could just come in and rip off the lab, he said.

Dr. Fitzhugh was talking about a plan to lock the outside doors after five. All the graduate students could have keys.

The dining room was very hot. The oven had been on for a long time. Mrs. Fitzhugh turned off the overhead light. "Is that too dark? Can everyone see what they're eating?" she asked. There were only a few candles on the buffet table and a light from the kitchen.

"Well, it's very romantic this way," Sandford Carver said, not taking his eyes away from Ron. Dr. Fitzhugh and Philip continued to talk about building security.

Jesse was listening patiently, his head bent toward Toy Ping

Huang. She spoke halting English in a teensy voice, so you always had to strain to hear.

Jay Levitt started talking about the security of the buildings when he was at Columbia University, how much better it was. Stephanie dismissed him, saying, "Don't be ridiculous, Jay. You can't compare Urbana with Harlem."

Sandford Carver leaned back in his seat, his eyes half-closed, still peering at Ron, who by this time was not looking up from his plate. At this point the student bartender walked around refilling the wineglasses and everybody else was talking, eating, nodding their heads. Mrs. Fitzhugh had just come in from the kitchen, fanning herself with her napkin. It was as if there was a ghost in the room that only I could see.

After coffee, I asked Mrs. Fitzhugh if I could use the phone. We had a new young baby-sitter, just going into sixth grade, and I wanted to check how things were going. Mrs. Fitzhugh directed me upstairs, to their bedroom, "So you can have some privacy, dear." The bright light in the upstairs hall made me blink.

The Fitzhughs' closed-up bedroom smelled like rotting bananas. On the walls were sepia-toned pictures of ancient relatives and glossy colored photos of new grandchildren. The phone next to the bed was black and heavy, substantial in my hand.

Melissa, the baby-sitter, said everything was fine; Libby had already been asleep for more than an hour. "There was a call, Mrs. Burke," Melissa said, reading efficiently from a note she had written. "Barbara called. She said call back if you're not too tired tonight. Otherwise she'll try you tomorrow."

"Thanks, hon. We'll be home before twelve," I promised. "See you soon." I put the phone back in the cradle and picked it up to dial again, not even realizing what I was doing. Just on impulse, I was dialing Barbara's number in Urbana, smiling to myself as I prepared to describe the scene downstairs. It was funny already, telling it in my head. Barbara, listen to this, I can't really talk, I'm at a dinner party at the Fitzhughs'. . . .

At the third or fourth digit, I remembered. Stricken, I sank down on the Fitzhughs' lumpy bed, the phone in my lap. I thought of Barbara, out in California, starting a whole new life without me. I thought of all the things I was never going to be able to tell her from now on.

Chapter 20

The second week of December, I drive to O'Hare to meet Barbara as she leaves the girls with David. She has arranged a three-hour layover before she goes on to see her sister in Pennsylvania. It is one of those picture-perfect Midwest winter days, with the air windless and crisp, the sun brilliant on the frozen fields.

It is mobbed at the terminal, but I see Barbara at the United baggage carousel where we said we'd meet. She is saying something to Jana, holding both the child's skinny shoulders in her hands, while David and Amanda watch for their suitcases. I kiss everyone, but the children seem shy in front of me and after the embrace move closer to David, the vacation parent.

I haven't planned to cry, but suddenly the tears spill over, as if there has been a reservoir waiting there. "Look how beautiful you both are," I say to Amanda and Jana. Amanda seems taller and thinner, and already has a pubescent look of sultry poutiness. She has a jean jacket on and big socks that puff around her ankles. Jana, though, is the real surprise. Her curly hair is cut short, boyish, and there is something athletic and perky about her. She grins, looking up at David, then back at me. I can't imagine the child in front of me whining or sucking needily on her fingers, the way she had done almost the whole trip across the country. "I wish Libby were here to see you girls," I say through my tears.

Barbara kisses them both. She gives last-minute instructions for calling, minding manners, taking medication.

"We'll see you soon," David promises me, steering them away under the protective arc of his arms. He is stiff in Barbara's presence, not even looking at her. "We'll get together for dinner with everyone, all right, Sharon?"

"Sure," I say quickly, uneasy making this arrangement in front of Barbara. David has been seeing Margaret, a researcher in his lab, since the end of October. She is nice enough, but so dull that during an evening with her my eyes water from stifling the yawns. Surprisingly, in Margaret's company David becomes more outgoing. He and Margaret share a lot of the same interests—they are both into camping and Thai cooking—and David talks a lot about these activities. I think I liked David better when he was more withdrawn.

David takes the two large suitcases and leads the girls through the electric eye; the doors heave themselves open, and Barbara and I watch as the three of them spill out into the cold, bright light.

"I could use a drink," Barbara says tremulously.

We sit across from each other in a dining room with plush rose velvet chairs in front of a plate-glass window that faces a runway. Gold brocade draperies are drawn back in thick, heavy folds. Barbara orders a vodka martini, straight up, and I ask for a fuzzy navel. "So you're still drinking those college-girl drinks," Barbara says, smiling.

"So you're still getting great haircuts," I say, also smiling. The sides rise in smooth, black poufs, but the top is a mass of gently tousled curls. She wears large, unusually shaped earrings of pounded silver, and a wide silver bracelet snakes its way up one tanned arm. High-impact accessories, Barbara used to say, make all the difference. We have talked on the phone nearly every other week since she's been gone, but there is something in her physical presence that overwhelms me.

"Do you and Jesse get together a lot with David and Margaret?" Barbara asks casually.

I deny any significant relationship. "Oh, no," I tell her. "Usually at dinner parties, that's all. I think the last time I saw them was at Ron Simone's party. He threw the biggest bash for himself when he turned forty last month."

"Nubile dancing girls? Virgin sacrifices?"

"Ron brought his parents up from Tulsa to live with him. His father has the beginnings of Alzheimer's and his mother has glaucoma and can't drive anymore. They both live with Ron. He's *real* nice with them, too. I see him grocery shopping with his mother, leading her down the aisle."

"Amazing!" Barbara says, plucking the olive from her martini. The waitress, an apple-cheeked girl with aggressively healthy looks, loiters over by the dessert table, waiting. "Split a chef's salad with me. I can't do all that chewing by myself."

"What about splitting a piece of quiche, too?"

"Sure."

"Vegetable or seafood?"

"Veggie. Living in California has spoiled me. I couldn't stand to eat those tiny canned shrimp now."

"Tell me what's happening with Andrew," I say after the waitress takes our order. For the last month, they had been having trouble, but Barbara was guarded. They were "working on things," she said. Over Barbara's shoulder, at the other tables facing the runway, I can see three men in dark suits with their backs to us. Each is sitting alone, reading a newspaper. Though one is bald and one is blond and one is fat, at first glance it seems as if I were facing a prism of reflecting glass.

Barbara sighs, massaging the space between her eyes with two fingers. "It's hard," she says finally, relieved, as if she is making a confession. "Sometimes I feel like he's sucking me up. Like he's sucking the life out of me."

"What do you mean?"

"I don't know, I think all the time I was talking myself into it, that his need revealed a great passion. That's what a real love should be—not being happy unless you're with that other person. When you're together, you fit. Then, you are complete. Do you know what I mean?"

"It's a very romantic notion."

"It's probably an unhealthy notion," Barbara says. "Andrew calls at work every day and he gets so upset if I'm busy and can't speak to him." Barbara begins to explain how at dinner Andrew commands her full attention, oblivious to the children's interruptions. "Well, not oblivious," Barbara says. "No, I wouldn't say he's oblivious. It's more like he just steamrolls over them conversationally. He wants to *pretend* they aren't there, so he just talks to me. I feel as if I were being pulled apart. I talk to the children, then I look back to Andrew and continue a completely different conversation with him, and then the girls say something else. It's exhausting."

When the food arrives, Barbara puts half the salad onto an empty plate. "Do you want some of this crumbled on top?" She points to a wedge of cheese mapped with spidery blue lines.

"Please." I run my knife through the middle of the quiche; it looks fluffy, but the crust is soggy and dense from being reheated in a microwave.

"We have sex every night," Barbara says, peppering her salad. "He comes over every single night."

I stop my fork in midair. "Why? Do you want to?"

"Well, at first . . . Andrew is such a very good lover. Very intense and passionate. But lately it has become this compulsion, I think. He says he doesn't 'feel right' unless we do it. And I can't stand it anymore."

"Oh, Barb. . . ."

She puts her hand up to stop me. "Now I know what you're going to say, Sharon. . . ."

"What?" I didn't know what I was going to say.

"You're going to say that that was one of my complaints with David. Not enough sex. Not enough connection. Right?"

"I wasn't thinking of that," I say truthfully.

A man walks by our table, pausing to look at Barbara, who stares back boldly. "Andrew scares me, actually," Barbara says quietly. "It isn't just the sex. He scares me with his need."

"I don't know if I should ask this," I say, looking down at my plate.

"You know if you say that, you *have* to ask."

I let out a ragged breath. "All right. I think about when you left and all. How fast everything went . . ."

"It seemed fast to you," Barbara interrupts. "I was thinking about leaving for a while."

"Okay. I know. Still, I guess I wonder sometimes, you know . . ." I paused for a breath. "Well, I wonder if you have any regrets. That if you could do it over again?"

"A depressed person doesn't make rational decisions," Barbara interrupts again, her forehead pinched up in thought. "I think I fell in love with Andrew because he made me feel alive. I know how corny that sounds—he made me feel alive. But he made me feel *necessary*. All those years with David, they were peaceful, I guess. And boring. But I didn't leave David because I was just *bored*. I mean, I know some people think that of me. Jesse probably thinks that. I know Jesse never really liked me, Sharon." I am about to protest, but Barbara puts up one hand to stop me. "It doesn't matter," she goes on. "But how can I explain why I left? Last summer, I know I was crazy, but even now I'm not sure I can explain it. I said I didn't love David. But it's also that David didn't make me feel loved. I was looking for something in other men. And then with Andrew, I thought I'd found it. I was just as needy as Andrew, two lost souls clinging together. So even if it doesn't work out with him, no, I don't think I regret leaving David."

"Barbara," I say, shaking my head. "How could you call yourself that—a lost soul? You're so smart and successful and beautiful. How could you think of yourself like that even for a minute?"

"You don't know, Sharon," Barbara says kindly. "You're lucky not to know. Because you've always had people who made you feel loved. Your parents, your grandmother, Jesse. Even old boyfriends. People who made you feel *necessary*."

"Oh, Barbara." I am crying again. In front of me, Barbara looks brave and resolute.

"Really, I'm all right. I'm not in bad shape at all. Listen, I'm learning a lot about myself living out there. And," she adds proudly, "I'm probably the only person in California who's doing it without a therapist!"

The waitress comes between us, silently pouring coffee from a silver pot. "It's you I miss," Barbara says, reaching for my hand across the table after the girl walks away.

Outside, the sunshine skating on the asphalt and the white mounds of snow creates shimmers through the cool glass. Along the runway, a plane, massive on the ground, like an enormous, ungainly animal, suddenly pulls itself into the air and rises gracefully, high, higher. Barbara and I sit like this for a while, watching the plane until it is only a silver speck in the sky.

"God, I wish you had never left," I tell her.

At night a light snow is falling and on the couch, in front of a not-quite roaring fire I am building, is Libby, still damp from a bath. Her skin is golden. She seems lit from inside.

Jesse comes over with an afghan and sits with her. He begins reading a book about a friendly dragon who uses his fiery breath only to cook fish or thaw snowy mittens. The book has too few pictures, but Libby is content, lulled by the sound of Jesse's voice, of the fire crackling in the background.

On a page of the newspaper that I have not yet crumpled and put into the fire is a headline about missiles in the Persian Gulf and a story about a group of English rock musicians who are organizing a benefit concert for the next African famine. I do not recognize this rock group nor have I heard the song that the article says has been on the charts for several weeks. The lead singer looks scruffy but hopeful. Just seeing his face suddenly makes me want to weep. I have the feeling that time is reeling full throttle, that the days are spinning themselves out like calendar pages in old movies. That there will always be an African famine. That people will always be surrounded by dangerous waters. The words come to me: "This is what there is. This is it." I wonder if I am necessary. If another woman could be sitting here by the fire. Another mother could have combed out Libby's tangled hair. Another wife could go with Jesse up to bed.

Jesse raises his head from the book and says to Libby, "Look at your mother. She is thinking deep thoughts." He says it without being ironic. It is purely a statement of observation— the way one might say, "Look outside, it is beginning to snow."

Obediently, Libby looks over to me and smiles. There is the heat of the fire. The smell of her clean, wet hair. The three of us drawn together as if by a magical thread. "This is it," I say aloud. The sound of my own voice surprises me, as if it has not been used in a long time.

"You don't *know*," Jesse says to me. It is one of the expressions that Libby uses when she is feeling growly. "You don't *know*, Mommy," she says when I affirm that yes, she will like squash, if only she would give it a try; or yes, she will have a good time at a birthday party, even though she is feeling shy. You don't *know*. Now Jesse and I use this phrase in a teasing way when one or the other is acting too adult, too definite.

"We don't know what?" Libby asks.

"Nothing, sweetie," I say, crumpling more newspaper for the fire. "Daddy's just kidding around."

"Yes," Jesse says, clearing his throat to begin again. "Where were we now?"